DREAM BOUND

Paranormal Romance by Kate Douglas:

Demonfire
"Crystal Dreams" in *Nocturnal*
Hellfire
Starfire
Crystalfire

Erotic Romance by Kate Douglas:

Wolf Tales
"Chanku Rising" in *Sexy Beast*
Wolf Tales II
"Camille's Dawn" in *Wild Nights*
Wolf Tales III
"Chanku Fallen" in *Sexy Beast II*
Wolf Tales IV
"Chanku Journey" in *Sexy Beast III*
Wolf Tales V
"Chanku Destiny" in *Sexy Beast IV*
Wolf Tales VI
"Chanku Wild" in *Sexy Beast V*
Wolf Tales VII
"Chanku Honor" in *Sexy Beast VI*
Wolf Tales VIII
"Chanku Challenge" in *Sexy Beast VII*
Wolf Tales 9
"Chanku Spirit" in *Sexy Beast VIII*
Wolf Tales 10
Wolf Tales 11
Wolf Tales 12
"Dream Catcher" in *Nightshift*

Published by Kensington Publishing Corporation

DREAM BOUND

Kate Douglas

APHRODISIA

KENSINGTON PUBLISHING CORP.

www.kensingtonbooks.com

APHRODISIA BOOKS are published by

Kensington Publishing Corp.
119 West 40th Street
New York, NY 10018

All Kensington titles, imprints, and distributed lines are available at special quantity discounts for bulk purchases for sales promotion, premiums, fund-raising, and educational, or institutional use.

Special book excerpts or customized printings can also be created to fit specific needs. For details, write or phone the office of the Kensington Special Sales Manager: Kensington Publishing Corp., 119 West 40th Street, New York, NY 10018. Attn. Special Sales Department. Phone: 1-800-221-2647.

Aphrodisia and the A logo Reg. U.S. Pat. & TM Off.

ISBN-13: 978-0-7582-6934-8
ISBN-10: 0-7582-6934-X

First Kensington Trade Paperback Printing: July 2012

10 9 8 7 6 5 4 3 2 1

Printed in the United States of America

*This one's for my husband, and not just because
he took me all the way to Hat Creek in the High Sierra
to tour the Allen Telescope array in preparation
for writing this series. No, it's because after
forty years and counting, the man still makes me laugh.*

Acknowledgments

My sincere thanks to my terrific, eagle-eyed beta readers Jan Takane, Lynne Thomas, Rose Toubbeh, and Karen Woods, for their insightful comments and great catches! Sometimes writing really does feel like walking a tightrope without a net, and these terrific ladies are there with the catch. Any mistakes are—quite obviously—my own.

Thanks also to my editor, Audrey LaFehr, and her *assistant extraordinaire*, Martin Biro. Audrey, for once again taking a chance on one of my totally out-of-the-box ideas, and Martin, for keeping me in line, though not necessarily in the box.

And, as always, to my fantastic agent, Jessica Faust, of Book-Ends LLC, who not only sees the forest through the trees but manages to keep me on the right path. Thank you.

1

If she'd had her human body—the one she loved with the violet eyes and long dark hair—Zianne would have wept. This one could only feel sorrow—not physically express it. She'd left Mac only moments ago—a few minutes for her and almost twenty years for him. It had been such a simple thing to make her nightly slip through time, passing from twentieth-century Earth and returning to the Gar's craft in its stationary orbit behind the twenty-first-century moon.

How had they discovered her absence?

She'd been so careful. Her fellow Nyrians had covered for her, yet somehow the Gar—their captors—knew. The Nyrian elders had warned her as soon as she materialized within the ship. They'd explained that her soulstone was locked away; that the Gar waited, ready to entrap her, should she come to claim it.

Once they knew which one of their captives had been stealing away and visiting Earth, they intended to make an example of her. She would die a very public and painful death, her energy slowly, painfully leached away until nothing was left.

Until even her soulstone crumbled into dust.

It was too soon. She and Mac were close, but she hadn't had time to teach him enough. The technology he was beginning to develop in Earth's year nineteen hundred and ninety-two was much too primitive. He'd had twenty years, but still, he couldn't possibly have learned enough to create the sophisticated equipment with the kind of power they needed to free Zianne and the few survivors of her race.

But she had no choice. She'd been away from her soulstone for twelve full hours. If she returned to the past, she'd use up what energy she had left. Her only hope—her people's only hope—was that somehow, some way, MacArthur Dugan had pushed Earth's technology far enough, fast enough, to have everything ready by now—*now* being twenty years later for Mac.

Had he loved her enough? Had he believed in her enough to embrace her goal as if it were his own? Did he still love her? It had been mere minutes for Zianne since Mac last held her in his arms, since he'd made love to her, but it had been twenty long years for her beloved Mac. Would he even remember her?

And if he remembered, would he forgive her for abandoning him without warning? At least she had hinted to him this might happen, that her absence might be discovered before their work was done. She'd worried that the truth might turn him away, but instead it had pulled him closer. He hadn't shied away from the truth at all—instead, he'd embraced her.

Embraced her cause.

He'd already guessed she wasn't human, that she was an alien being, so it wasn't a terrible leap to explain the rest, that she was one of the last few members of a dying race, a creature of pure energy given form through the power of his mind.

Most precisely, his amazing sexual fantasies, images so strong and true that they had given her a glorious body and so many wonderful *human* abilities.

Even tears.

He'd loved her then. She had to believe he still loved her. She had entrusted the entire future of her people to one brilliant man. A man she had fallen in love with despite the differences between them.

She would not give up hope. Her people could not abandon hope. With that prayer in mind, Zianne slipped into the engine room where her fellow captives surged and glowed, powering the Gar's vast starship with their sentient energy. Pausing near the heart of the ship, she sent her thoughts out to the ones who labored for their unrelenting masters.

I am returning to Earth. Mac may not have had enough time or enough knowledge to build the antennae and receivers for us. If he can't help us within the next couple of days, my energy will cease and I will die, but before I'm gone, I'll do my best to convince him to keep trying. I am certain he will do everything he can to save all of you. He's a good man. A loving man, but he's only human. He can only do so much.

She heard Nattoch's measured tones, the Nyrian elder who had trusted her to find a way to free them from bondage.

Dear Goddess . . . she hoped she had not failed.

Go with Nyria's blessings, child, and go with what soul energy we can share. You have done all you can and yet you continue to forge ahead. If you fail, your soul will return to our goddess. If you succeed, you will have saved these poor remnants of a once proud civilization. Our love goes with you. Our hopes and our dreams and what little strength you can carry. Now quickly, before you are discovered. Find your human, and bring us to our new home. Our refuge on Earth.

She might not be able to weep in this form, but her sorrow was every bit as real, her fear as profound. She felt it then, a powerful burst of energy as her fellow Nyrians fed her with what they could from their own souls. Shivering with the sensual wave of power flowing across her body, she took them into her, took their love and their generosity, and along with that, their hopes and dreams.

With a final glance at the few remaining members of her kind, Zianne slipped through the molecular structure of the ship into the endless darkness of space.

She searched for the one mind strong enough to call her.

Searched for him now, in the present.

It took longer than she'd expected. He was changed. Older now. Weary. So weary and alone, and yet he thought of her. Still loved her, longed for her, and dreamed of her.

With hope driving her onward, Zianne linked her energy to his, and followed the patterns that would take her back to Earth. Back to an Earth twenty years older than the one she'd left this morning.

Back to MacArthur Dugan. An older, more jaded, more cynical Mac Dugan, who, with Nyria's blessing, might hold the power and the knowledge to give her people their last shot at a future.

Rodie Bishop paused in the open doorway to the large conference room, hesitating as she might not have done just a few months ago. She forced her active mind to still, to expand and experience. The room was big and sterile and almost empty—a typical corporate meeting room designed to hold hundreds, not a mere handful. She'd been here for five prior meetings over the past two months. Those other times the room had overflowed with people, had been filled with a different energy.

This time, the occupants were changed, the mood altered, and so she used this new sense she had that occasionally allowed her to check things out on a different level. A more intimate level. Casting her thoughts forward, she studied the room and the few souls in it as she worked up the courage to go inside.

Stupid, really, the way she'd become such a damned coward almost overnight, but a violent assault on her way home from work had really done a number on her—that along with the world's worst breakup. Of course, that had been so bad it was almost funny.

Maybe someday she'd actually be able to laugh, though she couldn't see it all as bad. Not when the combination of crap had somehow kick-started this weird thing in her head. A new ability that allowed her to sense danger, to pick up on the various kinds of energy swirling about.

She'd always been a perceptive sort, but now? Now she took perception to an entirely new level that was beyond exciting. She just wished there was someone she could tell about it, but who the hell would believe her? Most of her acquaintances already thought she was nuts.

Casting her thoughts wide, she felt nothing that raised any concerns. She took a deep breath, focused on one of the empty seats, and stepped into the room.

So weird that there were only three others here, especially since the room was big enough to seat so many more. Though the gatherings had grown smaller each time, she'd still expected it to be more crowded. It was, after all, the final meeting. Tonight they'd find out who had been selected.

There was a young man in the third row, but he looked half asleep, slouched down low in the uncomfortable-looking chair with his long legs stretched out in front. His shaggy dark hair had fallen over his forehead so she couldn't really tell what he looked like, but the way his worn, paint-stained Levi's molded to his long legs and well-defined package caught her interest.

At least she was thankful the bastard who roughed her up only wanted her backpack and laptop. She wasn't sure how she'd feel if the attack had screwed up her appreciation for sex.

No, that was functioning as well as ever, thank goodness, in spite of the assault that happened shortly after that little incident with the ex-boyfriend. If catching him in her own bed with both a woman and another man hadn't screwed up her libido, she figured nothing would.

And it was almost worth it for the satisfaction she'd gained from running all three of them out of her apartment, so terrified of her Taser they'd escaped the place stark naked.

If only her neighbor hadn't caught the entire thing on his mobile phone. Unfortunately, that was the sort of video just crying out for mass distribution on the Internet, but the best part was, he'd focused on her naked ex-boyfriend, the woman, and the other guy. Rodie'd been little more than a mass of swirling dark hair and the zapping buzz of the Taser gun.

Yep. She bit back a smile. Some bad things were worth going viral, if only for the joy of revenge. She grinned for the first time today, and took another appraising look at the cute dude. Opened her senses to him. Nothing on the mental level beyond a soft buzz. Maybe he was napping, but she didn't really care. On second glance, he looked young—hardly out of his teens.

Jailbait wasn't on the menu.

Her gaze slid over to a really cute white girl in the front row. She had long brown hair—board straight—a perfect little nose and a big smile. Another kid. She looked too damned perky, as far as Rodie was concerned, but there was always one in every crowd.

Of course, now that she'd hit thirty, Rodie figured everyone looked younger than she did.

The only other person already here, another guy, sat in the very back row. Dark hair, long legs, and something about him that was so blatantly carnal she caught herself sliding her tongue over first her upper lip, then the lower. Hell, there was no reason for it—he was just sitting there with his back to her, but damn!

He'd turned his chair and had it tilted back on two legs with his feet planted firmly on the wall. Cords from his earbuds disappeared over his shoulders. It looked like he was listening to his iPod while playing with his phone.

Now this was a guy who made sense, even if her reaction to him didn't. He was here, but controlling his own space. She liked that. Forcing herself to look away, Rodie shoved her hands into her back pockets, sauntered into the room, and took a seat on the far side, fifth row back, so she could watch the door.

This couldn't be everyone. When they'd started the selection process, there'd been over a thousand applicants, originally meeting in three separate groups. Even though a lot of them had been dropped, there'd still been almost two hundred people the last time they'd met. Where the hell were they?

As Rodie scrunched into her chair, a tall, slim black girl, much darker than Rodie, paused in the doorway, looked around, and then stepped into the room. She practically oozed class, and Rodie bet the chick's snazzy little handbag alone probably had set her back a good six hundred bucks. She walked with long, purposeful strides and took a seat toward the back, on the side opposite the guy with his feet on the wall.

It appeared they were all staking out their territory.

Opening her senses, she realized the buzz of energy in the room felt charged—more like there were dozens of people here rather than just the five of them.

Rodie checked her watch. Four minutes after seven. Where the hell was everyone else?

A new guy strode into the room. No hesitation there. Rodie sat up and watched him. This one acted like he owned the place with his tousled dark blond hair almost artfully disarranged and bright blue eyes darting from one person to another as he checked everyone out. Another gorgeous guy? Damn . . . did the men get picked for their looks? He caught her watching him and flashed a bright grin, walked across the room, and sat a couple of seats away.

He leaned close and whispered, "Where is everyone? I'm never early, so . . ."

Rodie laughed. "I was just wondering the same thing."

At that moment, an older man stepped into the room and the energy sizzled. Rodie's breath caught in her throat. This guy actually did own the place. It was him—MacArthur Dugan—in the flesh. And oh, mama, but it was mighty fine-looking flesh. She flashed a grin at the guy next to her and straightened in her seat, eyes forward.

She'd heard so much about Dugan that she felt like she knew him, but she'd never actually seen the man in person. The prior meetings had all been run by other people within his company, but she'd followed media reports of Dugan for years. He was considered a god in the industry, his every move fodder for the evening news. In media clips he was usually at an opening of some play or speaking in front of Congress or doing something that required a suit and tie.

Sometimes he had a beautiful woman on his arm; other times he traveled with a well-known, openly gay news anchorman. Nils something-or-other. Tall guy, blond hair. Also gorgeous. No one knew if the two had something going, if Dugan was gay or straight, but as hot as the dude was, as much money as he had, did it really matter?

It appeared he was alone tonight, and he'd discarded the suit and tie for a more relaxed look. Holy crap, but the dude even looked hot in worn jeans and a sleeveless T-shirt.

The guy even had tats. A big stylized cross of some kind spread from his right shoulder almost down to his elbow. He was definitely better-looking than on TV, with that thick, dark-blond hair and absolutely brilliant blue eyes. Rodie knew he was in his mid-forties, but he didn't look more than about thirty or so. Probably all that money. Any guy rich as Mac Dugan had access to whatever it took to look hot.

He bounded up the four stairs to the stage, walked across to the podium, and glanced around the room. Then he frowned. "This won't do at all," he said. He crooked his finger overhead and pointed toward the door. "Follow me."

Rodie glanced at the guy beside her, shrugged, grabbed her backpack, and stood. Like a bunch of mismatched sheep, the six of them followed him through the door. Dugan waited just outside. "Break room's this way. It's a more intimate setting for what we need to discuss."

No one said a word, but they all followed him down the broad hallway into a smaller room with black granite counters, coffee machines, soft drink dispensers, and a tray of donuts that had probably been fresh sometime this morning. A large oak table with matching chairs all around dominated the space in the center.

Dugan took one of the chairs. The rest of them each found a seat around the oval-shaped table. Rodie glanced to either side of her. The smiley guy who'd been next to her in the first room was on her left; the one who'd had his feet planted on the wall sat on her right.

Good god, but she was surrounded by pheromones. At least earbud dude had removed the buds, turned off his iPod, and stashed his phone. Everyone appeared totally relaxed, but Rodie could feel the buzz, as if their curiosity was cranked up on high. She toned down her sensory abilities, thankful she'd at least learned how to do that much.

In the beginning, when this new ability of hers first appeared, picking up on everyone's mood had almost driven her off the deep end. She was still learning how to work it, how to make it work for her, not against her. She forced herself to relax, glanced at Dugan, and waited. He smiled at her and then planted both his hands on the table.

"This is better," he said. "I'm MacArthur Dugan, and you six are the only ones to make the cut out of over a thousand original applicants. I appreciate your willingness to hang on through what has to have been a frustrating and seemingly interminable selection procedure, but all those questions and tests were essential to my project. It's my hope that you'll decide to stick with it once you hear the details."

Wow. Rodie took a new look at the others and wondered what the six of them had that the other thousand-plus didn't.

Earbuds raised his hand.

Dugan acknowledged him with a nod. "Yes, Mr. Black. What do you wish to know?"

"You said there were over a thousand who applied. On what criteria were we selected? And what, exactly, have we been selected for?"

Dugan grinned at all of them and then focused on Black. "Why don't you introduce yourselves first and tell us why you applied, who you are, what you do. Then I'll explain everything, including the project. You go first. Age, why you're here, that sort of thing."

The guy nodded. "Fair enough. I'm Morgan Black. Thirty-five years old. Self-employed landscaper." He gazed at Dugan as if he were daring him to say something. "I clean up dog shit, pull weeds, and mow lawns."

Oh, my, but he had a sexy voice, and she loved the obvious chip on his shoulder. She could so relate, but that voice! So deep she felt the timbre of it touch her inside like a physical stroke between her legs. All her vaginal muscles clenched, leaving her so intent on the sensation, she barely heard what else he said.

"I got interested when I heard the rumor going around that this was closely tied to the SETI project."

"What's that?"

Rodie almost snickered. Wouldn't you know it, the classy black chick didn't have a clue. Probably spent all her time and energy finding the right shoes to match her handbags.

Dugan didn't seem to mind answering such a dumb question. "SETI, Miss Pearce, stands for the Search for ExtraTerrestrial Intelligence."

"Aliens?" She glanced at the others. "Really?"

"Really." Dugan chuckled. "Why don't you introduce yourself, tell us why you're here?"

She looked nervous. "Well, it's not to look for aliens." She laughed. "At least it wasn't. My name's Kiera Pearce. I'm twenty-eight, an attorney. I was originally hired by a group of religious fundamentalists that wanted me to find a legal basis to shut your project down."

She glanced at Mac Dugan and smiled. "Obviously, I couldn't find any way to file a lawsuit that wouldn't be considered frivolous, but when I saw that the ones you selected would spend six well-paid months living in the mountains, I figured it sounded like an interesting change of pace." She shrugged and laughed again. "I filled in the application more out of curiosity than anything. I never expected to be selected." Still smiling, she added, "For the record, no one said a thing about aliens."

"Aliens or not, you're actually highly qualified," Dugan said. When she raised her eyebrows, he added, "I'll explain in a moment." He looked at Rodie. "Ms. Bishop?"

Clearly, he'd done his homework. He knew all their names. She fought the impulse to squirm in her seat like a little kid. Something about Dugan got to her on such a visceral level that it was totally disconcerting. She took a quick breath. Let it out. Reached for whatever composure she could find.

"I'm Rodie Leigh Bishop. I'm thirty. I got my masters in computer science at Stanford. I'm in telecommunications, the research and development part, currently on a leave of absence for personal reasons."

She wasn't about to explain that the combination of assault and robbery just after the ex-boyfriend fiasco had really knocked her for a loop. She needed this. Needed to shake up her life a bit and get her confidence back, but Dugan was smiling at her, and it was obvious he wanted more.

"I applied because I'm fascinated by the telescope array you've been building," she said, which was part of it. "I mean, it's huge, even bigger than the Allen Array. From what I've read, it's a lot more sophisticated, though I couldn't find out everything I wanted to know." She flashed Dugan a bright grin. "Security on this project has been amazing, but you're going to tell us all about it, right?"

Smiling mysteriously, Dugan nodded. "Eventually." He glanced at the young-looking guy who was slouched in his seat, all bored attitude and shaggy hair. "Mr. Paisley?"

The kid sat up. "Uh . . . Cameron Paisley. I'm thirty, an artist." He glanced at the others and added, almost defensively. "No degrees. Lots of art classes, though, and I make a living."

Rodie got caught on his age. Sheesh . . . the kid looked about seventeen, tops. Even younger when he sort of puffed up his chest and added, "I do paintings of impossible landscapes."

"But are they really impossible?" Dugan steepled his fingers and rested his chin on his fingertips. "Or are they places you've possibly traveled to in your dreams?"

Rodie glanced at the kid. The attitude was gone. He stared wide-eyed at Dugan.

Dugan merely let the question hang there a moment. Then he turned to the blond dude. "Mr. O'Toole?"

"Finnegan O'Toole. Finn." He flashed a cocky grin that seemed to take in all three of the women. "I'm thirty-three, I can fix anything that breaks, including your satellite dishes. I've had every job imaginable from oil-rig roustabout to bank teller to a three-year stint as a professor of physics at UC San Diego. And yes, I do have a doctorate in applied physics. However, I'm mainly here to check out the women."

"I see." Mac chuckled. "Good enough, I guess. I'm sure we

all appreciate your honesty, if not your goal." He flashed a grin at the man. "Though I guess we can always use a good repairman."

Still smiling, Dugan shook his head and turned to the last one in the group, the young-looking white girl. "Miss Connor? Your turn."

She blushed. Rodie almost rolled her eyes. Talk about deer in the headlights . . .

Then she sort of shook herself, sat up straight, and spoke with a lot more self-confidence than Rodie'd expected. "I'm Elizabeth Connor. I prefer Liz or Lizzie. I'm twenty-five years old, and I'm looking for something new. I've specialized in satellite communications for the aerospace industry, but I'm really tired of the sexism and ageism in my field. I've been following the development of Mr. Dugan's project and actually had some input for the telescopes, receivers, and antennae. I'm thrilled to have been selected for this. Thank you, Mr. Dugan."

"You're more than welcome, Lizzie. I know you'll be an asset to this team. And, by the way, let's drop the 'Mr. Dugan' stuff. I probably won't be able remain on site all the time once you guys are comfortable with the job, but we'll be living and working together as a team enough to drop the formalities. My name's Mac, though I imagine there'll be times when it's something else, hopefully only muttered quietly under your breath."

He smiled at their laughter, then focused on Lizzie again, and Rodie tried to hide her disbelief that this little girl could be an asset to anything more sophisticated than the next routine on the cheerleading squad. Twenty-five? She looked about twelve.

Almost as if he'd read her mind, Dugan looked right at Rodie. "Lizzie may look young," he said, turning quickly to smile at the girl. "And she is, but she's also an amazing young woman. Lizzie was homeschooled before entering Georgetown at fifteen. She completed her undergraduate work at eighteen and had her doctorate in astrophysics from Princeton before she turned twenty-one. Lizzie's been heavily involved in research and development on the Mars project for the last four years. When she talks about satellite communications and design, it's for the new Mars lander that's under construction."

Rodie shot a quick glance at the girl. Then she chuckled. "Okay. I take back my wayward thoughts. Pretty impressive."

Lizzie blushed and mumbled something. Rodie thought it was a thank you. Curious, she asked, "What do you mean by ageism? I thought that was something directed at the over-fifty crowd."

Lizzie shrugged and shook her head. "You're doing it right now—looking at me and thinking I'm just a kid. I was the only woman on my team, and the only member under thirty-five. In the beginning, more than ten years under." She squared her shoulders and gave Rodie a level stare. "I know I'm young, but I'm far from stupid. I got tired of being treated like the resident bimbo."

"Ouch." Kiera Pearce chuckled. "I ran into that in law. The good old boys' network is tough to deal with sometimes."

"I've run into it, too," Rodie said. "And you're right. I'm sorry for doing the same thing to you. I should know better."

"Thank you for that." Lizzie shot her a bright smile, and Rodie suddenly had a whole new appreciation for both women. A sisterhood, of sorts.

Amazing how a shared problem created its own camaraderie. "I finished my masters in computer science at Stanford the year I turned twenty." Rodie sensed they wanted to know more. Was that why she felt a need to explain more than she would under normal circumstances?

But then, what was normal anymore?

"No one took me seriously. I didn't know whether to blame my age, my gender, or my indeterminate race." She'd grown tired of explaining. No, she wasn't black. Wasn't Asian. Wasn't

Hispanic. She was just a mutt. A perfectly happy mutt, if the idiots who needed a label would just leave her alone.

"Or all three."

She glanced up at Morgan's dry comment, unsure whether he was teasing or agreeing or just making fun. "Or all three," she echoed. Screw him. She didn't really care.

He stared at her a moment. One corner of his mouth was quirked up in what could have been either a smile or a smirk. He held her gaze a moment and then turned toward Mac Dugan. "So. Are you going to tell us why we're here and the others aren't?"

Mac had been quietly watching them. Intently, the way you might study a lab experiment, was Rodie's first thought. The silent buzz in the room grew stronger.

Mac nodded toward Morgan. "I am. I'm guessing you've already figured out some of the main points in your favor. All of you are incredibly intelligent. Off the charts intelligent, if you want the truth. You're all powerful type-A personalities. Driven, creative, unafraid of trying new things. You're all leaders, which could create a problem, except I'm the alpha wolf in this little pack and you will defer to me."

"And why, may I ask, will we be doin' that?" Finnegan's question had a whole lot of Irish along with an obvious thread of steel running through it. Rodie sat back so she could better observe Dugan's reaction.

"Because, Mr. O'Toole, this is my project and my money. My ideas." Dugan grinned at all of them. Rodie almost laughed out loud at the feral, almost wolf-like look of the man.

"And because you signed a statement agreeing that I was the one in charge and that all final decisions would rest with me when you filled out the original questionnaire. If you don't like it, you're welcome to leave." He folded his hands on the table and his gaze slowly swept over each of them.

No one moved.

"You've also got creative minds and you're physically healthy. That was important—no genetic health problems or weaknesses, no communicable diseases, venereal or otherwise. Your psychological profiles show no sign of major neuroses or other mental issues. Plus, the women have all agreed to implants for birth control, which you ladies will need to take care of by tomorrow. We have a clinic here on the main campus." He shrugged at the surprised looks from the guys. "What do you expect? I'm not about to put six sexually active, extremely attractive young adults together for six months and risk unwanted pregnancies."

He continued with his assessing gaze moving slowly over the six of them. "There's another thing you all have in common. It's probably the second-most important ability."

Now he focused on each of them in turn. Rodie held his gaze when he got to her. A shiver raced along her spine, a sense of knowing. Of some weird connection to the man, even though she'd never met him before.

And she knew. Just like that, as clear as glass, she knew what trait they shared. "You tested us for psychic awareness, didn't you?" She almost laughed as Dugan's smile grew. "I bet we all scored really high on the extrasensory perception part of that questionnaire."

"You were just in my head, weren't you? Telling me that we tested off the charts for ESP." Cameron's sulky attitude was gone. He laughed, staring open-mouthed at Dugan. "You just used telepathy with me."

Every single one of them—including Rodie—stared wide-eyed at Mac. She almost snorted when Cameron's head suddenly jerked one way and then the other, catching everyone's amazed expressions. Then he narrowed his gaze on Dugan again. "You talked to all of us. You were in our heads at the same time. How?"

Mac Dugan leaned back in his chair with a huge, obviously satisfied grin on his face. "The same way you're all going to be able to communicate with each other. Each of you has strong telepathic abilities. You merely lack the training."

"How does this fit in with the telescopic array you've built, assuming this entire process has to do with the array?" Rodie could still feel the mental touch of Mac Dugan's words in her mind. It was a disturbingly intimate sensation. Maybe she wasn't dealing with the assault or the boyfriend incident as well as she'd thought, but those things had happened weeks ago. Why was she thinking of them now? "ESP and big satellite dishes? I don't get it."

"First of all, yes, this is all about the array. As I said, telepathic ability is the second-most important trait you share. The first is more personal." Once again his gaze caught each of them independently, and the corner of his lips tilted slightly. "You are all, to one extent or another, sexually active and sexually very creative, very free about your sexuality. Mr. Black lives openly as a bisexual. He's had a number of short-term relationships with both sexes over the years. Kiera, you've been married, briefly. You're now divorced, but you said you identify as lesbian, maybe bi. You, Mr. O'Toole, wrote on your application that you consider yourself entirely heterosexual. You also identify yourself, and confirmed it a few moments ago, as a sexual predator." Dugan chuckled. "Pretty ballsy statement, if you're serious. Point being, you all have robust sex lives, and according to the tests we've run and the forms you've filled out, amazingly detailed sexual fantasies. With the telepathy, you have the ability to project those fantasies."

Lizzie snorted. She covered her mouth with her hand and glanced at Rodie and Kiera. "And with the array, we have the ability to project those fantasies into space." Laughing harder, she snapped her fingers. "Now that should bring any horny aliens in the universe racing our way. Wicked amazing!"

Laughing so hard she could barely catch her breath, Rodie glanced at Lizzie and started giggling again. This was so not what she'd expected, and it was obvious she wasn't alone. All of them were laughing and cracking wise.

All except Morgan. She caught the frown, sensed his anger as he settled his chair back on all four legs and slapped his palms down on the table. A little shiver raced across her spine. Damn, but the man was hot. Even more so when he was pissed off.

"You are fucking kidding me." He glared at all of them, growling in that deep, sexy voice of his. "You've pulled all of us together based on our ability to broadcast sexual fantasies? That's the stupidest thing I've ever heard."

"Actually, Morgan, it's not. Hear me out." Mac Dugan shoved back his chair and stood up.

Rodie sensed the alpha wolf had just raised his hackles and growled. The laughter stopped. Every single one of them sat straighter in their chairs and paid attention. Rodie took a quick glance around as another shiver snapped across her spine. Even Morgan appeared to have backed off.

The easy smile was gone from MacArthur Dugan's face. He shoved his hands into the pockets of his jeans and his gaze flicked from one to the next. And then, in a few terse words, he changed everything Rodie had ever thought about space and life on other worlds—and the power of the human mind.

2
_____

The energy in the break room was positively mind-blowing. Mac stood there for a minute without moving, but when he looked at the six young people in front of him, he felt like pumping his fist in the air and shouting.

They might not realize it, but he had his dream team.

An absolutely perfect team.

He'd never been surrounded by so many brilliant minds. Not in the classes he'd occasionally taught at Stanford, not in the research and development meetings held here in this same building, headquarters of the company he'd first envisioned with Zianne—their company, known around the world as Beyond Global Ventures, or BGV.

Only when he'd been with Zianne had he experienced this kind of connection. The thought slammed into him, left him shaken—these six reminded him of Zianne. Of her power, her strength, and her amazing mind. Their thoughts were so bright and strong, their questions tumbling one over the other, and yet at this moment, with him standing here before them, they were open. Receptive. Even Morgan was curious and waiting, despite his skepticism.

Mac wished he could tell them the truth, but they weren't ready. Soon. Soon he would tell them everything. But for now, he would merely whet their curiosity. Convince them that he wasn't crazy, that he really was offering them a chance to touch the minds of an alien race.

"I know you have questions because I hear them." He nodded at the varying expressions flitting across their faces. "Yes, I can hear and see your thoughts. Not crystal clear, but I do read them well enough to know that you're seriously wondering whether I'm completely crazy or just mildly nuts."

He folded his arms across his chest and perched on the counter beside the espresso machine. "I can assure you, there is no need to call the men in white coats."

Damn, but a good, strong drink would go great about now.

He glanced at Morgan Black and bit back a laugh.

"Morgan, I see that you and I are of a like mind. Believe me, if I had a bottle of Jack Daniel's within reach, I'd be pouring a double shot for each of us." He spoke over Morgan's soft "Holy shit," and added, "I should have planned ahead."

Leaning forward with his feet resting on the back of his chair, he planted his elbows on his knees and rested his chin in his hands. His memory of Zianne's beautiful smile, as clear now as on the last morning he'd seen her almost twenty years ago, settled in his mind. He ached for her now with as much pain as he'd felt when he first realized she wasn't coming back.

When he'd finally accepted that she wasn't returning because she couldn't, he knew it meant just one thing—her nightly escapes to see him had been discovered by her captors. His only hope now was that they hadn't killed her. That the Gar were still in orbit behind the moon, still within reach.

That the remaining Nyrians—including Zianne—were alive.

He sighed and focused on the six brilliant young men and

women watching him so intently. Six minds that were the hope of an entire race of alien beings, maybe even the hope of this whole damned world.

His hope as well, and with luck, his salvation.

For some reason, he thought of Dink—Nils Dinkemann, the one who'd been his closest friend and, with Zianne, his lover. God, it was so long ago. He'd been even younger than most of these kids. In so many ways, he and Dink had been little more than children, still finding their way, but they'd made a great team. Mac, Dink, and Zianne—a computer nerd, a young man searching for his sexual identity, and an immortal creature from another world. Ageless. Brilliant, and beautiful.

He still saw Dink on occasion, but damn it all, he missed Zianne so much he ached.

"There are some things I can't tell you right now," he said, shoving his memories aside. "Things that would make little sense out of context, but that you will learn once we reach the site. I can tell you that intelligent alien life does exist. I can promise that you will be contacting these life-forms, hopefully within the next few days, and that they will reply to you.

"That connection is the purpose of this entire project, which is similar to SETI, but not officially part of it. Once you sign on for the initial six-month program, you will be the core members of the DEO-MAP project, an acronym for Discovering Extraterrestrial Organisms through Mental Acuity and Projection."

He gazed from one person to the next, knowing their lives were going to change over the next few days, weeks, and months. He sensed their skepticism, but he also realized their minds were wide open, their curiosity spiking off the charts. "I am handing you the vehicle to connect with alien minds. All I ask of you is the power of your sexual energy, which is the strongest karmic force in existence. Give that freely, without reservation, and I promise, you will make contact."

"How do you know this?" O'Toole had an almost fevered look in his eyes. Mac saw his thoughts, spinning in so many directions it was obvious none of them were registering.

"I know this, Mr. O'Toole, because I have made contact. I have spent time with, have spoken with, and have learned from an alien being."

He didn't tell them he'd fallen irrevocably in love with that alien being. Not yet. They'd know soon enough, but at their muttered gasps of surprise and disbelief, he sat back and planted his hands on the counter. "I am a very wealthy man, as all of you probably know. I have gained my wealth over the past twenty years through my innovative software and hardware developments. My inventions, my unique discoveries . . ." He smiled and shook his head. "Did you ever wonder how I know the things I know? How the technology I developed was so far ahead of the curve?"

Kiera Pearce stared at him, wide-eyed. "You're saying that you learned all that stuff from aliens?"

"I'm saying, Ms. Pearce, that you will all be learning things you never imagined possible. You will see things you thought only existed within the realm of science fiction and fantasy. All you have to do is agree to join me on the most amazing adventure of your lives. Become a member of my dream team, and I promise to show you things you never in your wildest fantasies believed could exist. I will, quite literally, take you where no man—or woman—has gone before."

Mac poured a shot of Jack Daniel's, stared at the glass, and then tipped the bottle again and made it a double. He stared out through the big plate-glass window with the view of Silicon Valley spread out below. The last couple of days had been hell. Waiting for the team members to tie up their lives in order to join the project was killing him, and time had dragged.

Over a thousand applicants, and only six of them had the

skills he needed. He'd originally thought he'd be turning away qualified people, but instead he'd ended up with exactly the number he needed. Hopefully, that was a good sign.

An omen of success.

But what if some of them decided against going? Would any of them drop out at the last minute, figure he was nuts and they wanted no part of his stupid project? Shit. He couldn't think like this. Not now, not when he was so damned close.

He focused on the lights spreading across the valley and searched for calm. *Impossible.* Not with his heart pounding and his mind practically tied into knots. Tomorrow was the beginning.

"Or maybe it's just the fucking end." He tipped the glass back and took a big swallow, choked down the fiery liquor, and breathed deeply through his nose. Getting drunk probably wasn't the smartest thing, not with the long drive tomorrow, but he knew he'd never fall asleep sober.

He'd come home from the office tonight, still wound tight after talking to the kids a couple of nights ago. He was energized by their excitement, tired of waiting, and ready to head out *right now.* He'd grabbed a bite to eat, showered, and realized he was wide-awake. Put his jeans back on along with a warm flannel shirt and poured his first drink.

It wasn't going to be his last.

He upended the glass and finished off the rest of the Jack, stared at the empty glass a moment, and then refilled it. Grabbed the bottle and stepped out on to the deck, flopped down in one of the redwood chairs, and stared at the stars.

He hated to admit it, but he was living proof a heart really could break.

"Are you up there, Zianne? Did you realize, when you left my bed that last morning, that you weren't coming back? I can't imagine you knew and didn't tell me, so I have to believe that somehow, something went terribly wrong."

The stars blurred and his eyes stung. Angry, frustrated, scared half to death, he ran his arm across his face, wiped away the tears he'd not allowed to fall for almost twenty fucking long years. Twenty years. It seemed almost impossible now.

He'd been drunk the first night she came to him. God, it was still so clear, like it had happened yesterday. She'd just appeared out of nowhere—naked in his shower, her long dark hair swirling over her shoulders, her violet eyes sparkling, her lips . . . oh, damn, her lips were like a dream, which was exactly what she was—his fantasy woman brought quite literally to life.

He'd imagined her, described her to Dink while they'd gotten quietly drunk that night. First Dink had given Mac a perfect description of his fantasy lover, which, as Mac had expected, described him perfectly. Mac had described Zianne, a woman created totally out of his fantasies. Not an hour later, she'd materialized on her knees in his shower, perfect down to the long dark hair and violet eyes.

He'd never forget how one minute she wasn't there, and the next she was kneeling in front of him, taking him in her mouth and giving him a blow job unlike anything he'd ever experienced.

He didn't learn until days later that the power of his imagination—his sexual fantasy—had given her form and substance, but her intelligence, her heart, and her amazing inner beauty had been all her own. That night had marked the beginning of the most amazing four months of his life.

Four months of Zianne, of learning who and what she was, and even more important, discovering just who he was, what he was capable of, how his mind worked.

Four amazing months that would shape the rest of his life, which prepared him for the challenge he faced now and would continue to face in the coming days.

But what if they failed? What if there was no one to contact? What if the Gar had discovered Zianne's subterfuge and pulled their huge star cruiser out of orbit, had disappeared into space, too far for Zianne or her people to connect with Earth?

Had she been left, stranded in space? Was she still alive?

Too much could go wrong. Might have already gone wrong. His mind spun in too many directions to pin down any particular problem to worry about, and then . . . "Well, shit. One more thing." He stared at a set of headlights winding up the long private driveway to his house. Where the fuck did they come from?

Who in the hell could have come through the locked gate? Only a couple of people knew the combination—his attorney was in Washington on business, and Dink had called just this morning from New York where he was shooting a news special about global climate change. No way either of them could be here.

Quietly, quickly, Mac stood and slipped inside, grabbed the .45 automatic he kept by the door, and went out on to the front porch. Standing under the porch light in full view of his unknown visitor, he waited while the headlights drew closer. He heard the soft growl of an expensive engine as the vehicle took the last switchback below the house and then rolled into the driveway.

Security lights flashed on as the vehicle pulled up to the garage, and recognition struck like lightning. Laughing, Mac opened the door and put the gun away. Then he strode quickly across the lawn as nationally famous news anchor and Mac's closest friend since forever, Nils Dinkemann, unfolded his lanky frame and crawled out of the little Mercedes sports coupe.

"You're supposed to be in New York!" Mac grabbed him in a tight hug and fought an uncharacteristic need to burst into tears. Damn, but he'd missed this guy.

Dink hugged him, and then stood back and looked him in the eye, something not that many men were tall enough to do.

"No, I need to be here. I didn't realize you were this close, that you're headed up to the site tomorrow. You're going for it, aren't you? You're going to find Zianne."

Stunned, Mac stepped back, out of Dink's grasp. "What? What do you mean?" He'd never told anyone the truth about Zianne, not even Dink. Never once had he given away her secret, that she wasn't just a beautiful, brilliant computer geek who'd loved him and then dumped him for no reason, that she was instead an alien creature from not only another world in another galaxy but from another time.

Dink shook his head. His smile didn't reach his eyes, and exhaustion marred his otherwise youthful appearance. "It's okay, Mac. You don't have to lie to me. We both suspected from the beginning that Zianne wasn't human." His lips tilted in that familiar grin Mac loved.

"It used to bug me, that you didn't trust me enough to tell me what you knew, but I figured you had your reasons, that Zianne had her reasons. When she disappeared . . ." He shrugged and shook his head. "You gonna invite me in?"

Mac stared at him, trying to take in the fact that Dink knew, had known all along. One of the top investigative reporters of all time, and yet he'd sat on a secret like Zianne? It made no sense, but Dink's profession was the only reason Mac had never said anything. As much as he loved the guy, he knew how important Dink's work was to him. How much he'd always loved ferreting out a story. It hadn't been worth the risk.

Except Dink knew. He'd known all along.

Mac nodded. Brushed a shaky hand across his eyes. "Yeah, I'm gonna invite you in. And you're going to get roaring drunk with me while I tell you a story you can't tell anyone, especially on the six o'clock news. Do I have your promise?"

He stared into Dink's silvery blue eyes and saw his own reflection in their depths. Dink just smiled at him—the same smile he'd given Mac when they were just little kids trying to stay sane in a totally screwed-up world.

A world where they'd each lost their parents much too young and ended up in foster care, tossed into a system that wasn't prepared for a couple of little boys with brilliant, totally screwed-up minds. They'd kept each other sane, in a few cases kept each other alive. Over the years they'd forged a link that not even Dink's unrequited love for Mac or Mac's love for Zianne could break.

Dink was looking at him now like Mac had taken leave of his senses. Then he sighed, and the sound spoke of so much pain, Mac really didn't want to dwell on it.

"I wish you could have trusted me enough to tell me the truth." Dink gazed into Mac's eyes, almost as if he could see his thoughts. "That hurt, but at the same time—ah, hell, Mac. Who's to say what I might have done while I was selling my soul to make it." He chuckled softly. "Well, I've made it now, so I think you can trust me. You know I'll do anything for you, Mac. Whatever it takes, but I'm not leaving you alone tonight."

He reached into the car and pulled out a well-worn leather travel bag, threw an arm over Mac's shoulders, and steered him toward the house. "And yes, I will get drunk with you, and I will listen to your story, and I will believe it, because I know that whatever you tell me will be the truth. And I promise to carry your secrets to my grave."

Mac shot him a quick glance. That was a new twist on an old promise. "And then what?" he asked, because there was something else going on, something he realized he wanted as much as Dink.

Dink kept walking, but he turned and shot Mac a grin that reminded him of some of the trouble they'd gotten into as kids. "Then we're going to get naked and we're going to spend the night fucking until neither of us can get it up again."

There was no answer to a promise like that.

They stepped into the house. Dink closed the door behind them. Mac took a deep breath, remembering. Twenty years ago, he and Dink had become lovers or, as Dink had described it, fuck buddies. While Dink had openly loved Mac, Mac had loved Zianne. Dink accepted it. He'd said he was happy with whatever Mac could give him. They'd only had sex a few times, but the best of those times had been with Zianne.

The three of them, together. It made Mac hard, remembering.

Then Dink went off to San Francisco for a shot at his dream to become a newscaster and investigative reporter, while Mac and Zianne started work on the projects they hoped would lead to the rescue of Zianne's people, the Nyrians, who were held captive on a ship in orbit behind Earth's twenty-first-century moon.

She'd risked traveling back in time to 1992 to find Mac when he was young enough and there were years enough to develop the technology they'd need to mount a rescue in 2012. She'd planned to work with him, juggling time while moving between Earth and the Gar star cruiser, but it hadn't worked that way.

Zianne had disappeared, and Dink's star had risen as he'd followed assignments around the world, reporting on wars and famines, international corruption and third-world politics; Mac had continued working on the project, working on DEO-MAP, knowing he had just twenty years to get it right.

Twenty years to bring Earth's technology to a point where he stood now—so close to attempting the rescue that had become his life's goal.

Not nearly as close as he now stood to Dink. They'd stayed friends all these years, gotten together whenever they could, but never again as lovers. Not since Zianne disappeared. Mac stared at his friend, fighting a smile that somehow seemed totally inappropriate. "It's been a damned long time, Dink."

His buddy shrugged. A curl of dark blond hair slipped over his forehead and his mouth curved up in that familiar, rakish grin that made him look twenty-six, not forty-six. "I know. Twenty years. But I've never forgotten. Not you, not Zianne, not the way you made me feel." He sighed and swept a hand across his forehead. "Look, I've been traveling for hours. I need a shower and we need to talk. Then later, if it feels right . . ."

Mac stopped in the hallway, turned, and cupped Dink's face in his palms. He felt the roughness of a day's growth of beard against his fingers, saw the exhaustion in his friend's eyes, the concern. And the love. Always, with Dink, there was love. "Damn you, Dink. It will always feel right with you. Always." Then he leaned close and kissed him, pressing his mouth against Dink's, obviously catching him by surprise.

He heard the leather bag hit the floor, felt the shift in Dink's body as he strained close, wrapped his arms around Mac, and held him tightly.

And kissed him back.

Mac hadn't kissed anyone with this much emotion, this much love, since Zianne had disappeared. The times he and Dink had gotten together had been as old friends, both of them ignoring the sexual tension that always simmered in the background.

Not tonight. He felt Dink's tongue against his lips, parted for him, drew him inside, and tasted mint and male, tasted the familiar flavors of long ago.

Finally, breathing hard, heart pounding, Mac broke away. "Get your shower. Have you eaten?" When Dink nodded, he said, "Good." Then he glanced at the bag on the floor. Cleared his throat, said as casually as he could, "Put your things in my room, okay?"

Dink smiled. Leaned over without another word and grabbed his bag, and headed down the hallway toward the master bedroom.

Mac watched him go, still breathing hard, his heart still pounding, but now his cock was straining against the zipper on his jeans. Twenty years seemed to melt away as he tasted Dink on his lips. They'd both been kids; now they were grown men. Men with histories, with a lot of life well lived. Then he thought of all he had to do tomorrow, of the long drive ahead. The project. The team.

And he put it all out of his mind. Took a long, calming breath, and followed Dink down the hallway.

The bedside lamp left most of the big room in shadows. Mac was waiting, sitting on the edge of the bed with a glass of Jack in his hand when Dink walked out of the bathroom wearing nothing but a dark green towel wrapped around his slim hips.

He paused in the doorway, whether for Mac to look his fill, or maybe to give himself a moment to consider what they were going to do tonight. For whatever reason, he stood there with the bright overhead light from the bathroom glistening off his wet hair. It was slicked back, framing his face, emphasizing the sharp cut of his cheekbones, the fullness of his lips, the dark brows and lashes around his spectacular steel-blue eyes.

This was so much more than the face the nation saw on the nightly news. This was a side of Nils Dinkemann that Mac knew very few were privileged to see.

Dink was and always had been a spectacularly beautiful man.

He still had a perfect body—toned and well muscled, as lean and fit as he'd been twenty years ago. More muscle, and the hair on his chest was thicker, darker than it had been, his eyes a bit more world-weary, but while he was Nils to the world, to Mac he would always be Dink, the one Mac had counted on during all those tumultuous years when they'd been so damned young, so terribly vulnerable.

The one he knew he could count on tonight. Dink grinned and walked across the thickly carpeted floor.

Mac handed him a drink. "Jack on ice. Hope that's okay."

Dink laughed. "It is, but do you expect to talk here, like this? Do I get to put my pants on?"

Slowly, Mac shook his head. "I thought we'd talk later. I know you—you won't pay attention if you think you're going to get laid." It was only a small lie. Mac hadn't been able to think of anything else. He'd fought the urge to join Dink in the shower. It had been all he could do to sit here, waiting impatiently until Dink had finally shut off the water and come to him.

Laughing, Dink took a swallow of the whisky. "You're right. So why are you still dressed?"

Mac shook his head once again, but he didn't look away. Kept his gaze trained on Dink's face and wondered what was going through that amazing mind of his. He'd never been able to read Dink. "I don't know. Started to undress, felt sort of foolish. Decided to wait."

Still clutching the towel at his waist, Dink slowly shook his head. He glanced around the room, focused once again on Mac. "Don't ever feel foolish with me, Mac. We've got too much history, too much between us for that."

Mac stared at him. So many images crashed into his mind, so many memories, and the words came spilling out, unfiltered and painfully honest. "I watch your show every night. Did you know that? I mean, I see you here the way you are now, standing in my bedroom wearing nothing but a towel with your hair all wet and slicked back, your eyelashes spiky, and I'm picturing you on the damned TV, not a hair out of place, makeup perfect, wearing a suit and tie." He laughed, feeling even more awkward.

Dink smiled softly. Not the practiced news anchor smile, but the one Mac remembered from long ago. His fingers moved nervously over the knotted towel. Water beaded on his shoulders and in the mat of hair on his chest. "Behind that desk, I'm wearing faded jeans with that suit, if it makes any difference."

Mac stared at him a minute, felt his heart rate speed up. His voice cracked, sounded unusually hoarse when he said, "There are nights, sometimes, when I picture you naked behind that desk. I've never forgotten what it was like between us, Dink. Never."

Dink sat beside him, enveloping Mac in the familiar smell of Mac's soap overlaying the subtle scent that was uniquely Dink. He stared at Mac for a moment and sighed. "I wasn't going to, but I have to ask. Have there been many others?"

Mac shook his head. "No. No men. Very few women." He felt foolish, admitting the truth, but he could always be honest with Dink, even when it hurt. About everything but who and what Zianne really was. He'd not been honest about that. He would, though. Tonight he'd tell him everything.

"Zianne was always there, in my head. I tried dating, but it was a long time after she left before I even attempted to go out with another woman. No good. Tried seeing a few women just for sex, but I was better off with my own hand than trying to fuck someone who wasn't her. I even thought, for a while, that I'd be better off if I tried to forget her."

He laughed, but his laughter choked off, like a sob. Not what he wanted at all. Not tonight. "That lasted about an hour. She owns my heart, Dink. She always has. But you?" He reached out and placed his fingers against Dink's chest. Felt the steady *ka-thump, ka-thump, ka-thump* beneath his fingertips. "You own a part of me that even Zianne can't touch. You have from the beginning."

Dink downed the drink in his hand and set the glass aside. Then he leaned forward and started working at the buttons on

Mac's flannel shirt. Mac watched him—not helping, just watching—and concentrated instead on the way Dink chewed on his lower lip, the intense focus he gave to each button.

He was as nervous as Mac. There was nothing now of the famous anchorman, the reporter who'd terrified Mac with his stories filmed in dangerous war zones around the globe, who sat before a camera and calmed a frightened nation with his smooth, unruffled approach to whatever crisis occurred. No, right now there was none of the polish or the finesse. He wasn't Nils Dinkemann, America's eye on the world. Not here, not now.

Not with his fingers trembling as he worked the buttons free down the front of Mac's shirt. Not with his audible swallow as he slipped the soft flannel over Mac's shoulders. Mac finished taking it off. Then he kicked off his shoes, unzipped his jeans, and slid them over his legs.

He'd skipped shorts after his shower earlier, and there was no hiding the erection that curved up thick and hard, almost touching his belly. Dink didn't say a word, though he had to know it was all for him. Because of him. He slid to the floor and grabbed Mac's thighs in both hands, leaned close, and nuzzled the thick, dark hair at his groin.

Mac closed his eyes and let the sensations course through him, but he wanted to watch. Had to watch.

He opened his eyes. Dink's were closed. He hummed softly as he ran his lips over the smooth tip of Mac's cock, a soft sound of pleasure as he licked and gently stroked Mac's sensitive skin with his tongue. Slowly, so slowly, spreading soft, sucking kisses over the silky crown, his fingers digging into Mac's thighs with enough pressure to leave bruises. Mac sighed and lay back on the bed with his legs over the edge, but he propped himself up on his elbows. Watching.

Dink took him deeper, sucked harder, used his teeth and tongue, his lips and his hands to give Mac the kind of pleasure he'd not experienced for the past two decades.

There were unexpected calluses on Dink's hands. Calluses that snagged lightly in the thick hair curling at the base of Mac's cock. Groaning, Mac collapsed his elbows, lay back, and arched his back. So close. He'd not expected to feel his control slipping this quickly, but he was so close. "Dink. I'm not going to . . ."

Dink pulled back. His cheeks were flushed, his normally silvery-blue eyes dark as midnight. "I know. I don't want to finish you yet." He laughed. "Hold on a minute."

He stood, loosened the towel, and let it drop. Mac sucked in a needy breath. Damn, Dink was even more beautiful now than he'd been all those years ago. Where he'd been so lean he was almost skinny, now his body rippled with well-developed muscle. His erection stood hard and proud, curving out from his sleek hips, thick and dark, with a single pearly drop at the tip.

Mac licked his lips, imagining the salty taste. Remembering.

Dink wrapped his fingers around his cock, squeezed tightly at the base, and then slowly stroked upward. Mac forced himself to look up, to watch the expression on Dink's face.

Dink was breathing through his mouth, eyes shut, body flushed with need, but he held himself for a moment, obviously struggling for control. After a moment, he let out a deep breath and grinned at Mac. "Close, damn it." Chuckling, he walked across the room to the bathroom and his overnight kit.

Propped up once more on his elbows, Mac watched Dink's reflection in the bathroom mirror as he reached into the kit, pulled out a small packet, and ripped it open. As Dink carefully sheathed himself, Mac sat up and wrapped his fingers around his own cock.

His erection was still damp from Dink's mouth. Hard and curving upward, the crown brick red from blood pounding its length. Veins pulsed, thick and ripe along his shaft. Cupping his balls with his left hand, Mac merely held himself, holding on but not stroking while his blood throbbed beneath his fingers in time with his thundering heart.

Just holding himself, waiting as Dink smoothed the condom along his full length.

Then Dink was back. His cock stood high, thrusting up out of a nest of springy dark curls, curving toward his flat belly. He carried a tube of lubricant in his hand.

The spit dried in Mac's mouth. It had been so long. Twenty years since . . .

Dink tossed the lube on the bed beside Mac; spoke Mac's thoughts aloud. "I've waited so damned long for this, Mac. I wasn't sure it would happen again, but I've hoped. Dear God, how I've hoped." He pressed his hand against Mac's chest and gently shoved. Mac lay back on the bedspread without any resistance.

Dink knelt between Mac's legs and once again used his mouth, nipping at Mac's inner thighs, running his tongue the length of his erection, suckling first one ball between his lips, then the other.

Mac groaned when Dink wrapped his lips around his sensitive crown, tongued the small slit at the end, and then sucked him deeper into his mouth. Dink groaned. Then he swallowed roughly as he worked the broad tip past the back of his throat.

Panting, fighting for control, Mac bent his knees and planted his feet on the edge of the bed, lifting his hips, forcing his cock deeper down Dink's throat. Dink took everything, swallowing him down, gently squeezing Mac's balls with one hand, with the other running his fingers along the crease of his ass.

The lube came next, and the slick slide of Dink's fingers over that sensitive ring of muscle almost took Mac over the top. Dink must have sensed how close he'd come once again. Slowly, he pulled back and slipped Mac's cock free of his mouth.

Then Dink sat back on his heels. "Up and over," he said. He took a deep breath, then another. "On your knees, Mac."

Mac obeyed. No questions, no hesitation. He knelt in the

middle of the big bed, arms folded with his cheek resting on his forearms, butt raised, and he remembered the first time they'd done this, how vulnerable he'd felt. How embarrassed, to have someone back there, looking at his ass like this.

He felt no embarrassment now. No, this was Dink and he trusted him with his life. With everything important to him. It was all good, and he waited, relaxing himself, preparing his body and mind for Dink's first thrust.

So hard to believe it had been twenty long fucking years. Fingers first. Long, slow strokes between his ass cheeks, then the coolness of the lube, the sensual slide of fingertips through the thick gel, gliding over millions of screaming nerves.

He moaned when Dink paused, slightly swirling a single fingertip over Mac's anal ring. Then he groaned with the long-remembered pain and pleasure as he felt first one, then two, then three thick fingers when Dink pressed them through Mac's taut sphincter, stretching tender tissues that hadn't had this kind of use for way too long.

Mac pushed back against Dink, concentrating on relaxing, on not fighting the intrusion. Welcoming the pain along with the dark rush of pleasure when Dink slipped his fingers out and pressed the sheathed head of his cock against Mac.

Pressed, and carefully pushed against him.

Mac grunted and involuntarily jerked against the burn of entry. "Oh, fuck. I forgot how that felt." He gasped when Dink chuckled. Then he forced himself to relax, pressed his cheek against his arms, and pushed back against the pressure, pushed until he felt the fiery stretch and give as Dink entered, the smooth, somehow forbidden pleasure as Dink's swollen cock slid forward and filled him.

His cock was thick and hard, larger than Mac remembered, but Dink moved slowly, carefully, until he was completely seated deep inside. Both of them sighed. Mac snorted a short bark of laughter, bit back the sound, and then almost laughed out loud at himself.

He'd needed that laugh. For a minute there, he'd wondered how well or even if Dink was going to fit.

Mac was still congratulating himself when Dink wrapped his lube-coated fingers around Mac's erection and began to thrust deep and slow, stroking his full length in time with each rhythmic penetration. In, out, and back in again, the rhythm took hold of Mac, the sense of fullness held him, engulfed him in pleasure, in a sense of homecoming he'd not expected.

This was Dink. The one he loved, the one who loved him. The man who knew all there was to know about MacArthur Dugan.

All except those details he would learn tonight.

Later. When they were both sated. When there was no longer this driving need to find completion, to fuck and be fucked, to love, to forget . . . and then to remember.

Dink's steady thrusts were coming faster now, his deep breaths harsh against Mac's neck, his balls slapping close up against Mac's ass. His cock filling Mac with heat and strength and a sense of connection Mac hadn't realized he'd missed so much.

Dink's fingers tightened around Mac's cock. His breath stuttered in and out of his lungs and he drove deep, hard and then harder still, taking Mac with him, both of them crying out, cursing and laughing as they climaxed. The two of them, in sync as they'd been in everything they did so long ago.

Max felt the hard pulse of Dink's cock deep inside, answered it with the thick rush of his own, spilling his seed over Dink's fist, feeling the hot splash against his own belly.

Coming and laughing, rolling to their sides still connected, bodies covered in sweat and semen, and in Mac's case, at least, face awash with tears.

They lay there, lungs heaving, hearts thudding in their chests, and Mac realized the fear was gone. The tension that had been his companion for so many long months as he struggled to find the perfect team, to finish the project, to do any one of a million things, was gone. Entirely gone.

Sated, at first he wondered if it was just the sex, but he knew better. It was the connection with his oldest friend, the only one who remembered. Dink had known Zianne almost as intimately as Mac. His memories were proof that she wasn't merely a dream, a sexual fantasy come to life. She was real—as real as the man who had made love to Mac while he'd made love to Zianne. The three of them, in bed together.

Born of fantasy, yet so very real. A time almost too good to believe, but it was a time shared. It had been amazing, but this was damned good, too. And lying there with Dink's arms wrapped around him, with Dink's cock still deep inside his ass, Mac told his friend all of Zianne's secrets. Told him about the Gar, the creatures who'd not only captured Zianne's people but had also destroyed her world.

A brutal race of aliens now hiding behind Earth's moon, considering ways to plunder the earth, to steal what this world had to offer unless Mac and his team of unsuspecting kids could stop them.

Stop them, and rescue the final remnants of an entire race of people held captive on an alien starship. It was the biggest story of his career—of his life—and Dink couldn't say a word.

He couldn't tell a soul what Mac was planning to do.

3

The sun was a brilliant orange ball shimmering through morning smog when Rodie stepped out of her cab in front of Beyond Global Ventures headquarters. She glanced at the sign in front of the main building and realized that *Beyond Global* meant something entirely different to her now.

Dugan really was talking about going beyond global with the DEO-MAP project. About as far beyond the globe as they could. She still couldn't believe she'd signed on for this, but how could she not have agreed to be part of Mac's team?

She paid the cabbie and handed him a hefty tip after he dragged her unwieldy duffel bag out of the trunk and dumped it on the curb beside her backpack.

Dugan had told them to pack for all climates. She didn't know jack shit about the site where they'd be working, other than the fact it was isolated, a hell of a long way from San Jose, and temps dropped well below freezing in winter.

It was already August—winter in the mountains wasn't all that far off.

"Hey, you're Rodie, right?"

She turned away from the cab driver and flashed a quick smile at the good-looking blond. "Yeah. And you're Finn, our resident sexual predator, if I remember correctly."

Laughing, he nodded. "At your service. Guess I'm never going to live that down, am I? Need help with that?" He gestured toward her heavy duffel.

"I do. Thank you. I tried to pack light, but . . ."

Finn gave an exaggerated groan as he lifted the bag. "Yeah, right. I can tell." He started toward the double doors. "We're waiting in the same break room as before, but this time the donuts look fresh. Dugan had security let us in. He'll be back in a few with our transportation, but he said to leave the heavy stuff just inside the doors."

"Is he driving?"

Finn shrugged as he carefully set the heavy bag with a pile of others. "I'm not sure, but it sounds like it. He said something about gassing up the monster—I'm guessing he must be."

"You must have gotten here early." She shot him a quick grin. "I thought you said you were never on time for anything."

Finn rolled his eyes.

Sparkling green. Damn. For being such a jerk, the guy was definitely a hunk.

"Generally speaking, but for this? I couldn't even sleep last night. All I could think about was getting started."

"Tell me about it." Rodie hitched her backpack over one shoulder and followed Finn down the same hallway they'd taken just three nights ago. Hard to believe they were leaving so soon—she'd barely had a chance to find someone to water her plants while she was away. Dugan had said he didn't want to waste time, but she still felt as if her head was spinning.

The door to the break room was open. She followed Finn inside.

"Hey, Rodie."

It took Rodie a moment to respond. "Kiera?"

Kiera Pearce didn't look anything like the sharply dressed attorney she'd met Wednesday night. Sturdy hiking boots, faded blue jeans, and a comfortably worn sweatshirt changed her from classy to laid-back, and with her long dark hair tied back in a ponytail and threaded through a Giants baseball cap, she was definitely a lot more approachable.

"Yep." Kiera spread her arms wide. "This is the real me." She laughed, and it was a deep, throaty sound that had Rodie laughing with her. "I get so tired of acting like a grown-up," she said. "I'm really looking forward to nothing but play clothes. Here's to blue jeans and sweats for the next six months." She raised her coffee cup in a toast. "We're just waiting on Cameron and Morgan. Lizzie's here somewhere."

"I'm here. What about our exalted leader? Has Mac gotten back yet?" Lizzie walked into the room and went straight for the coffee. "Morning, Rodie. You ready?"

"I am." Rodie took the cup Kiera offered to her. "Anyone know where we're headed?"

"To the farthest, northeastern corner of California. The northern reaches of the Warner Mountains."

Rodie spun around as MacArthur Dugan walked into the room. Like the others, he was dressed in comfortable jeans, a faded T-shirt, and sturdy boots.

"What's up there?"

He flashed a brilliant smile that Rodie felt right between her legs.

So not a good response to the boss.

"A little over a thousand acres that I bought about twenty years ago," he said. "Back when I first envisioned this project. We'll be at about seven thousand feet elevation and far enough from civilization that the air is some of the clearest in the country. I've built the satellite array on a high plateau where we won't have any interference from outside light or power sources.

Power lines are underground and everything is shielded so that we've got a clear shot at the sky."

He took a couple of swallows of his coffee. Then he rinsed the cup out in the sink and left it on the sideboard. "Cameron and Morgan are out front. Grab your bags. We've got well over eight hours of driving ahead of us. With stops for breaks and food it'll be at least ten hours travel time before we're there. Let's get this show on the road."

"Wow." Finn flashed Rodie a big grin as he grabbed up another bag. "A lot of cows gave their lives for this rig." His comment seemed almost sacrilegious as they waited beside the big silver Cadillac Escalade parked in front of the building.

Large enough to seat all of them comfortably on butter-soft leather, it appeared to have every accessory imaginable. The dash looked like something out of a high-tech control center with GPS and touch-screen maps, USB ports for their computers front and rear, and a backup camera and computer screen that must run directly off the battery—they were already lit up and blinking like the rig was preparing for takeoff.

Of course, a man with Dugan's reputation in the computer and software industry was bound to be wired no matter where he went, though at first glance, he really didn't look or act the part of a mega-billionaire computer geek. It was cool how approachable he seemed this morning. How normal.

Rodie'd fully expected him to have hired a driver. Instead, he and Finn were squeezing as much of the gear into the back of the SUV as they could fit. Morgan was the tallest, so he had the job tying more bags to a rack on the roof. There was a lot of typical guy talk, cussing and teasing, but they got everyone's stuff loaded and tied down in a matter of minutes.

Rodie grabbed a seat in the middle, while Kiera and Lizzie sat in the back. Mac stuck his head through the open window on the driver's side.

"Okay, ladies. Any last potty stops? I plan to drive straight through until we hit the rest stop north of Sacramento on I-5."

Kiera snorted. "You notice he only asks the women?"

"I saw that." Lizzie shrugged. "And so it begins . . ."

Laughing, Mac took his seat behind the wheel. "Don't come whimpering to me when you want to stop and there's nothing but a dry bush and no TP."

Rodie rolled her eyes. "He only says that because the guys can pee on the hubcaps. They don't need a bush."

"Or the TP," Kiera added. "We're fine. Let's go."

Cameron snagged shotgun, claiming he'd puke if he sat in back. Finn crawled into the rear seat and took a spot between Kiera and Lizzie. Mac raised one eyebrow and then laughed. "Starting in on the women already, Finn? Have you thought of trying a more subtle approach?"

Finn put an arm around Kiera's and Lizzie's shoulders. "Hell, Mac. You already blew my cover. It's too late for subtlety."

Kiera leaned around him and whispered, "I doubt he'd know subtle if it bit him in that tight little ass of his."

Lizzie laughed. Finn's eyes lit up. "You like my ass? Mac, Kiera likes my ass. See? It's working."

Kiera rolled her eyes. Rodie snorted, but the teasing definitely seemed to take the edge off. She glanced out the window and almost swallowed her tongue. Morgan had moved around to her side of the car to check something on the roof rack. His arms were stretched over his head and his T-shirt had come untucked, baring a perfect set of taut abs with a darkly inviting happy trail disappearing below his belt line.

The first thought that entered her head was rolling down the window and licking her way along that enticing dark path. Thank goodness the windows were electric and Mac hadn't turned on the ignition—yet. Holy crap. Taking a deep breath, she turned away from the window and stared straight ahead.

Rodie had no idea what it was about Morgan, but as far as

she was concerned, he absolutely radiated sensual appeal. He was pure eye candy to look at, but she really liked his attitude. He came across as pure bad boy—all mouth and swagger—but she was sure there was more substance underneath.

By the time he finished checking the ties on top she was practically humming with arousal. When he got in, Rodie scooted to the right and Morgan took the empty seat to her left, close to the window. Her first thought was that she wanted to lean close and just inhale.

Not good. Not good at all.

As soon as the doors were all shut, Mac started the engine and pulled out of the parking lot. It was barely seven. Rodie leaned back and planted her feet on the console between Mac and Cameron.

Any nervousness she'd felt earlier about taking this leap along with Mac Dugan and his merry band of oddballs had totally disappeared. In fact, this was the most relaxed she'd felt in weeks, and the thought flittered through her mind that the laid-back atmosphere might help her shed some of her baggage over the assault and the ex-boyfriend.

Wouldn't that be nice? Right. Sighing, she settled back for the ride as Mac expertly maneuvered through the heavy rush hour Bay Area traffic. It took them almost three hours to cover the distance between San Jose and Sacramento, where they headed north on Interstate 5 for the long haul to the exit that would take them into the mountains.

They all talked non-stop the entire way. Normally, Rodie wasn't all that comfortable with new people and new situations, but she was reveling in the connection she already felt with this group. The comfort level among them was so easy it felt totally bizarre. She'd never felt as if she fit anywhere, and suddenly she was surrounded by a bunch of geeks who actually seemed to *get* her. It had to be from their shared psychic abilities.

For the first time in her life, she honestly felt as if she wasn't the odd one in the group, since all the others appeared to be just as crazy as she was. Which made her wonder—if they were so perfectly in sync, did that make them all totally weird?

No matter. Even listening to Finn as he made his moves on Kiera and Lizzie was totally entertaining. One thing about the guy—he was definitely persistent. So far the girls were taking it all in good humor. It appeared they gave as well as they got.

The chatter died down as their surroundings grew more interesting once they got off the freeway and headed east into the mountains. Rodie hardly noticed. She'd been practicing her newly discovered telepathy, not that she was all that proficient, but talk about a bizarre combination of thought processes! Enough information from the others' thoughts flitted in and out of her mind that she was assured she wasn't going to be bored over the next six months.

Mac hadn't said much, though Rodie'd been almost preternaturally aware of him in the driver's seat. The guy absolutely radiated sex appeal, along with something else she couldn't really describe but certainly couldn't ignore.

It was more than charisma—more a sense of leadership that was undeniable. He hadn't been kidding when he'd said he was the alpha of this pack. Not even Morgan Black tried to push that boundary, and if anyone was going to, Rodie figured it would be Morgan. Of the three guys on the team, Morgan was definitely the one to watch—there was something dark and edgy about him. Something that made him terribly attractive to her.

And that voice didn't hurt a bit. Shit. She could sit back and listen to him talk for hours. She'd immediately tagged him as a guy who wouldn't walk away from a fight, and wouldn't have any problem with fighting dirty. He'd maybe lived harder than the rest of them, had to stake his claim to whatever he wanted in life, yet even as strong a personality as he had, Morgan still deferred to Mac as naturally as the others.

Her respect for Mac Dugan went up another notch.

Finn was cute, sexy, and funny and not kidding a bit when he'd said he was a sexual predator. The guy was constantly on the make, like it was as much a part of him as breathing. Before they'd gone a hundred miles, he'd managed to hit on all three of the women and hadn't backed off a bit when Morgan—and Rodie was almost sure he was kidding—told Finn to quit wasting his time on the women and check out the guys.

Finn had given Morgan a thoroughly assessing look, and then he'd turned his charms on Cameron. The poor artist didn't have a clue what was going on—either that, or he did one hell of an act. Rodie was still trying to figure him out, but he was definitely easy on the eyes. In fact, all four of the men—Mac included—were absolutely beautiful. Tall and lean, athletic without being over-muscled, hair a bit longer than the norm—pure eye candy. And smart. Damn, but they were all so smart, something that was every bit as sexy as their appearance.

If nothing else, Rodie figured she'd have plenty of fodder for sexual fantasy, which was, of course, what Mac wanted, right?

Lizzie'd been a surprise. She had a wicked sense of humor and no problem at all with being the butt of a joke—as long as she was free to turn it back on the jokester, which she did with a lot more finesse than Rodie'd expected.

The really weird thing was that Rodie found herself watching Lizzie and getting hot. She never jonesed over women, but for some reason she was feeling a powerful sexual vibe from both Lizzie and Kiera. Feeling it, and not fighting it.

That was, after all, more of what Mac wanted, right?

Kiera was smart and funny and not like any lawyer Rodie'd ever met. Of course, nothing about today had been as expected, not that she'd really had a clue what to expect. She'd thought she'd feel awkward with six complete strangers, but they'd laughed and teased and kidded around like they'd known each other for years. Even Mac, as quiet as he'd been, had joined in on occasion.

His zingers were always right on target, though Rodie had a feeling he had a lot on his mind. Of course, the guy had a ton of money invested in this project. Millions of dollars, and his success all depended on the six of them.

Six odd ducks good at sexual fantasy. Try putting that on a résumé, but it was something too powerful to ignore. Buzzing just beneath the surface of everything any of them said or did was that truly powerful sexual undercurrent. On occasion it had grown stronger, enough that Rodie's nipples beaded up and grew taut with arousal. Even her panties got damp, which was downright embarrassing. She wondered if any of the guys were hard, if anyone else felt the same thing.

And there was always that weird telepathy thing. Not that she could read anyone's mind—not clearly, anyway. But Rodie'd been aware of a connection with these guys—Mac included—unlike anything she'd ever felt in her life. And it wasn't the least bit scary. No, it was actually kind of comforting to feel a personal link like that, though it made her arousal even more pronounced.

She'd never thought of her brain as an actual erogenous zone in spite of what all the studies said, but having another mind touch hers . . . wow. Just, wow. Every once in a while she'd get an almost physical sensation from one of the guys, as if their thoughts were sliding over her mind—and on to parts beyond.

Like now? Was that . . . ? *Oh, shit.* So light she had to focus to find it, and then it was there, touching her mind so sweetly, so seductively. She shivered, aware that her clit was beginning to swell, that once again her panties were getting damp.

But who? It had to be one of the guys. One of them capable of a feather-light touch of pure sensation so intense that she tightened her thighs together to trap the feeling. Then she had to bite back laughter, wondering if she was going to spend the next six months with her legs locked together, or maybe just screwing anyone she could catch. Hell, with her luck, she'd end up frigging herself alone in her cabin. She'd always had a healthy libido, but the way she felt right now was so far off the charts she wasn't sure how to describe it.

Or if she even wanted to. Hell, she was already along for the ride—she might as well enjoy it. That thought had just slipped through her mind when the sensual feeling lingered, the sense of someone touching her became more pronounced, and her arousal flashed through the roof.

She bit back a surprised gasp as invisible fingers slowly parted her labia, softly stroked her clit. Her breath caught in her throat. She tightened her thighs again, pressing her knees close together when all she really wanted to do was spread her legs wide and enjoy.

Oh, man . . . this was real, not merely a fantasy of her own. This was definitely someone else touching her. Someone else slipping a finger deep inside, then using her own moisture to gently rub over her sensitive clit.

Talk about giving the term *mind fuck* a whole new meaning!

Finn was the most obvious, but she sensed that this was someone else, someone more subtle than the playful Irishman. Biting the insides of her cheeks to keep from panting, Rodie glanced at Cam. He seemed to be asleep in the front seat, his body perfectly relaxed. She cast out with her mind. At least she thought that was what she was doing, but it was hard to know if she was doing it right.

Nothing from Cam.

She chanced a glance at Morgan sitting quietly beside her.

From the intensity in his dark eyes—his gaze was locked on Rodie—to the bulge in the crotch of his faded jeans, she knew without any doubt at all it was his mind touching hers. His thoughts ratcheting up her arousal. His imaginary fingers caressing her clit, slowly slipping past her swollen lips, and curling deep inside.

She sucked in a sharp breath and stared at him, unblinking. He watched her just as intently, but his expression didn't change a bit, and she wondered if he even saw her, or if he was totally focused on whatever scenario played out in his mind.

Everything around them seemed to fade away. Kiera's and Lizzie's laughter over something Finn had said, the wind whistling through Cam's partially open window, the soft sound of something by the Dave Matthews Band on the SUV stereo system.

Rodie gazed straight ahead to hide her intent, but she wanted to send the same sense of arousal back to Morgan. First she needed a visual, so she imagined the hard root of his cock where it jutted from his groin. Then she pictured the wrinkled skin covering his balls, doing her best to sense how it would feel to wrap her lips around his sac, to slide her tongue along the silky skin over his erection.

Then she slowly turned her head, looked directly into his dark eyes, and let her thoughts fly—directly at Morgan.

He blinked. His head jerked back, and the link between them snapped. Rodie almost wept. Her vaginal muscles pulsed and clenched, searching for Morgan's lost mental touch. He'd left her hanging on the edge of climax, all sensation of contact gone.

Morgan stared straight ahead, his body rigid, everything about him shrieking *Don't touch.* She didn't look at him again. Not for a long time. Not as the road climbed ever higher into the mountains, as the voices in the seat behind her blended, one into the other with the soft music on the car stereo. She turned away from Morgan and stared at the thick forest passing by outside the window, trying not to think about that amazingly sensual touch she'd felt between her legs. She couldn't look at Morgan.

She wouldn't.

But they still had a long drive to get to the site.

* * *

"Hey, Mac? You gonna feed us sometime today?"

Lizzie poked Finn in the side. She'd discovered it was fun to touch Finn because he always responded, but his plaintive request had all of them laughing. Kiera stretched her long arms over her head and yawned. "I think the plan is to starve us into submission. We'll be easier to control."

"Submission?" Finn leered at Kiera. "I can do submission. You the domme?"

"In your dreams, Irish boy." Kiera laughed and elbowed him.

Lizzie bit back a chuckle. Instead, she gravely patted Finn on his hard belly. "It's okay, Finn. I'm good with a whip. I packed my fleece-lined cuffs, too."

"Holy shit." Finn leaned away. "I hope you're not kidding."

Lizzie just smiled.

"I hate to interrupt the foreplay, Finn, but there's a Subway just up the road." Mac checked the GPS map on the console. "Five more minutes. Can you children behave for that long?"

Lizzie laughed. "Hell, no, Mac. I didn't sign anything that said I had to behave."

Rodie poked Morgan with her elbow. "Reminds me of my mom telling me to quit complaining when I was a little kid."

Morgan looked startled by the contact. Lizzie thought that was pretty odd, because he'd seemed interested in Rodie from the beginning. Not that he was all that obvious about it. Morgan was much too cool to be obvious about anything—at least that was the vibe Lizzie'd picked up. Then he seemed to catch himself and he winked. It was the first sign of humor she'd seen in him.

"I know," Morgan said. "I think Mac's afraid of a mutiny."

"I'm terrified." Mac's dry comment had all of them hissing and booing in response, but since they were pulling up in front of the restaurant, focus changed immediately to food.

Curious, Lizzie kept her eye on Morgan and Rodie, but she managed to stay within touching distance of Finn. The guy was driving her nuts, but he was damned hot.

And he didn't treat her like a little kid.

Mac followed the six of them into the restaurant and waited in line while everyone ordered. His head was still full of the night he'd spent with Dink, and even if he'd wanted to forget, he had a constant reminder. His ass hurt. He probably should have thought about that when they'd spent the night fucking like a couple of kids.

Damn. He hadn't had that much sex in twenty years, but he definitely owed his buddy. He'd slept like the dead when they'd finally gotten the need to screw out of their systems, though Mac knew he'd never be totally free of the feelings he had for Dink.

No one else in his world cared as much for him as his old friend. Fame hadn't changed Dink a bit. More polish maybe, a maturity that hadn't existed twenty years ago, but the man was still the same loving friend he'd always been.

He'd known Mac needed him, and he'd made the long trip from New York to California to be there for him, even though it meant crawling out of bed at four in the morning and catching an early plane back to New York. Knowing Dink cared that much had left Mac feeling more than a little maudlin today. All the money in the world couldn't buy friendship like that. He'd known it on an intellectual level, but Dink had given the concept form and feeling.

Thanks to Dink's visit, Mac was seeing his project and his chances of success much more clearly. After talking about the project, laying his plans bare in front of his friend, things looked even better to him than they had at any time before.

The most interesting thing has been the way Dink took the news about Zianne, about her identity and the fate of her peo-

ple. He was curious—hell, Dink was curious about everything—but there'd not been a moment's doubt. No hesitation
over any of the things Mac told him.

Too bad the jerks at the Pentagon hadn't been as open.

Dink had given a solemn promise not to say a word to anyone, though he did insist that, once Mac had rescued Zianne
and the other Nyrians, if they ever went public, it was his story.

Just the fact that he said *when,* not *if,* made it easy to
promise.

Mac glanced up as the line moved forward. Lizzie had been
first with Finn right behind her. Now she reached for her purse
to pay for her sandwich. Mac had been curious about that,
whether they'd just assume he was paying—which he was—or
if they'd expect to pay for their own.

Little stuff like that told him a lot about people. None of
these guys expected a free ride. They were all going for wallets
and purses, which told him they were in it for the adventure,
not for a free ride. "Put your money away, Lizzie. I'm getting it."

She flashed him a quick smile. "Oh. Thanks, Mac. I didn't
expect that."

"Expect it. Don't forget, I own you guys for the next six
months. I figure that makes me responsible for feeding you."

Finn leaned over Lizzie and whispered *sotto voce,* "That's
why he picked such an expensive, upscale joint for lunch."

"Watch it, O'Toole, or I'll make you choose a little one."
Mac stared meaningfully at the foot-long sandwich the employee was carefully assembling in front of Finn.

Finn sighed dramatically. "C'mon, Mac. We all know bigger
is better."

Mac shook his head and chuckled. How could he possibly
answer that one without getting himself into trouble? If they
only knew how he'd spent the night. He bit back more laughter.

Dink certainly proved bigger was better.

They shoved a couple of tables together so they could sit as

DREAM BOUND / 53

a group, and the laughter and teasing never let up. Mac sensed the cohesiveness, the sense of camaraderie building much faster than he'd hoped—along with some obvious sexual tension. The original plan had been to fly everyone to the site, but he'd chosen the long drive, thinking that maybe they could get to know each other before they finally arrived at their destination.

It seemed to be working, and all of them appeared to be thoroughly enjoying themselves. So was he, for that matter. He hadn't expected to, not when the culmination of so many hopes, of so many years of planning and working on this project, was this close, when twenty years' of struggle, of successes and failures were all coming to a conclusion.

One that could go so terribly wrong. All that effort, that time, money, and literal sweat and tears coming down to the next few days—to contacting Zianne and her people.

Yes, he'd told them six months, and he expected them to remain at the site, taking that time to help acclimate the Nyrians to this new world once they were rescued, but he'd know in a matter of days whether or not their effort would succeed.

Would they be able to project enough sexual energy to bring the Nyrians to Earth? To free them from slavery and give them the corporeal bodies they'd need to survive on this world?

Zianne had explained how she'd traveled through time when she visited him in 1992. She'd given him enough information to go on that he had a fairly good idea what the corresponding date for her time had been that last morning she'd left his bed.

Even though the two of them had prepared for such a horrible event, he'd never dreamed she wouldn't return. It had taken days of watching for her before he fully accepted the fact that she wasn't coming back. But he'd feared it could happen, and weeks before Zianne disappeared, he'd already put a plan into action.

He'd put a down payment on a large tract of land in the isolated, high desert country of northeastern California, in an area where he knew he could build the transmitters and antennae he'd need to contact the Nyrians and bring them to Earth. Then he had worked on the programs, pushed the industry to improve the technology by leaps and bounds. All of it on a very precise schedule, readying himself for this moment in time.

The only moment they might have to save Zianne and her people. They were cutting it close, but he'd timed it this way on purpose—and if his calculations were right, Zianne should be arriving at her ship within the next twenty-four hours or so after leaving his bed in 1992.

He had no idea what had happened to her, but somehow the Gar had found out she'd been leaving. He didn't think they would kill her—from what she'd told him, there were too few Nyrians left to power their ship to put any to death. He had to believe she was still alive, that she would remain alive.

As connected as they'd been, wouldn't he know if she ceased to exist? If he was too late, if this didn't work . . . no. He couldn't allow himself to think of failure. How could any man survive, knowing he'd doomed an entire race of people to slavery and death? Knowing he might be responsible for his own world's end, if the Gar were truly as powerful as Zianne believed.

He wanted to feel excited about finally putting all his plans into action. Wanted to feel more hopeful than he did, but instead he was aware of an almost smothering sense of dread when he allowed himself to think of how slim his chances were of finally pulling this off.

He'd explained his fears to Dink, how he almost felt as if it was better to be working toward the ultimate goal he'd carried for the past twenty years than to actually put it into action—and discover he'd failed.

Dink had set him straight. *Failure isn't an option. It's not just Zianne we're talking about—it's the potential damage the Gar can do to our world. We're talking Earth's future. This isn't just about the woman you love. You've always seen the whole pic-*

ture. See it here, Mac. He'd paused then, wiped his hand over his eyes as if the concept of failure was too much to consider.

Then he'd grinned at Mac, shaking his head. *Hell, Mac. For you, failure isn't even a possibility. Don't worry about it, don't consider it. You won't fail. You're too damned much of a perfectionist to fail.* Then he'd kissed him soundly and added, *not to mention, stubborn as a mule and just as hardheaded.*

Thank God for Dink. His impassioned words still resonated with Mac this morning. Last night, Dink had helped settle his nerves in more ways than he'd imagined, but unloading the whole convoluted tale had done even more. Sharing the story of the Nyrians with Dink, seeing his unwavering acceptance, his support for all of Mac's plans, had made a huge difference.

Dink was right. He couldn't allow himself to consider failure. Not with the lure of Zianne's love, the safety of her people, the proof he'd not been tilting at windmills for all these years with his plans so close now to fruition. So close and so dependent upon this group of brilliant young minds, currently uniting in a goal they truly didn't understand.

"Mac?"

He glanced up from his sandwich. Kiera smiled expectantly at him. "Yeah?"

"When do we start our shifts? You said we'd be working around the clock. Will we start tonight?"

He shrugged, but inside he was singing. "If you're not too tired from the trip. If you think you're ready. Each of you will want to get settled into your individual cabins when we arrive, but you're more than welcome to work out a schedule that feels most comfortable. I know some of you are night owls, others better in the morning." He shrugged. "The length of your shifts, the timing . . . it's all up to you."

"Any suggestions?"

Cameron had been so quiet all through the ride, Mac was glad to see him at least contributing something. "Probably that you not plan on working too long a shift. If you've never done anything that's kept you in one spot for a long time focusing all your concentration on one thing in particular, I can tell you it's more exhausting than you might think."

Cam rolled his eyes. "Mac? I'm a painter, remember?" He laughed. "Concentrating on one thing in particular for a long time is how I make my living." He shot a quick glance at the others. "If we figure on four-hour shifts, the six of us can cover the entire twenty-four. Is four hours too long?"

"I'd say we give it a try, see how that works," Morgan said.

He glanced at Mac. Checking to be sure he hadn't over-stepped? Yep. The man learned fast. Feeling more satisfied than he should, Mac nodded. "That makes sense. Midnight to four, four to eight, and on through the day. Pick times that work best for you."

"I want midnight to four." Cam grinned almost shyly at Mac. The kid was a hard one to figure out. "That's when I'm most creative in my painting," he said. "Probably when my fantasies are most vivid."

"I'll take four in the morning to eight." Finn was carefully folding up the paper over the crumbs of his sandwich.

Mac cocked an eyebrow in Finn's direction. "Why would you purposefully choose that one? That's a tough time frame for most people to stay awake unless you're an absolute night owl."

Finn leaned back in his chair and tossed his bag of garbage at the trash can by the door. The tightly compacted wad of paper and plastic sailed neatly through the slot. "Because I imagine the women will be sleeping then. I hate the idea of working when I could be doing something more productive."

"Give it a break, Finn." Rodie stood to clear the rest of the bags off the table and carried them to the trash. "We've all had advance warning. You haven't got a prayer of getting laid."

"I dunno." Lizzie winked at Rodie. "I think he's kinda cute, in a desperate sorta way, and six months is a long time to do without."

"Lizzie, he's all yours." Kiera stood and brushed crumbs off her sweatshirt. "Back in a minute. Put me down for twelve to four during the day. I am most definitely not a morning person." She leaned over and kissed Finn on top of the head. "Behave, scoundrel," she said, heading for the restroom.

"I'd like the morning shift, from eight to twelve." Lizzie patted Finn's knee. Then she leaned close and planted a big kiss on his lips.

His eyes went wide, but he didn't hesitate to kiss her back. Lizzie grinned at him and quickly pushed away from the table. "We can pass like ships in the night," she said. "And no, don't even dream about getting lucky."

Morgan snorted. "I'll take either four to eight or eight to midnight. Rodie? Which would you prefer?" He glanced her way.

Rodie shrugged. "I'm a night owl. Eight to midnight works for me. I want to see the stars while I'm talking to them."

"I hadn't thought about that, but yeah. I like the idea of knowing who I'm talking to." Morgan glanced at Mac. "Or projecting. Sending . . . whatever."

"All of the above." Mac pushed his chair back and stood. "If you want to refill your soft drinks or you need a restroom stop, do it now. We've still got four or five hours to go, and not too many towns in between. I've got a crew at the site who'll have dinner for us when we arrive." He tossed his soft drink cup in the trash. "I'll be out in the car."

His cell phone rang as he headed out the door. He checked the screen, took the call. Listened to the head of security at the site for a moment before giving him an estimated time of arrival.

Then he ended the call and stared at the screen. "Crap." It appeared things were already going to shit.

4

Lizzie curled up against the window with Finn next to her and Kiera on the opposite side. For the past half hour or so, she and Kiera had tried communicating without words. Already they were forging the barest of telepathic links. It wasn't easy, but it was working.

Mac hadn't been kidding.

For some reason, though, when she tried to see Finn's thoughts, she came up against nothing but a wall of sensation. It took her a while to figure out what was going on, but she finally realized the guy was immersed in sexual fantasies. Vivid, kinky, over-the-top fantasies, and both she and Kiera were right in the midst of all of them.

He was simple enough to block. She'd discovered that if she thought of a one-way mirror that would allow her images through but keep his away, it worked.

That was all it took—if she pictured something, it was so.

Now, if she could link with Kiera, if the two of them, together were to . . . oh, my. Inspired, aware of a new sense of focus even as she bit back an incipient case of giggles, Lizzie tried to reach Kiera once again. An idea was forming, one that could certainly make the long drive go by faster.

Suddenly, Kiera's dark eyes went wide. *Lizzie?*

Amazing! It was almost as if a window had opened between them. *Yes! You can understand me?*

I can. This is the clearest you've been.

I've got an idea. She sent her thoughts to Kiera, wondering if they might be too abstract for the other girl to understand, but Kiera's devilish grin was all the confirmation she needed.

Finn was leaning back against the seat, his lips curved in a mysterious smile, eyes shut, and a huge bulge at the crotch of his jeans. Dozing—not really sleeping, but not wide awake, either—and obviously enjoying his fantasies.

It was time to take this to the next level. He'd started out as a tease, but then, after their lunch break, he'd gotten a little more touchy-feely than either Lizzie or Kiera appreciated. Maybe it was the long trip, or boredom, or just his natural impulsiveness, but since lunch Finn had gone from cute to merely irritating to acting like a horny teen without any controls or concept of limits.

They'd responded by giving him the silent treatment until he'd retreated. Now that Lizzie knew he'd merely slipped into his own little fantasy world—one starring both her and Kiera—she figured it was time to set some boundaries for the dude.

Lizzie and Kiera had talked a bit during one of their stops along the way—if they didn't put the brakes on Finn now, he could be an absolute pain in the butt once they reached the site. Cute only carried creepy behavior just so far.

Lizzie opened her thoughts fully to Kiera. Next she relaxed and let her eyelids drop so she'd look as if she were asleep.

Then she sent her thoughts to Finn.

Setting her imagination free, she broadcast a vivid image of Finn standing in a forest glen, naked, arms bound and stretched over his head, feet spread wide, his ankles shackled to stakes buried in the dirt. At first she pictured a blindfold covering his eyes, but after she thought about it a moment, Lizzie decided she wanted him to see what she was doing.

She projected an image of herself, standing in front of him. Then she slowly removed his blindfold and posed for him.

Clothed at first, wearing the same things she had on now. Slowly, methodically, she disrobed. It took only a few moments until she was naked, except this was, after all, fantasy, so she made her breasts a little larger, her nipples darker. She added a few glistening drops of moisture around her fully shorn pubes and made certain he could see her swollen labia and the pink shimmer of her distended clit.

And damn, but this was fun, especially when she noticed a hitch in Finn's no-longer-steady breathing beside her. Was he aware this was not entirely his own fantasy?

She knew immediately when Kiera joined in—her visual slipped easily into the fantasy, all tall, lean, and dark next to Lizzie's short, fair self. She flashed a smile at Lizzie and received one in return as the two women smoothly meshed their fantasies to create a single projection. Finn's fantasy eyes opened and he watched them both, and Lizzie knew that, for now anyway, he still wasn't sure if this was his fantasy or theirs.

Kiera imagined walking closer to Finn and running her hands along his sides. Then she knelt in front of him and cupped his balls in her palms.

The real man in the seat beside her groaned softly.

Grinning, Lizzie imagined herself behind him. She pressed her flat belly against his taut butt cheeks, ran her hands down his lean hips. He jerked—both against his bonds and beside her in the backseat—but it was Lizzie and Kiera's fantasy, and he was bound tight and couldn't move far.

Would that restrain Finn's imaginings? Or was he strong enough to break free of their fantasy and make it his own? Did he even realize he was no longer in control? Lizzie pressed closer.

Here, in the backseat of the SUV, she felt his body tense and jerk against her side. When Kiera fantasized wrapping her lips around his engorged cock, the real Finn moaned again.

Just like the one in the fantasy.

Lizzie wanted to cheer. Instead, she snuggled closer into the curve of her seat and let her body totally relax. If Finn pulled out of their fantasy, she didn't want any doubt that she was sleeping.

She poured on the images and shared the sense of her fingers stroking between his taut buttocks, trailing all the way down the crease to the sensitive perineum, then on to where his sack was pulled up tight between his legs. The fantasy was so real, she felt his slightly sweat-damp skin along that warm valley, smelled the musky man smell of him. When she knelt behind him, there was warm dirt beneath her knees. Her fingers stroked firm flesh as she parted his cheeks, bared his puckered, dark-rose-colored anus, and ran her tongue across the sensitive ring.

Finn whimpered, both in her fantasy and in real life.

This was so cool, doing things in her mind that sort of grossed her out in real life. Empowered, she used her tongue on him, licking and jabbing against him, moistening the entire area around his anus with her saliva. From the rhythmic pull to his body and the images Kiera shared with her, she knew her partner in crime pictured herself kneeling in front of Finn, swallowing his cock down her throat.

He was getting it from both women at once. She wondered how he was interpreting everything, if he even had a clue where this was all coming from.

The best part was the fact that this was all make-believe. They'd both pictured him huge—long and thick with heavy veins running the length of his cock, but again, since this was fantasy, Kiera easily swallowed him down, milking him with her mouth and throat, tugging at his balls with both hands.

The man sitting between them had given up all pretense of ignoring the two women, though neither of them acknowledged him at all, other than with their minds. Finn's body shuddered and twitched, his breathing had gone shallow and fast. He fell deeper into their fantasy, his body shivering with the input from two feminine minds devoting all their energy to his pleasure.

Lizzie continued licking all around his taut sphincter, wishing she had a big dildo to use on him. If nothing else, they really wanted to teach Finn a lesson. He'd been grabbing breasts and rubbing butts and pulling whatever shit he thought he could get away with, and enough was enough.

Lizzie really wanted him to pay, and if embarrassment would do it, she was all for making Finn feel like a fool. A dildo would fit her plans perfectly, except . . . well, shit.

This was a fantasy and she was in charge, so she imagined the perfect dildo, and there it was, clasped in her hand. Even larger than she or Kiera had pictured Finn, the damned thing was well lubed and perfectly textured.

She hadn't planned on purple, but purple she got. And just so Finn would know what to expect, she showed it to him. Held it up in front of his face long enough for the shock to register.

Then she was back, kneeling behind him with the thing clutched in her left hand. She rubbed her fingers down the crease of his ass, pressing against his sphincter as if she planned to penetrate. She teased him while Kiera sat back on her heels and merely licked the tip of his cock.

Finn bucked and twisted in his restraints, but he remained silent. Maybe he couldn't talk back to them if they didn't allow it. She really had no idea exactly how this worked, but whatever they were doing definitely had an effect on Finn.

Lizzie grabbed his hip and held him in place. The man beside her went still. Then she pressed the smooth tip of the big purple dildo against his sweet spot and pushed. She pictured the way his taut sphincter tightened up, fighting the intrusion. Then she let it give way, stretching a little before clenching against the dildo once again. She continued pushing and Finn slowly began to loosen, to weaken against her persistent pressure.

She imagined that it burned like fire, because she really wanted it to hurt him enough that he'd think before he grabbed her breast again. The man in the seat beside her grunted. Then he softly moaned as she kept pushing, twisting and turning the thing and adding to the tension, the fullness she wanted Finn to experience. Finally, she put all her imaginary weight behind the dildo and shoved hard, burying the massive thing clear to her fist.

"Fuck!" Finn jerked beside her, arched his back, and groaned. A moment later a large wet spot formed in the crotch of his jeans, spreading wide as Lizzie went back into his mind and pulled the imaginary dildo out of his ass and then shoved it back one more time, pushing it deep.

She just left it there, jammed all the way in to the thick knob on the handle part that held it in place. Then she pulled herself out of the fantasy and glanced at her partner in crime.

Kiera sat quietly laughing on Finn's other side. She glanced up and Lizzie caught her eye, raised her hand, and high-fived her right in front of Finn's nose.

Finn looked like he'd just lost a fight. Sweat covered his face and his eyes were glazed. Morgan and Rodie had both turned in their seats to see what all the commotion was. Lizzie grinned and gave them an innocent shrug.

Cameron slept in the front seat, but there was no ignoring Mac's laughter.

Finn shook his head, took a deep breath, and then shot a furious glare at Kiera before he focused his steely gaze on Lizzie. Her heart tumbled into overtime. Had they made an enemy with their head games? Finn was physically big and strong. What if he was really angry with them?

Lizzie sent a worried glance at Kiera, but Finn suddenly threw his head back against the seat, laughing hysterically.

"Oh shit, mama," he said, catching his breath. "You gonna pull that thing out or leave it there? I know it's not real, but damn! Remind me not to mess with you two again."

Morgan frowned. "What happened?" He glanced at Rodie. She shrugged and then he stared at Finn again. "You okay?" He glanced meaningfully at the wet, sticky spot beside the button fly on Finn's worn jeans.

Finn reached out and grabbed Kiera's and Lizzie's hands before either one could move out of his reach. "I'm fine," he said, squeezing lightly. "But I can honestly say, I've never before been attacked by someone else's sexual fantasy." He nodded to each of them in turn. "Ladies. You win. I apologize, and I promise to behave."

Lizzie smiled, leaned close, and kissed his cheek. "Thank you. I guess we proved our point."

Chuckling, Finn nodded. "That you did. And you have my permission to prove it again, any time you want."

"In your dreams, smart-ass." Kiera leaned close and kissed him as well. Then they all settled back against the leather seats.

Morgan stared at the three of them for a moment. Then he shook his head, turned around, and settled again beside Rodie.

For all intents and purposes, Mac appeared to stay focused on his driving. He never once turned around, but Lizzie could still hear him softly chuckling long minutes later.

Kiera kept her mouth shut. Of course, she was an attorney.

They were good at knowing when to talk and when to keep quiet. Lizzie took one last glance at Finn. Then she closed her eyes.

But she didn't even try to wipe the smile off her face.

Stunned, Finn lay his head back against the soft leather and tried to figure out exactly what he'd just experienced. He knew it had been fantasy, knew that no one had actually touched him, though try telling that to his cock.

Or his ass. Holy fuck. Thank goodness the sense of the dildo had finally faded away. He'd been afraid he'd be stuck with the thing—literally—until whoever put it there pulled it out.

He couldn't remember the last time he'd come that hard. In fact, here it was a full two minutes later, he was still pumping out spunk and his fucking dick was still hard.

It was going to make for one hell of an uncomfortable ride.

He glanced at Kiera and then Lizzie and chuckled softly. Sitting there, heads back, eyes closed, as innocent as newborn babes. What a couple of bitches! And he had to admit, he was at least half in love with both of them already.

He could still feel Kiera's hands moving over his balls, the smooth glide of his cock down her throat. But Lizzie . . . good goddamn, but she was amazing. That smile so sweet, sugar wouldn't melt in her mouth, but he'd felt her tongue rimming his ass, felt the shivers even now the way he had when she'd slipped through.

Holy shit. He'd always been so sensitive there, and while he'd never let a guy fuck him, he'd played around a few times and knew what it felt like to have a woman's fingers making him nuts.

But Lizzie's tongue? Wow. Just . . . wow. Except, how come his butt actually hurt? Logically, he knew it had been nothing more than a shared fantasy, but the dull ache in his ass right now was definitely uncomfortable, the way he imagined he'd feel if someone really had shoved a foot-long purple dildo up his butt. He shifted against the soft leather, trying to get more comfortable, but the pain persisted.

Not really terrible, but enough that he'd remember for a while what the two had done to him. Even if he'd deserved it, after harassing the girls all morning, Finn still had to figure out a way to get them back. You didn't let something like this just slide. Not when retribution could be so entertaining.

Smiling, he relaxed and let his mind wander over all the myriad ways he could make Lizzie and Kiera pay.

And, funny thing. His ass didn't hurt anymore.

Morgan stared at the thick wall of trees on either side of the road. Damn Finn. What a jerk! It was obvious he'd just shot a load in his pants, but why? What the hell had the girls done to him? No question they'd pulled something, and from what little he knew of Finn, the bastard probably deserved it. He'd have to ask him. Later, when he didn't have so many other things going on.

He didn't usually get hung up on chicks, but for some weird reason his thoughts were totally locked on to Rodie. It bugged him, because he wasn't sure why. She wasn't the prettiest of the three women. Not the most outgoing or even the sexiest, but there was something about her.

Something that grabbed him by the balls and wouldn't let go. The feeling had been growing since that first night he saw her—it must have been close to two months or so ago, at one of the first gatherings of applicants, when he'd spotted her coming in a bit later than the rest of the crowd. She'd seemed flustered, a bit nervous, and he'd been curious then.

He'd asked around about her, and it took him a while to find out, but he'd discovered that night she came in so shook up that she'd been the victim of an assault and robbery just that afternoon. Some jerk had roughed her up and stolen her backpack and laptop, and that was just after she'd had a pretty ugly breakup with some guy. That story—with film—had been all over the Internet, how she'd caught the dude in her bed with another guy and a woman and Tasered the three of them.

But she hadn't said a thing about any of that.

She'd had her world turned upside down, and yet she'd still made it to every one of those damned meetings. And here she was, acting like the whole thing was a big adventure, which, he figured, it was, but she'd had some really bad shit in her life and she hadn't let it stop her. He admired that about her. A lot.

Then this morning, when he'd been trying out his newfound telepathy without a clue as to what he was actually doing, damned if she hadn't turned the tables on him.

He had no idea what she'd been feeling when he imagined sliding his fingers over her clit and deep inside her pussy, but he could have sworn her lips were wrapping around his balls and her tongue was licking his shaft—utterly impossible since she was sitting there, staring at him.

Had the feelings he sent her way been as intense? He wished he had the balls to ask her. He was still sorry he'd broken the connection, though coming in his jeans would have been about as embarrassing as anything he could imagine. Especially since he'd have had to sit in his own spunk all the way up the mountain.

Just the way that idiot O'Toole was doing now. He wished he knew what those two chicks had done to the guy, because it was more than obvious they'd pulled some kinda shit.

But Rodie . . . goddamn. If she'd made him feel her tongue and her hot mouth, that meant he must have succeeded with his concentration on her clit. Had she felt his fingers inside her? He couldn't know for sure, but she'd looked like a woman on the edge of orgasm.

He'd been so close to losing it, but he had to admit, knowing they had this link made her even more fascinating. And the fact that she'd turned the tables on him meant she wasn't all that averse to trying out this new power they seemed to have.

He wondered when Mac was going to teach them more about it. He felt like he was scrambling for answers but had no idea where to look.

So he leaned back against the soft leather seat and looked at Rodie. And let his imagination fly.

The closer they got to the site, the more Mac felt his excitement build, though he honestly couldn't say whether it was because he was finally going to go after Zianne or if it was the result of all the sexual head games going on in the car.

He'd gone along for the ride with Kiera and Lizzie. Thank goodness he'd pulled himself free of their fantasy in time or he'd be riding up the mountain in sticky shorts, just like Finn.

Those girls learned fast. He'd tagged on to Morgan's and Rodie's fantasies for a while, but again he'd had to pull back before they sucked him in entirely.

He'd have to teach them how to block that sort of thing before it got out of hand, but for now it gave all of them something to entertain themselves with during the long trip.

All but Cameron. He knew the kid had a vivid imagination—his paintings made it more than obvious that he'd traveled the realm of fantasy and learned to make it pay in a big way. But he'd been quiet most of the day.

Quiet, or possibly blocking Mac's curious questing thoughts? Maybe Cam had already figured out what the others had yet to learn. If so, it might mean his mental acuity was even stronger than Mac first thought.

He glanced at the GPS, watched for the familiar break in the forest off to the right, and slowed down for the turn. The sun had disappeared behind the mountains, but it was still light out, and he was glad that the team would get to see the site for the first time in the light of day.

He was damned proud of all he'd accomplished over the years, but this satellite dish array was beyond anything he'd ever imagined so long ago when he and Zianne first made their plans.

He glanced in the rearview mirror and saw that everyone was awake and paying attention. They had to be wondering about the turn from the two-lane highway to the narrower county road, or maybe they felt his excitement, sensed the edge he was riding.

Or maybe a bit of both. "The site is less than a mile from here," he said, taking another tight turn as they followed the county road for a short distance. "We'll be turning on to GEO-MAP property in just a bit and starting the climb up the side of the mountain. We don't go all the way to the top—our site is on a rather large plateau that's at the seven-thousand-foot elevation point. We're in national forest land, and this was one of the few places I was able to purchase privately that fit my criteria."

"We're a hell of a long way from the closest bar."

Finn's dry comment had everyone laughing.

"No problem." Mac glanced over his shoulder. "I happen to appreciate a glass of wine or a good stiff drink once in a while. I think you'll find everything you need at the site."

"Including protestors. Wow! Who are those dudes?"

"Well, Cameron . . ." Mac had been hoping they'd be gone by now. Obviously, security hadn't been successful at clearing them away, but at least they were outside the gates. Unfortunately, they had every legal right to be there.

"What the hell's that all about?" Morgan leaned forward.

Mac slowed the vehicle as they got closer to the small group of men and women gathered on the road. "That's the gate to the array. It's locked, and I doubt they want trespassing charges, but this isn't the welcoming committee I was hoping for."

Cameron read the largest of the signs aloud. " 'No mere man may map God's heavens'? What the fuck? I don't get it."

"That, my friend, is how narrow minds find fault with the name of a project they haven't even tried to understand. They're convinced DEO-MAP, which they've dubbed the God Project, is my attempt at mapping the heavens to disprove the existence of God."

"You're kidding, right?" Morgan shook his head, laughing. "I'm amazed there are enough people living around here to get this many together for a party, much less a protest."

"I'm beginning to think it's their version of a social life." Mac turned around and grinned at Morgan. "Like Finn said, we're a long way from the closest bar."

Finn just shook his head. "How do we handle this, boss?"

"We ignore it," Mac said. "Security called me when we stopped for lunch in Burney, so I knew they might still be here, but we should have someone from the sheriff's department before too long. There's no reasoning with narrow minds. Besides, if they knew what we were really planning, they'd probably call for reinforcements."

"How far are we from the actual array?"

Rodie sounded concerned, but Mac had heard about her assault shortly after they'd started the selection process and wondered if this sort of thing might upset her. "Your living quarters and the array itself are another half mile up the road. The entire area is fenced and monitored, so they can't get any closer than this gate. We've got good security, so once we're on private property, we shouldn't have any trouble with them."

He drove forward slowly, and most of the dozen or so men and women moved aside. Three men, however, blocked the entrance and stood in front of the electric gate.

Mac rolled down the window. "Move aside, please."

"Sorry, Dugan, but we can't allow that." The largest of the three men planted the stake to his sign on the road in front of him and leaned on the top. His long gray hair curled over his shoulders and he wore a loose shirt that gave him the appearance of a modern saint—or possibly a pirate. "We condemn this hellish project. Do not bring more people here to do the devil's work. Not in God's country. Do not desecrate our beautiful mountains."

"Well, Mr. Roberts, you're standing in front of my gate to my part of the mountain right now. If you don't move, I'll have to call out the sheriff again. We've had a long drive and we'd like to get home."

"Looks like reinforcements are already here." Finn pointed at the four-wheel-drive SUV pulling up behind them.

"Good. I had security tell the sheriff when we expected to arrive, that we might need help." Mac climbed out of the car and met the deputy. "Hi, Ted. If you can get us through the gate, we'll be fine. They're welcome to stay out here, as long as they stay off my property, for as long as they want."

"Not a problem." The deputy, a tall, lanky guy with short, cropped hair shoved his hat firmly on his head and walked around the Escalade while Mac got back inside. Within moments, the small group of protestors had moved out of the way. Mac punched in the code for the gate and they were through.

"I had hoped they would already be gone." Mac adjusted the rearview mirror and watched the gate close behind them. "We've had trouble with them since the project was first announced. Bart Roberts objected on general principles in the beginning when I applied for the permits to build, but once the name was made public, he pulled in the others and started in on the religious aspects. In fact, I suspect he was the one behind Kiera's lawsuit. What's frustrating is that they're not associated with any church, and I've heard that Roberts is paying folks to stand out there and wave signs. With the economy as poor as it is, especially up here, people will do anything for a paycheck, but he's whipping up an issue that doesn't really exist."

"Personally, I like the name," Lizzie said. "There's something sort of wonderfully pretentious about 'the God Project.' "

She laughed. "Not that I don't like DEO-MAP, but you have to admit, it is sort of catchy."

"Catchy is fine," Mac deadpanned. "Blocking my gate isn't." He followed the narrow road up the switchback, concentrating on the drive during the steepest part, before adding, "Protesting and threatening my people rubs me the wrong way, especially when my gut tells me something else is going on, but I can't figure out what it is. Hopefully, they'll get tired of waving signs at no one and go home."

He took the final steep turn, drove over a small rise, and pulled out on to the plateau. As it always did, the view made him catch his breath. Twenty years to reach this point. Twenty long fucking years, and damn, but it was so beautiful.

The array spread out before them, fifty large satellite dishes all pointing at the heavens. Dusk had settled in around them, turning the sky from pale peach at the horizon to darkest navy overhead. Pale moonlight reflected off the huge white dishes so that each one seemed to glow as if the light came from within.

The view was unworldly, ethereal. Best of all, it was functional—the tools to bring Zianne and her people to Earth.

Mac pulled himself back to reality, felt the excitement, the sense of disbelief as the six young men and women took in the sight of what most of them had only imagined. He thought how young they seemed, but then he realized he'd been even younger when he and Zianne first imagined this project, long before he knew she'd not be working by his side while he got it built.

Had he been this ready for adventure? This excited about everything around him? This open?

Damn. He felt so old beside them. Old and jaded. He wanted that excitement back, and then he realized that it was here for the taking. Here, on this plateau, with their dreams and his experience and the hope of an entire race of people.

He couldn't help but think this must look like something

out of the latest science fiction novel, but wasn't his love for Zianne exactly that? Something that belonged in a fantasy, not real life? He gazed at the first stars just beginning to show and wondered where she was now, if she was all right.

No. He couldn't worry about that. Not if he wanted to bring her safely home. He had to believe she was fine, that she was getting her people ready for the rescue that he hoped would happen over the next few days.

He turned in his seat and studied his team as they stared out across the silent array. The plateau was huge—almost a mile across with forest covering part of it, a view of the mountain to the west and the Nevada desert to the east. All of it bathed now in that mystical half-light between daylight and dusk with the full moon rising through twilight along the eastern edge.

No one said a word. Mac sensed their awe, knew they were as overwhelmed by the sight spread out across the plateau as he always was. He heard the back doors open, then the passenger side as the six silently crawled out of the Escalade and walked around to the front. He joined them, standing quietly in the background, soaking up the myriad thoughts swirling among six amazing minds.

After a long moment, Morgan turned to Mac with an unexpected look of wonder. He seemed so cynical and jaded most of the time, but now his eyes were wide, his senses so tangled that he projected thoughts that bounced all over the place.

"This is beyond anything I imagined. I've seen the Allen Array, but this ... holy shit, Mac. How long did it take to build?"

Mac let out a deep breath. Pushed thoughts of Zianne to the back of his mind. "Six years for the array, though it's taken almost fifteen to get the roads in, the fences built, wells dug, and power brought in. Fifteen years and almost sixty million dollars, and yes, I've done this without any outside funding."

He almost laughed at Morgan's raised eyebrow. "I know. A

lot of money to follow a dream, but trust me, it's money I fully expect to recoup. I just wish I could get back some of the years." He laughed softly, shaking his head at the memories. "I've had to deal with terrible weather, bad roads, and endless government permits. Now I've got a bunch of nuts out front who don't understand what I've built or why we're here." He shook his head, amazed by the hurdles he'd had to jump to reach this point, but it was done and the site was as ready as it was going to be.

He was ready, and with any luck, the six of them were ready. "It wasn't easy," he said. "But it's done. Just waiting for the six of you." Then he turned back to the car and stood beside the open door. "Get in. I'll drop you off at your cabins. Take some time to get settled, and then we'll meet in the main lodge for dinner in about half an hour. I'll give you a quick rundown on what I want you to do. With any luck, you can start working your shifts tonight."

5

Cameron Paisley put his belongings away in the bank of drawers built into the large closet in the bedroom. He'd figured they would be living in some kind of glorified dorms, but the log cabin Mac had brought him to was fantastic. There was a small kitchen complete with a sink, refrigerator, microwave, and toaster oven, a living area that was twice again as large as the kitchen with comfortable furnishings, and in the back, a separate bedroom and bathroom.

The six cabins were identical, each with its own front porch, built all of logs with a small woodstove as well as a heating system for winter nights. They had tin roofs equipped with solar panels, and all six of the cabins were arranged equidistant around the main lodge where they'd be meeting later for dinner.

Mac had said his rooms were upstairs in the lodge. They'd take their meals on the main floor, and there was a fully equipped gym in the basement with a lap pool for year-round use, plus a separate bunkhouse for security people and the few technicians and staff who would remain on the site.

They were responsible for keeping their own cabins as neat

as they wanted, but housekeeping would provide fresh linens and towels. There was a laundry at the back of the lodge and even a fully stocked bar.

Hell, he didn't have it this good at home, and he had one hell of a nice place. This was really sweet.

Kiera was in an identical cabin on one side and Lizzie on the other. Finn's cabin was next to Lizzie's, then Rodie's, Morgan's, and back to Kiera's. The array spread out across the huge plateau to the east of them, with all those big dishes pointing skyward and covering all points visible in space. Mac had explained that once any form of contact was made, the dishes would turn in unison to lock onto the signal.

Trapping even the most distant pulses of energy, even as they sent energy outward from whomever was on duty at the time.

Mind-blowing didn't come close to describing it.

Cam shoved the last of his clothes into the drawers and glanced at the bed. King-sized beds in all the cabins. That had certainly caught his attention. Kicked his already healthy libido into overdrive as well when he imagined things he could do with a willing partner and all that room.

Any one of the women along on this project would be more than welcome. All three of them were gorgeous, each in her own way. Gorgeous, with open minds when it came to sex.

Why did he feel as if this was a surfeit of riches?

Grinning, Cam wandered out of the bedroom and checked the main living area. Even with the big leather couch and comfortable chairs, there was plenty of room to set up his easel. He'd been assigned the southernmost cabin. Mac explained he'd picked this one for Cam because it had the best daytime light for painting.

He checked a storage closet in the main room and found tarps and cleaning supplies for his brushes and stacks of stretched canvas, all ready to go. Amazing.

Mac's foresight was impressive—and thoughtful, too. Cam hadn't even thought of what his workspace would be like when he'd packed his supplies—he'd only known he needed a break, that his dreams weren't coming to him as regularly as he needed, and Mac's project sounded far enough out of the ordinary to maybe kick-start his brain.

He glanced up at the perfect skylight over his head. He'd have exactly the light he needed to paint during daylight hours.

Then he checked his watch. No time now to unpack the rest of his stuff. He'd deal with it after dinner. His shift didn't start until midnight.

Cam fully expected to start work tonight—on both projecting his fantasies into space and the newest painting. He gazed skyward and freed his thoughts, staring at the dark skylight and emptying his mind, the way he did when he drew on his fantasy images to paint.

"Oh, shit." He snorted, laughing out loud when instead of one of his fantasy scenes, the perfect image of Finn's butt stuffed with a purple dildo filled his mind.

Definitely not the image he expected, but it probably served him right. He'd managed to piggyback on Kiera and Lizzie's fantasies with Finn, just as he'd done earlier with Rodie and Morgan. As far as he could tell, no one suspected a thing. It hadn't been easy to keep his features slack while watching the fantasy Lizzie and Kiera worked on the Irishman. Everything was so damned vivid, including the stretch of muscle and the more intimate details of Finn's cock and balls, that he'd had trouble controlling himself.

He wondered how close the girls' imaginations had come to the real thing. He wasn't usually into guys, but he'd had to consciously fight his arousal or he'd have come all over himself right along with Finn. Then there'd be no hiding the fact that he'd figured out how to tap into everyone else's minds, and that was a secret he wasn't prepared to share, at least not yet.

He'd never been around so much intelligence in his life, never had the opportunity to actually peek into another person's thoughts, but now . . . he shook his head, laughing. Did Mac Dugan realize the kind of power he'd brought together? Did he even have a clue what the six of them might be capable of, should they ever combine their mental strength?

Cam hoped so. He hadn't been kidding about getting carsick, so it had been easy to play possum most of the way up the mountain. In fact, he'd taken his Dramamine and had slept some of the way, but he'd also pretended to sleep while he slipped in and out of the five other minds in the car. The only one he'd avoided was Mac's, but that was because he wasn't yet certain of his own abilities.

Or, for that matter, Mac Dugan's. The man was brilliant and Cam didn't plan to make the mistake of underestimating him.

He stared out the window at the ghostly shapes of the huge satellite dishes marching across the plateau and felt a shiver crawl along his spine. He'd dreamed vividly last night and the night before—ever since he'd accepted the fact that Mac wasn't kidding when he said they all had extrasensory abilities.

Cam had always dreamed of worlds beyond imagination, sensual dreams of scenes beyond anything that had ever existed. Or, as Mac so succinctly had asked, did they exist? Were they real, and not mere fabrications of Cam's mind? He'd suspected for years that his dreams took him to places that, while beyond reality, were not totally impossible. Places that had to exist somewhere, somehow, in order for him to experience them.

Now he was here, in a place designed to connect his mind with other creatures, other worlds, other amazing scenes. Not as imagination but as reality. Not merely his own reality but one that truly existed.

His art was recognized worldwide and hung in some of the most prestigious art galleries and museums around the globe, but many critics still saw him as nothing more than a weird, quasi-talented geek with an offbeat, fantastical view of life.

Maybe that was about to change.

Chuckling, Cam took one last glance at the ghostly satellite dishes shimmering beneath the rising moon. Then he turned on the porch light, stepped out, and closed the door behind him.

The lodge glowed from gaslights positioned all around the big covered porch surrounding the entire log structure. Morgan and Rodie were standing outside, leaning against the porch railing. Looked like each of them had a drink of something. Kiera, Lizzie, and Mac stood off to one side, deep in discussion. Finn walked across the open ground toward the lodge.

Cam noticed he'd changed his pants.

"Pretty cool, eh?" Finn paused, waiting for Cam.

"It's bitchin'." Cam shook his head and glanced at Finn. "Is this what you expected?"

Finn shook his head. "No. Are you kidding? My imagination is good, but not this good." He spread his hands wide, taking in the array of satellite dishes, the cabins, the big mountain looming a darker black against the deep blue-black of the evening sky, and let out a long, low whistle. "I'm not usually into the kinky ESP stuff, but I swear that if something weird's going to happen, if we're going to connect with alien lifeforms, this is the place for it."

Nodding in agreement, Cam followed Finn up the stairs to the porch. He suddenly felt well out of his comfort zone. Something would happen here, something big. He knew it.

He just wished he had some idea what to expect.

Mac stood at the head of the long trestle table while the kitchen staff cleared away the empty plates. Six sets of eyes focused on him, and he realized he already saw them as family.

Funny, when he thought about it. He didn't feel that connection with anyone he worked with, nor with any of his friends. Only two others in his world fit the term: Dink and Zianne. Now these six had become part of that very select group whether they wanted membership or not.

He hoped none of them came to regret it. "Okay, guys. First, I hope you enjoyed your dinner. I was lucky enough to convince Meg and Ralph Bartlett to move up here and take over the cooking and maintenance. If you have any housekeeping questions, check with Meg, and if anything breaks, call Ralph. Their numbers are keyed into the phones in each cabin."

He nodded toward Meg and Ralph and they accepted a round of applause from the kids. When they'd left the room, Mac planted his palms on the table and leaned forward. "Looks like we're starting tonight. Rodie, you're going to go first, in about half an hour, if you're okay with that. We'll stick with the schedule you guys developed, try it out for a week and see how it works."

Kiera raised her hand. "Mac, will you be taking a shift? I mean, if you've already made contact, wouldn't you be the one to connect again?"

He chuckled, shaking his head. "No. The thing is, I can connect without the array. I'm already linked to one mind, though we've not connected now for twenty years—at least for me. For her it was today." He took a deep breath, forced a sense of calm he didn't feel. "But that's because she'd traveled back in time to reach me." Damn. When would he be able to talk about Zianne without this frickin' lump in his throat?

He paused, cleared his throat, and took a breath. "When she left it was to return to her time, which, if my calculations are correct, is today. I'm hoping I can reach her on my own while the six of you will try to connect with the rest of her people. They'll be expecting contact after tonight."

Rodie stared at him. "Are you saying you scheduled this whole thing to begin on this exact date? Tonight? You set it up like this twenty years ago?"

He nodded. "I did. Twenty years and four months ago, I met an amazing woman named Zianne. She told me she was not only from another world but another time. Twenty years in my future, to be exact. She said she'd linked to my mind in Earth's past because she knew the world didn't have the technology needed to bring her people to Earth, and she was there to teach me how to build it."

"Shit." Morgan shook his head, the look of disbelief in his eyes warring with his obvious sense of wonder. "That's a bit hard to swallow. Why was it so important that you bring her people to Earth?"

Mac sighed. He didn't want to lie, but he hadn't really planned to tell them everything so soon. He wasn't sure how much of the truth they could handle right now, but when he gazed at the six expectant faces, he knew he had to be honest. They deserved the truth, the way he'd deserved the truth from Zianne.

She'd chosen when and where to explain it to him, and he'd believed, but that was because he already loved her. Would they believe him now? He sure as hell hoped so.

"What I tell you cannot leave this site." He held up a finger for silence and walked back to the door leading to the kitchen. Ralph and Meg were finishing up the dishes.

"We have some classified work to go over," he said. They'd been told that much of what happened on the site had to remain private, and Ralph's classified status from his years in the military were sufficient for Mac to know the man wouldn't talk—or listen where he'd been asked not to.

When they both nodded, Mac quietly shut the door and returned to the dining area. "Twenty years ago, a very close friend of mine and I got drunk." He chuckled at the grins around the table. "Yeah, I know. I was twenty-six and doing my grad work, and no, getting toasted was not all that unusual. But what happened later that night was."

Lord, but he remembered it all like it was yesterday. Picturing his fantasy girlfriend—describing her to Dink in such intimate detail—long dark hair, tall athletic build, violet eyes. Going home almost too drunk to walk and stepping into his apartment, smelling the sweet scent of honey and vanilla.

Having her appear in his shower, kneeling before him, taking him into her mouth. "She was exactly as I'd described her to Dink, but I might have written off the event in the shower as not enough sex and too much cheap beer if I hadn't awakened a few hours later with her beside me in bed. She stayed with me for four months, leaving during the day to return to her prison."

"Prison? Where?" Morgan glanced at the others and back at Mac. "I thought you said she was on a spaceship."

Mac let out a deep breath. Saying it out loud ... hell, it sounded unbelievable to him, too. "Zianne told me that she and the remnants of a once proud race of people were held prisoner aboard a star cruiser commanded by a ruthless people she called the Gar. Zianne is a Nyrian—she claimed that her planet Nyria was sentient. Nyrians are creatures of pure energy—she was able to take corporeal form merely from the strength of my sexual fantasy. That graphic description of the perfect woman I'd laid out for Dink had given her a physical body, though she could convert to her energy form at will."

"Have you seen her like that?"

"I have, Kiera. She looks like liquid lightning, if you can picture such a thing. It's an utterly beautiful form, but it can be deadly as well."

Cam frowned. "You said her planet was called Nyria. Past tense. Is it gone?"

Mac nodded. "It is. She was able to show me the destruction of her world through a mind link. It was my first real experience with telepathy. The Gar lured hundreds of Nyrians aboard their ship and then destroyed the planet and the millions of people on it. They've used the Nyrians ever since as their power source."

"If Zianne could come to you, why haven't all of them found a mind to link to and escaped?"

"They're held hostage, Rodie. The only solid part of a Nyrian is their soulstone. Zianne described it as pure carbon, like a diamond that they keep at their core. The Gar have taken their soulstones and locked them up on the ship. The Nyrians who are working as the power source do so without the stone. They get it back while they rest and recharge, then turn it in again when they're put back to work."

"How do they recharge?" Finn asked. "Where do they get their energy?"

"From the planets they pass by, from suns, from the energy of people inhabiting other worlds. Right now they're using our sun to recharge, but I don't know how long they're going to remain, or what the Gar plan for Earth before they go."

"What do you mean?" Morgan glanced at the others before turning his attention to Mac. "Are they a threat to us?"

Nodding, Mac checked his watch. "They are. Zianne said their usual action is to find a planet rich with natural resources where they stay in orbit long enough to allow the Nyrians time to recharge. Then they attack the world. Their ship is designed to take what resources are available—atmosphere and water included. Once there's nothing left, the worlds are left to die."

"Shit, Mac." Morgan was shaking his head as if he'd absorbed just one too many details. "Isn't this something you should be telling the President?"

Mac sighed, remembering the frustration, the conversations ignored, the incredulous, disbelieving looks. "I have. I went directly to the Pentagon because of my business contacts with the military, figuring I had enough credibility to make them listen. No one believed me. If anything, my credibility is probably hanging by a thread. It's up to us to rescue Zianne and her people, give them refuge here, and somehow destroy the Gar's ship before they attack our world."

Lizzie snorted. "And we're going to do this how, oh fearless leader?"

Morgan laughed. "Haven't you been paying attention, Liz? With our sexual fantasies, that's how. Newest weapon against alien attack."

Finn just shook his head. "My old man always said I'd probably screw myself to death." He glanced at Kiera and Lizzie. "I just never thought he meant that quite so literally."

There was a lot of laughter, just as many off-color jokes, but the one thing Mac had expected hadn't materialized at all. There was no sense of disbelief, not one of them looking at him like he had a screw loose.

Maybe later, when they'd had time to think about what he'd told them. Maybe that's when the disbelief would come. He hoped not. He glanced at his watch again. Almost eight. "I know you've got to have a million questions, but I need to get Rodie settled in first. We'll see how this first night goes and take it from there. You may not make any contact right away, but if you do, I want to know immediately."

Rodie glanced at the others. "Why do I feel like a lamb being led to slaughter?"

Finn leaned close. "Baaaaa."

Lizzie bopped him on the head.

Morgan stood and pulled Rodie's chair back. "Because you are?"

"Gee, thanks." She stood. "I'm ready. I think."

"Good." Mac grabbed her hand. "C'mon, lamb." He glanced over his shoulder. "The rest of you, too. Might as well come and see how this thing works. It's time I introduce my dream team to the dream shack."

6

"Are you okay?"

Mac stood beside Rodie, who was seriously wondering how she was going to manage to stay awake in the world's most comfortable reclining chair. "Oh, yeah." She scrunched her butt into the soft leather and stared at the high-tech-looking bank of instruments covering the panel in front of her.

The other five stood quietly just behind Mac, listening as he described the various buttons and gauges on the console. The dream shack building itself looked like a concrete bunker from the outside, but inside it was more like the interior of a space-ship. The name seemed totally apropos, too, when she thought of what she'd be expected to do in here, though Rodie really hoped she didn't fall asleep. That could be totally embarrassing.

But after all the shit Mac had just laid on them, she figured she'd be too terrified to fall asleep. Aliens made of pure energy? A starship filled with creatures out to destroy the earth? Hell, she could have just stayed home and watched monster movies if she wanted to scare herself half to death.

Except, in spite of his story, Mac wasn't a nut. His excitement over the project and his fear felt all too real.

She pulled her head out of the gazillion scary scenarios she'd been formulating and concentrated on what Mac was explaining. How the hell would she ever remember all this stuff?

He handed a headset to her—a fine mesh of silken wires with tiny disks all around. "This one is yours, Rodie."

She shot him a quick glance. "Do we each have our own?"

Nodding, he turned it so that the light caught the small disks. "Remember all those measurements we took at one of those final meetings? This one is designed to fit perfectly against the various transmission points in your brain. There's a cap here for each of you in the drawer." He flipped a little tag on the mesh with Rodie's name on it as she took it from him.

"This really is amazing." She lifted the headset and slipped it over her head. It stretched over her hair and then formed itself perfectly to the shape of her skull. Dials on the console suddenly came to life. "Do I have to speak aloud, or does it pick up my thoughts?"

Mac grinned like a kid showing off a new toy, and in a way, Rodie figured that was how he must feel. "Either. If you're comfortable speaking your thoughts aloud, feel free. There's no recording device to pick up what you say, though it will all go out via the array, but if you'd rather just imagine stuff, it can grab your thoughts as easily as vocalizations."

Okay. Even though she'd never heard of technology like that, Rodie figured she'd accept his word, which was just weird, because she'd been doing a lot of that tonight. Generally she was more of a skeptic. Smoothing the netting over her hair, Rodie studied the various LED screens in front of her. "Do I need to do anything with these?"

"No. As I explained, they're each tied to an individual dish and will be recording any incoming signals. This gauge here will measure your output, as far as the telepathic strength of your personal signal, but that's merely to let you know if you need to push harder with your thoughts."

He pointed to a small dial in front of her. The needle hovered at just about two o'clock. "You'll want to keep your mental signal in the mid-range at least—down around six o'clock. If you're having a problem with that, let me know and I'll see what adjustments we need to make. If you feel anything unusual, any contact at all, press that button. It's a direct link to me."

He pointed to a red button, larger than the others, within easy reach.

Rodie laughed. "Why do I want to refer to that as a panic button?"

This time Mac chuckled. "You don't think you'll panic if you're sending out sexual fantasies and someone answers?"

The others standing behind her laughed. Rodie'd totally forgotten they were in the room, but she turned and stared at Mac. Shit. She hadn't thought of that at all. "You believe that's going to happen, don't you? That we're going to make contact."

Mac leaned against the bank of screens, folded his arms across his chest, and raised one eyebrow as he gazed steadily at her. She felt like squirming in her chair. Of course he believed it. He'd sunk almost sixty million dollars and twenty years of his life into the fucking project.

"Guess that's kind of a stupid thing to say, huh?" Chagrined, she settled back in the chair.

Smiling, Mac shook his head. "Not stupid at all. To be honest, I'm surprised at how well all of you have taken my story. I hesitated to tell you all the details because I was afraid you'd think I was totally nuts, but I fully expect at least some of you will make contact within the first week. Maybe even tonight."

With that mind-boggling comment, Mac shoved away from the panel. "You're on your own, Rodie. I want you to feel free to let your thoughts go in as many kinky sexual directions as you can, and it'll be a lot easier if you know you're here by yourself."

She laughed. "Yep, just me and however many Nyrians are listening in, right?"

"Well, there is that." He straightened up and looked around the small room, and she wondered what he was thinking. She couldn't imagine working on a project for twenty years without any guarantees that anything would ever come of it. "Good luck, Rodie. Restroom facilities are in the back and there's a small refrigerator with cold drinks and bottled water. Granola bars and other snacks in the overhead cabinet. If there's anything else you'd like to have in here, let me know as soon as you think of it. Meg or Ralph will be making a trip to town at least once a week for supplies."

He glanced at the others. "Well, I guess that's it. I'm going back to the lodge. You guys can come with me or take the time to get settled in to your cabins. Cam, you'll relieve Rodie at midnight, right? Good. Rodie, remember, if you have any problems, questions, anything at all that is not of an emergency nature, that green switch connects directly to the main lodge and to my room. Anything scary, the red switch next to it will bring security. We'll have someone on duty twenty-four seven—don't hesitate to use it if you feel at all threatened by anything. And if you want me here without security, any time, day or night, that large red button I showed you will light a fire under my butt. I'll come immediately."

Then he leaned over and kissed her. His lips were soft and warm, the contact terribly brief, but Rodie felt the connection all the way to her toes. Before she could think about responding, he'd ended the kiss and pulled away. "Thank you, Rodie. I know you're here with your mind wide open and more questions than answers, but I can't begin to tell you how much I appreciate what you . . ." He glanced up at the others in the room.

"What all of you have committed to. This project means more to me than anyone can possibly comprehend."

He turned away, but paused once again. With his hand on the door he added, "But I promise you, if this works the way I expect it to, it won't be long before all of you understand why I've devoted my life to this. I promise you that you will believe, every bit as strongly as I do."

He held the door as the others filed out. Then he closed it behind him. It took Rodie a moment to gather her thoughts, to turn around in her comfortable seat, and get past the sense that she'd just spoken aloud to a man who was communicating on more than one level. Her mind had picked up something beyond his words, a longing that went beyond pain.

Needs, memories, and a sense of loss that left her shaken and wondering what she'd just missed. His comments had been so positive, so filled with hope, but there was more going on than she'd realized. He'd admitted to a sexual relationship with Zianne, but she hadn't really thought about the implications. Had Zianne been more than just a partner? Did he love her?

Could a human fall in love with a creature from another world? If so, she and the other members of Mac's dream team were part of what could end tragically for Mac, should they not succeed in rescuing his Nyrians or the woman he loved.

And that was only one of her concerns. If what he'd told them was true, this was more than a search for extraterrestrials. This was an opening salvo against an alien race out to rape and pillage their world.

If they rescued the Nyrians, they were essentially stealing the power supply to an alien starship. Would the ship crash if the Nyrians left it? Could this get any more bizarre? She wondered about Mac's hidden thoughts, the way he seemed to carry an extra layer of something around the stuff he was projecting.

Was she getting better at reading his thoughts, or was this

silken net linking her to the array somehow strengthening her abilities? She leaned back and stared at the stars through the skylight overhead. Crap, how the hell was she supposed to fantasize when there was so much going on inside her head?

A crystal-clear tempered glass dome covered a large part of the roof of the dream shack. She stared through the glass, at the stars spread across the sky like diamonds scattered over black velvet, and tried to settle her mind. Mesmerized by the beauty, still a bit unsettled by the connection she'd felt with Mac, and more than a little bit overwhelmed by the events of the past day—including the link she still felt with Morgan—Rodie set her thoughts free.

Images of Mac were quickly supplanted by a likeness of Morgan Black. She brought back the sensation of his mental caresses on the way up the mountain today and took them a few steps farther.

If there were any aliens listening in, she fully intended to give them something to think about.

Mac walked slowly across the yard to the lodge. The others had headed back to their cabins to finish unpacking and most likely to think about what he'd told them tonight. They probably wanted to make up their minds whether or not he was a total psych case.

He didn't blame them. There had been times over the past twenty years when he'd wondered the same thing, but memories of Zianne kept him going. Memories and a love that seemed to grow stronger over the years. It hadn't faded in the least.

He stared at the huge log structure that he'd had built before anything else. It had housed his workmen over the years and provided a place to stay when he wanted to be on site during construction. Some nights it had rocked with loud parties, too much drinking, and more testosterone and bad jokes than was probably healthy, but those days had ended just a week ago when the final work had been completed.

Now the lodge was quiet. A few lights illuminated the main room downstairs, but he'd head up to his apartment in a few minutes and hope like hell he could get a decent night's sleep. He was exhausted from the long drive and the emotions that had been all over the map these past few days, not to mention the night he'd spent with Dink.

Sighing, Mac realized he was grinning, that his mood had lifted immeasurably with merely the thought of his old friend. The fact that Dink had flown all the way from New York to California so Mac wouldn't have to be alone last night—now that was proof of friendship.

And, if he was perfectly honest, it was proof of Dink's love as well. Mac had always known Dink loved him. What he hadn't realized until last night was how much he loved the guy back.

That love would keep him going until he finally contacted Zianne. Dink understood. He'd been there in the very beginning. Had known exactly how it was between Mac and his amazing woman.

He'd shared laughter and love. He knew Zianne. Knew her as a warm and brilliant woman, as the perfect mate for Mac. Just knowing there was someone out there who understood how he felt was more important than Mac had realized. It was the one thing that had given him the strength to bare his soul to the kids tonight.

Kids. He had to stop thinking of them as kids, but they seemed so damned young, while he felt old as the hills. Would Zianne even recognize him, the way he'd aged?

Hell. One more thing to worry about. He was such a fool.

The air had grown cool. Mac gazed at the quiet lodge and then paused near the front steps and stared at the night sky. It was so clear and beautiful up here at elevation. The stars glistened like bits of white fire sparkling with life, filled with promise. The scents of pine and sage and sun-warmed rocks filled his senses, and he could almost imagine Zianne standing beside him, looking up at the sky and talking about a future neither one of them had been sure of.

Damn, but he missed her. Missed her amazing mind, her sense of humor, the way she understood who and what he was, what made him tick. She'd known him inside and out, quite literally, and he shivered, remembering the time she'd become pure energy and had melded her body to his.

He could still feel the crackling energy, the sense of connection as she found a place within his bones and muscles, within his very cells, a living mass of energy with a heart and a soul. He thought of her the one time he'd brought her up here, before the ink had even dried on the papers giving him ownership of this thousand acres of land.

They'd stood here together, just the two of them holding hands and staring at the same sky. It had been late afternoon, maybe a week before she'd disappeared. Over the past few weeks, she'd been worried about getting caught, about not making it back to him. She'd said they needed a plan, something she could hold on to if they were ever separated.

He hadn't told her he'd already been working on it, that he'd found a piece of property that would be perfect, so he'd brought her up here to look at the land. They'd driven most of the day and she'd loved the trip, the chance to see more of the earth outside of Silicon Valley.

They'd stood in the same spot where he'd eventually built the lodge, holding hands and staring at the rocks and sand and scraggly Jeffrey pines. Zianne had raised her eyes to the heavens. She'd gazed at the sky as the sun slipped behind the mountain and he could still remember the way she'd sighed.

When she'd turned back to him, her eyes had glistened like amethysts. There'd been tears on her cheeks and a smile on those beautiful lips. She'd spoken in his mind, the words as intimate as a kiss.

You'll do it, Mac. I know you will. You'll save us all.

God damn, but he hoped she was right.

She should be at her ship now. He tried to imagine what was happening at this moment. He'd known for the past twenty years that she must have been caught or she would have returned, and yet now, on this date, maybe at this very hour, she would be arriving aboard the ship.

Whatever had prevented her return twenty years ago was happening now, possibly at this very second. His heart ached. He worried for Zianne's safety; he feared for her life should the Gar capture her and choose to make an example of her.

Even worse, he hoped like hell the Gar hadn't decided to head to another solar system, but he doubted that. This planet was too ripe for the picking, too vulnerable to an attack from space, but if Zianne had returned to find the ship gone, she could be dead. Without her soulstone, he knew she couldn't survive for long. But if the Gar had gone, somehow she would have returned to Mac, wouldn't she?

He blinked away the sudden rush of tears. He had to quit thinking of all the worst-case scenarios, but if Zianne was already there, why hadn't she tried to contact him? Their mental link had been so powerful, their ability to connect absolutely unshakable. Why hadn't he heard from her yet?

The dates had to be right. They'd used the stars in the sky as their calendar, the phases of the moon and what Zianne had remembered about the process of linking to Mac and finding him in the past. Considering the number of days she'd been with him, the many trips back and forth that she'd made over the four months they'd been together, they should have nailed it.

He'd keep sending out his thoughts, continue calling to her. And hope like hell she appeared. His arms had been empty for too many years. His heart hadn't quit aching. He needed her.

Needed her more now than in all the years she'd been gone.
Needed to know that the dreams he'd had for the two of them
being together forever were more than mere fantasy.

Dreams of life with Zianne had kept him alive for the past
twenty years. What if he failed? What would become of him if
the dreams proved false?

What the hell did a man do when his dreams died?

Face flushed, heart pounding, Rodie stared at the stars
twinkling through the skylight above her head. "Holy. Shit."
She let out a huge breath and clamped her hands down on the
arms of her chair. Her vaginal muscles twitched and clenched and
she could actually smell the scent of her own arousal.

"How the hell did that happen?" She glanced at the dials and
various readouts in front of her. Nothing. No sign of contact,
though she hadn't been watching when it happened. According
to the readouts, there was nothing out of the ordinary, but
she'd never, not once, climaxed alone without touching herself.

Past tense, because the orgasm she was coming down from
right now had been one hell of a rush. She could barely remember the fantasy. Something about Morgan and another man and
her, all three of them naked together, which was just weird, because after the trauma of finding her boyfriend in bed with a
strange guy and another woman, the last thing Rodie figured
she'd ever want to fantasize about was a threesome.

Playing it back in her mind had her growing aroused all over
again. Shit. What the hell had happened? She'd almost fallen
asleep, she'd been so relaxed, and then her mind had started
spinning tales of Morgan. She tried to find that same sense of
relaxation again, and as her breathing slowed and her heart rate
returned to normal, the memories returned.

He'd been naked in her imagination, and since she'd never
seen him without clothes, the fantasy Morgan was hotter than

hell. Probably best if she never really saw him naked, because reality was never as good as the real thing, but her fantasy Morgan had been perfect.

Lean and muscular, his eyes flashing with desire, and it was all aimed at Rodie. Then the other guy had appeared. He'd never been all that distinct, though he had Morgan's dark hair—at least on his head. Unlike Morgan, there didn't appear to be any body hair on her fantasy third guy—not anywhere, including on his groin. Just dark, hot, sleek, sexy, male skin.

Somehow, she'd ended up on top of Morgan, rubbing her nipples across his chest, teasing his lips with hers, and finally settling herself down over his long, thick cock for a ride. She'd taken him all the way inside until he'd bottomed out, had felt the stretch and burn as he'd slowly worked his way deep, with her muscles tightening around him, gripping his full length.

Then the other guy—where the *hell* had he come from?—had run his big hands over her neck and shoulders, along her bare back, because this was, after all, sexual fantasy, right? He'd left shivering skin wherever he touched.

She felt the shivers now, as if he still touched her. Insane. This was absolutely insane.

Good lord. She remembered the rest. The images were there, slamming into her with the clarity of reality, but it was the weirdest thing, what happened next. She never fantasized about guys touching her back *there.* That was something her ex wanted, but she'd never let him. A girl had her standards, right? But this fantasy guy had not only touched, he'd used his mouth on her and then on Morgan's balls, and while she couldn't get the logistics right in her head, it had somehow worked just perfectly in her fantasy.

She'd been so hot, so primed by the time he'd used his fingers to penetrate her that it had felt wonderful, like the only thing that could make her happy. Then he'd used his cock.

Oh, mama! Rodie let out a huge breath of air, aware of a new clenching, a tightening of muscles between her legs. Hell, she was coming again, just from the memory of sensation!

It had been just that—a real sensation. The stretch and burn of entry had been absolutely real and the details in her head amazing. He'd been so hot. The skin over his hard shaft had been soft and smooth, and the tip was sleek as silk and so soft and pliable. She'd felt him slowly pressing and pushing through her tight anal sphincter. She'd been so relaxed she'd opened for him. She hadn't felt pain beyond that initial stretch and burn. None at all.

Which was the only reason she figured it had to have been a fantasy. No way any of it had happened. Except it felt real. Her climax had sure been off-the-charts real!

She pulled up the memory and felt him again, pressing, filling her up in back as Morgan slowly stroked in and out of her sex. She felt the two men sliding over one another with nothing but the thin sheath between her vaginal wall and rectum separating them, and she'd arched her back, whimpering with pleasure.

When her climax hit . . . she'd never experienced anything like it. Never, but remembering now left her feeling flushed all over again. Rodie wiped the back of her hand across her brow and it came away dripping with sweat. Her sweatshirt was stuck to her body. Her nipples looked like bullets, the way they poked against the soft cotton.

Even her jeans felt wet. Oh, shit. She crawled out of the comfortable leather recliner, careful not to tear the mesh cap covering her hair, patted her crotch, and almost giggled with relief when she realized she hadn't soaked through, that the leather seat wasn't wet.

She'd absolutely die of embarrassment if she'd left a wet spot. Sighing, she plopped back down and stared at the displays once again. She hadn't noticed if they'd altered at all during the fantasy, but she hadn't really looked, either. Maybe Mac had a readout somewhere that she could look at. Right now they were all normal, showing no sign of contact.

So what had made her fantasize like that? Why would she think of things she was positive she didn't like? How could those same thoughts turn her on so much?

Must be the setting. It had to be. The setting and all the talk about sex and the fantasizing and sharing their thoughts on the way up. Yeah . . . that had to be it.

She settled back into the chair and got comfortable again, but she couldn't get back into fantasy. It was like all that sexual tension she'd been feeling all day was gone. Hell, maybe she wouldn't be spending all her time alone in her cabin frigging herself. Not if she could sit out here and come all by herself without even touching!

Thank goodness there weren't any recorders. Lordy, if someone had caught her on camera she'd feel like such an idiot.

She closed her eyes and examined the way her body felt. She'd never had sex that left her feeling this replete, and she'd had a lot of sex over the years.

She'd never had a fantasy with quite the same result, either. Nope, her fantasies were usually pretty good, but it always took either a set of new batteries in her favorite vibrator—which she'd remembered to pack, thank goodness—or the judicious use of her fingers.

And doing it on her own never left her with the same after-glow she had now, though she wished she could get that feeling back, the way it had been when she'd felt Morgan slipping deep inside the front of her, and her fantasy man filling up the back. That first deep slide had been exquisite.

But how had she known? How could she possibly have pulled a fantasy like that out of nowhere?

A soft tap on the door had her spinning in her chair to see who was coming in. Cam poked his head through the door. "How'd it go? I'm here for my shift."

"Already?" She hadn't even glanced at the clock, but Cam was right. It was exactly midnight. "Wow. It went great. I mean, time really flew by." She released the raised leg rest on the recliner and planted her feet on the floor. "It's nice and quiet in here; the temperature is perfect." She pointed at a row of buttons next to the arm of the chair. "You can adjust the chair, the lighting, the temperature—all of it, right there. I checked out the restroom in the back and it's even got a shower. There's a small room next to it with a refrigerator with bottled water and drinks, and all kinds of snack stuff."

Cam glanced around the small room. "Cool," he said. "This really is sweet. I can't believe we're getting paid for this. So, did you send any great fantasies winging off into outer space?"

Rodie forced a soft laugh as she peeled her mesh cap off her hair and put it back in the little drawer where Mac had found it. No way was she going to tell anyone about tonight's fantasy.

Especially not a guy she didn't even know—one who was sexy enough to take a starring role in any of her fantasies. Cam shot her a grin as he grabbed the mesh cap with his name on it. He stared at it like he wasn't quite sure how it fit.

"Here." Rodie took it out of his hands and showed him the tag with his name. "This goes in the back, right at the base of your skull. That will position all the little sensors where they belong."

"Thanks." He leaned forward and she slipped it on for him, checking to make sure everything was in the right place.

"That looks good." She stood and watched while he settled himself into the chair and adjusted it with his feet raised.

He scrunched his butt around right where she'd been sitting. "You left it nice and warm for me. Thanks." Then he winked and added, "That's going to be my first fantasy. What was Rodie really thinking of out here all alone in the night?"

She felt the rush of heat over her chest and throat, knew it rose all the way to her eyebrows. "You just do that," she said. "Have fun. I'm outta here."

Then, for whatever reason, she leaned over and planted a kiss on his mouth. The moment her lips touched his, she had a panicked *What the fuck am I doing?* moment.

Then Cam kissed her back, and the panic melted away. His lips were soft and warm, and his left hand slid around her waist and up her back until he cupped the back of her head, holding her closer for his exploration as he took control. She felt the damp sweep of his tongue across the closed seam between her lips, sensed the question in him, but she kept her mouth closed.

Kept her mouth closed and her mind open. Cam's thoughts spilled into her head, and it was hard not to smile against his lips. He didn't push it, but he didn't end the kiss all that fast, either. No, he nibbled at her lower lip and brushed his tongue over her upper one until she could hear nothing but the blood roaring in her ears, feel nothing but the firm pressure of his palm against her skull, his lips on her mouth.

She was the one to end it. Thank goodness she managed to do it without sighing. The boy could kiss. Damn, but he could kiss!

"So," he said, tilting his head and smiling at her. "What was that for?"

She shrugged. Kept it light. "I just wanted to give you something to think about."

His grin was definitely cocky as he rubbed his right hand over the erection straining the front of his jeans. "You most certainly have, sweetheart. And I thank you."

She flipped him a jaunty wave. "Hope your shift goes well," she said. Then she was closing the door behind her and stepping out into the crystal-clear night, where she stopped long enough to suck in a few huge, deep breaths.

Stars shimmered brilliantly overhead, shining through air so clear and cold she felt as if she could reach out and touch each one. The moon had already disappeared behind the mountain to the west, and the air smelled deliciously clean—like sage and pine and sun-heated stone.

Rodie took another deep breath and listened with her entire body attuned to the world around her, absorbing the night, the last few hours she'd spent in the dream shack ... and Cam's kiss. She still tasted him on her lips, and while he might look like a sexy teenager, he kissed like a man who knew what he wanted.

Of all the guys, Cameron was the one who'd interested her the least, and yet he was the first one of their group she'd really kissed.

And damned if she didn't want to do it again. "If this is what the first night is like ..." Shaking her head, she jammed her hands into her back pockets, chuckling softly at how small her voice sounded. The next few months—hell, the next few days—could really prove to be interesting. When she considered their goal, her mind almost refused to believe what her heart so easily accepted, but it had to be this place as much as Mac and his dream. There was something about this country, about the satellite dishes marching across the plateau and the huge sky overhead, that made her feel almost tiny—tiny and totally insignificant, even as it fired her imagination.

She'd never spent a night in the mountains. Not this far from civilization and all the noise and stench of humanity. There was no smog. No sound of traffic. Not a police siren or the crash and bang of garbage trucks. No voices, no screech of brakes or barking dogs.

Surrounded by mountains and a sky that went on forever, she could have felt like the only living creature, but it wasn't silent by any stretch of the imagination. She cocked her head and listened for the natural sounds of night. An owl hooted. Then something squeaked overhead, and she was almost certain it was a bat. Way off in the distance she heard the howl of a coyote, followed by a series of sharp yips and more howls as others joined in. Wind made a soft shushing sound in the trees. The air was cool, though not uncomfortably cold, and Rodie couldn't remember ever feeling so isolated and yet so much a part of anything in her life.

She felt it with a powerful sense of certainty—this job was going to change her. In fact, change already had begun. Her telepathic skills were blossoming. She'd sensed Cam's arousal, but she'd heard his thoughts, so clear and vivid, he might have spoken them aloud. Except she knew he hadn't, or they probably both would have been embarrassed. She knew now that he found her attractive. She'd been certain he was gay, but now she knew he was pure heterosexual male with enough curiosity about guys to at least wonder what it was like.

And he really wanted to get naked with her.

And with Kiera and Lizzie, and Morgan and Finn while he was at it. She should have asked him why he didn't add Mac to the mix, but then she'd be giving herself away.

No, it was nice to know what someone was thinking, but probably safer all around not to admit it. At least not until she got to know him better.

That was going to happen. She was almost positive. After that kiss, Rodie was absolutely certain she'd like to get naked with Cameron Paisley, too.

And with Kiera and Lizzie and Morgan and Finn as well. But she'd invite Mac along. You couldn't have an orgy and leave out the guy who bought the beer.

Walking across the open area to her cabin, Rodie stopped, trapped once again by the beauty of the stars overhead. Was there really a star cruiser loaded with captive aliens up there?

Had anyone heard her? Did that fantasy of hers—along with her orgasm—make it to Mac's Nyrians? She hoped so, though there was no way to know.

He had said he really didn't expect anyone to make contact until each of them had spent at least one shift in the dream shack.

He'd told them to think of it as introducing themselves. It was the first step in letting the Nyrians know someone was down here actively wanting to help, that these human minds were receptive and that the power in the array would help the Nyrians draw the strength they needed to come to Earth.

The biggest problem, as far as Rodie could tell, was figuring out how to get the Nyrians' soulstones before they escaped. Maybe just knowing there was a whole group of people with telepathic abilities waiting to help them, they'd be able to come up with a workable plan.

Mac was so certain they'd make contact. Was he basing his feelings on fact, or on his dreams of lost love?

She wondered if he'd heard from the one he knew, from Zianne. And then she thought about the kind of love a man could carry for twenty years, focusing his entire life—his professional career along with a fucking fortune—on finding his lost love.

It said a lot about the kind of man Mac was—one capable of loving with absolute certainty, with a deep emotional connection and no promise that he'd ever again see the woman he loved.

It would take a very special man. And it changed everything she'd thought about MacArthur Dugan. He was definitely much more than a very wealthy, very smart man. He was suddenly so much more human, his emotions, his absolute loyalty to Zianne and her people a huge part of the whole package.

And it was probably the most romantic story Rodie'd ever heard. Blinking back tears, she sent a private little thought winging off on its own. Sent it to Zianne, just to let her know that Rodie hoped she was okay, that they would all do their best to bring Zianne and her people to safety.

Then, trying not to feel foolish over the tears streaming down her cheeks, she slipped inside her cabin and locked the door behind her.

She probably didn't need to lock it, but she couldn't get that fantasy out of her mind, and she couldn't help but wonder if that third guy hadn't been more than a mere figment of her imagination.

What if he'd been one of Zianne's fellow travelers? Had Rodie made contact without knowing it? Maybe she'd ask Mac tomorrow when she saw him. It wasn't the sort of question she was ready to ask in front of the others. Not yet.

She stripped out of her clothes and took a quick shower, but before she climbed into bed, she checked the lock on the door one more time. Satisfied the cabin was secure, Rodie pulled the blankets over herself and drifted off to sleep.

7

Mac stared at the illuminated dial on the clock. Midnight. Seven minutes later than the last time he'd looked. Rodie would be heading to bed and Cam should be hooked up to the array. He didn't worry about anyone missing their scheduled time—there'd been so much excitement that the kids practically buzzed with it once they'd left Rodie inside the dream shack.

He thought about walking over to her cabin, about asking how her shift went, but they'd had a long day, and he imagined she'd head straight to bed.

He'd love to be inside her head right now, but that was one of the problems with telepathy. He had to be really close to people to pick up their thoughts. Except with Zianne—they could communicate from a fairly good distance, though his abilities weren't anything like hers. She'd found him through time and space, though they couldn't actually communicate across that distance.

Still, she'd followed her sense of him in the beginning, some sort of psychic imprint that she'd picked up, and the closer she'd gotten, the easier it had been for her to find him.

Then she'd latched on to his sexual fantasy and the rest was . . . unbelievable. Good lord, but he missed her.

He'd tried calling her for days now, sending his thoughts out on a direct line to Zianne in the hope she might answer, but there'd been nothing. He wasn't discouraged. Not yet—she might just be arriving at her ship—hardly long enough to find him and come back in his time.

Time. It was all so confusing, and yet as far as Zianne was concerned, she'd just left his bed and returned to the ship. She wouldn't know the loss he'd experienced, the sense of being so damned alone for almost half his life. Hell, he didn't even look the same. He'd been a young man of twenty-six, still in his prime, still filled with hopes and dreams and so much in love with her that nothing else had really mattered.

He still loved her, but he was so different. When he looked in the mirror Mac saw a middle-aged man who'd worked his ass off for the past twenty years. A man who'd known both success and failure, who had followed a dream for two decades—a dream powered by hope. That sense of hope was there, though not nearly as fresh and shiny. Some of his dreams had come to pass, others waited out there, but that's where hope came in.

The love hadn't changed. If anything, he loved her more now than he had so many years ago, back when he thought he'd always have her. Loss had a way of doing that. When you loved someone as much as he loved Zianne, and then lost that love . . . well, it changed a man. Changed him in too many ways to count.

Would she even know him now? He wasn't that bright-eyed youth who had fallen head over heels for a beautiful, mysterious woman. No, he was a grown man, jaded, a bit world-weary and definitely world-worn. He'd fought more battles than he'd ever imagined, had lost more than a few, and yet the warrior in him would never rest. Not until he brought Zianne home. Not until he brought all of her people to safety.

But what if he failed? What if . . .

He flipped over to his side and punched the pillow. Damn, but he was tired. So physically and mentally exhausted that his mind seemed to be spinning in circles. He really needed sleep, but nervous tension had him strung like an overstretched rubber band. Hell, he needed a drink or he needed to get laid if he expected to sleep.

"Well, fuck." Where the hell was Dink when he needed him?

He'd been in the same shape last night before his buddy arrived, but the two of them eventually slept like the dead. He'd forgotten how effective sex was at relaxing a guy, but unless he wanted to handle the problem himself, that was out of the picture tonight. Except he knew jerking off wouldn't work. He might get a moment's relief, but he'd still be just as wired and every bit as worried.

Disgusted, Mac threw the covers back and sat on the edge of the bed. The wood floor was like ice against his bare feet and it was too dark in here. Rubbing absently at his chest, he gazed about the room, fascinated by the fact that it was so dark that he couldn't see anything beyond the green numbers on his clock.

Twelve-oh-four. It was going to be a long night. He held up his hand just inches from his face. Nothing. He might as well have had his eyes closed. He'd forgotten what it was like in the mountains—without the glow from the city, there was absolutely no light at all.

And, like an idiot, he'd neglected to put in a bedside lamp. First thing tomorrow morning . . . "Right. Along with a million other details I probably screwed up."

Grumbling, he ran his hand over the covers and found the pair of sweats he'd left at the foot of the bed. He slipped them on and walked carefully in the direction he thought the door should be. Took three steps and stubbed his toe on one of his boots. "Crap." He lifted his foot and rubbed the offended toe, then flipped on the light switch once he found the wall.

He really needed a bedside lamp. He'd had them put in the cabins, but hadn't given much thought to his own room. He hadn't planned on staying here for the project, but why? Like he was going to leave if there was any chance at all of finding Zianne?

He'd never really thought ahead, had he? Never thought of the actual search. He'd put all his energy into creating the array, but it was like he'd been afraid to think beyond that part of the project, mainly because that part was out of his control.

He hated this phase of a project, when the physical work was complete and everything depended on someone else getting the job done. It was like this at BGV and it was even worse here, where he was depending on his dream team—young people he'd hand-selected but still didn't know all that well.

He hated it more than he'd imagined.

He opened the door and stepped out into the dark hallway. The main floor just below had a couple of low-wattage lamps burning so the stairs were visible. The lodge was quiet. He'd left the main doors unlocked in case anyone wanted anything.

Sort of like he wanted something now. He thought of going downstairs to the gym, getting in some laps in the pool, but a drink sounded like a lot less work. He should have brought a bottle of Jack up to his room when he first went to bed. At least the kitchen was well stocked.

A drink would help him relax, maybe get some sleep. He had to sleep.

The long drive today had been exhausting. The selection process, going through everyone's records, figuring out exactly who was going to work, who wouldn't. Too many sleepless nights, too many details to keep track of. A company to run, politicians to lobby, the pompous jackasses at the Pentagon. Shit. The list was endless. There'd been too damned much of everything.

Hell, the last twenty years had exhausted him. He went

straight to the liquor cabinet, grabbed a new bottle and a shot glass, and headed back up the stairs, but his mind was still spinning, still working through the question that, once broached, now seemed to have captured his mind.

Why hadn't he planned to stay up here? Why had he given so little thought to remaining on site? Like he was going to leave when there was a chance of making contact. Was it his fear of failure? If he'd made plans to stay during the search and nothing was found, would that somehow make things worse?

Was it the lack of control, the fact that he'd been in charge of the development, but now it was out of his hands? So many screwed-up reasons.

He stepped inside his room and closed the door behind him. He'd ordered king-sized beds for all the cabins, including his own. If he'd been so sure of failure, there'd be a damned twin bed in here, right? But he'd gotten one big enough to share with Zianne. Hell, big enough for Dink as well, should the occasion arise. Grinning, he flipped off the light switch and walked across the room in the dark.

At least this time he managed to avoid tripping over his boots. He poured the glass full of the whisky and sat on the edge of the bed in the dark, sipping the fiery drink. Finished it and poured another.

Even without the lights on, he didn't spill a drop.

After the third, he set the bottle and the glass aside and stretched out on top of the covers. A minute later he pulled the comforter over himself. He'd forgotten how cold it got at night, too. Dark and cold, and lonely without Zianne beside him, but that was nothing new.

He'd been lonely for twenty fucking years.

His head was slightly muzzy, but at least the buzz of nerves and too much adrenaline was gone. Closing his eyes, Mac consciously relaxed his taut muscles, felt sleep claim him.

It couldn't have been more than a minute later when he

smelled that familiar sweet scent he'd always associate with
Zianne—vanilla and honey—and the moment his mind recognized her seductive aroma he lurched upright, heart pounding
double-time, and stared into the darkness.

"Zianne? Where are you? I know you're here, sweetheart,
but where?" He shoved the blankets back, stumbled across the
room, and scrabbled for the light switch. It took a minute, but
he finally found it and flipped the damned thing and stared
frantically about. Nothing. He couldn't see her, but she was
here. He knew it. He sensed her presence, her nearness. Her
scent filled his nostrils, so rich he could practically taste her, but
where the hell was she?

"Zianne? I know you're here. Don't do this, sweetheart.
Show yourself to me. Please?"

God, was he losing his mind? Was it the booze? Three shots
shouldn't have him hallucinating, but where the fuck was she?

He stood there, body rigid, heart thudding in his chest. He
had one hand on the light switch, the other flattened against the
wall. Air rushed in and out of his lungs in huge, desperate gasps
for what felt like forever. The scent of honey and vanilla slowly
faded. His heart rate finally slowed. After a while, Mac slid
down the wall and sat on the floor.

Nothing. No sign of her. Not even a lingering bit of her
scent. He must have dreamed it. Dreamed her, like he had so
many nights before, but damn, not now. Not tonight. The array
was finished, his team was in place, the time was right, and if
she was going to return to him, she should be here now.

Zianne. Not a fucking fantasy. Not just a memory.

"Zianne? Where are you?" His voice cracked. He gazed
about the big room, his eyes lingering on unfamiliar shadows,
the dark corners, but she wasn't here. She wasn't anywhere.

Wrapping his arms over the back of his head, Mac cried out,
a harsh, painful howl of pain. Then he pressed his forehead to
his knees and wept.

* * *

Frantic, Zianne hovered in the air just above Mac's sobbing form. Her heart was breaking—or it would, if she could manifest a heart, but she couldn't afford to use the energy it would take to become the woman he knew. It had weakened her to give him her familiar scent, but this wasn't what she wanted! Not Mac sitting on the floor, arms wrapped over his head, sobbing as if he'd lost her. She wanted to scream at him, tell him she was here, but she couldn't. Not without form. Not without burning up what little of her energy she held in reserve.

When it was gone, she would die. How could she reach him?

Before, when they'd been together, she'd shown him what she really was, how she looked on her own world as nothing more than energy, and he'd loved her even then. But they'd discovered that, while Zianne could understand Mac, he couldn't hear her telepathic voice when she was in her natural state. They were just too different.

To take on human form, she'd have to use energy—energy she couldn't replace without the soulstone. Even to take on her normal form would quickly burn out what few reserves she had. She was essentially little more than mist, a shadow among shadows, but at least she was close by, and somehow she'd make her presence known to him.

His mind was so different. He was different, and though she'd seen him just this morning, it had been twenty long years for Mac. Unlike Nyrians, who were immortal as long as they had their soulstones, humans aged.

He was more beautiful to her now than he'd been as a young man. His face had character—a strength she'd recognized in him before, but now it was etched into his appearance, a part of him no one could deny. But the changes in his mind—that was going to make it harder to link. She hadn't thought of that, the fact that with time and experience his brain—his personal mental signature—would actually change.

Somehow, she had to find a way to communicate, or possibly she could get one of her fellow Nyrians to do it for her. The others were coming. She'd sensed Bolt's visit earlier in the evening. He'd come much as she had first visited Mac, arriving as a fantasy, storing up the life-giving energy as he gave pleasure and then returning to the ship. Others would make the journey, learning the minds of the ones here who had come to help.

Once all of them had found a host, a mind that could call them to this world and give them corporeal bodies, then somehow they'd have to secure their soulstones and escape. She hoped they could find hers. She so wanted to live, if only to thank Mac. She'd only been away from him for a few hours, and yet the pain of missing Mac was a powerful ache deep inside.

How had he managed for twenty long years? She understood time. Knew how long a day was. Mac had waited for her for well beyond seven thousand days.

No wonder he wept. She settled her consciousness over him and held him close. Seeped into his warm flesh and merged within his very cells. He wouldn't even know she was near, but at least this way, in her own way, she could hold him. Offer him comfort and love, and the hope that somehow, some way, his plan to save all of them would work.

And somehow, she had to find a way to speak with him, to tell him she was here. It was important for him to know, that even if she didn't survive, her love would last forever.

Mac awoke stiff and sore. His eyes burned and his butt ached from sleeping on the cold floor. Blinking away the fog of dreams, he slowly shoved himself to his feet. Back propped against the wall, he reached around and flipped off the light before stumbling across the room and collapsing on the bed.

It was a little after two. Hell, he couldn't believe he'd been on the floor for almost two fucking hours. What an ass he was.

How could he have possibly thought Zianne was here in his room? Here, yet not making herself known to him.

That didn't make any sense. None at all, but somehow . . . he stared into the darkness, opening himself to the sounds and scents in the room. He did feel her. He was almost certain he sensed her presence.

It was subtle, but he couldn't deny the sense of warmth, the feeling that Zianne was nearby. Had something happened that kept her from announcing herself? Was there a reason she couldn't materialize?

Closing his eyes, he tried to relax and let his mind work unencumbered. Sometimes his clearest thoughts came to him when he wasn't trying to think.

If Zianne were caught in her energy form, they couldn't communicate. That much they'd proved while she was still with him, but he could see her in that form. He'd not been able to see her at all, no matter how clearly he'd scented her. So what could have happened? And if that was the problem—that somehow she couldn't take on a corporeal body, how could he help her fix it?

There was always a solution. You couldn't have a problem without a solution. Answers weren't always easy to find, but they were out there. Somewhere. Just like Zianne.

Once again he felt sleep claim him. Hopefully, the answers would come to him then. Hopefully, he would awaken to find Zianne.

That was all he really had right now, wasn't it? Hope.

Rodie heard the soft tapping on her front door and rolled over. Sun blasted her through the open blinds. She blinked, squinting at the brilliant light.

Note to self—remember to close the frickin' blinds before you fall asleep.

The tapping came again. Grumbling, she crawled out of bed and shuffled across the cold floor, walked through the front room, opened the door, and squinted at the figure just outside on the porch. "Kiera? What are you doing here so early?"

Kiera grinned at her and walked in without an invite. "C'mon, Rodie. It's almost nine. I'm dying to hear how your shift went."

Bemused, Rodie stood back from the door and waved her inside. Kiera put a steaming cup of coffee in her hand as she walked past.

"Oh!" Sighing, Rodie held the cup to her nose and inhaled. "Why didn't you say you had coffee? You're officially forgiven." Blinking owlishly, she closed the door, headed straight to the living room couch, and curled up against the big leather pillow at one end.

Kiera ignored the couch and flopped down in the overstuffed recliner closest to Rodie. She took a sip of her own cup. "I figured I'd have to bribe you if I woke you up. How'd it go? Was it fun or boring? What was it like?"

Rodie took a long swallow. It was almost worth burning her tongue for the wonderful taste. "It was . . ." Frowning, she took another sip.

"Rodie!"

"I'm thinking! Interesting. Yep. Definitely interesting."

"Do I have to take your coffee away?"

"Over my dead body." Carefully, she took another swallow. "Okay. I don't know how to explain what happened, but I'll give it a shot. Remember . . . this is on only a few swallows of my drug of choice. I was sitting there in my comfy chair, funky little cap on my head, staring at the stars through the skylight. I had turned off all the lights in the dream shack so I could see the stars outside, and it was just gorgeous."

"So? Was it hard to let yourself loose to fantasize? I mean, that's got to feel so weird—thinking about really personal sexual stuff and knowing your thoughts are actually going somewhere."

The caffeine was beginning to hit home. Rodie straightened up and drank a couple more swallows. "I figured, with all the good-looking guys around, there was plenty to think about, so I started in on a fantasy with Morgan."

"Morgan?" Kiera's voice went up a notch. "Why him? He's sort of scary."

"Yeah, but he's hot, too. Really hot. So I was just thinking of him naked, and it was working. I mean, I could feel my body getting into what my head was doing, so I sorta went with the flow." She gave Kiera a meaningful look and grinned.

"And?"

"Next thing I know, there's another guy in my fantasy."

"What? Who?" Kiera leaned forward.

"Haven't the foggiest. He was a complete stranger, but he was just as hot as Morgan and . . ." She paused, lost for words. How did you explain something that had never happened before? How could she describe her experience without sounding like an idiot?

"What happened?"

Kiera held her cup in both hands. Rodie took another swallow of her coffee and realized the cup was almost empty. Shrugging, she said, "I climaxed. Didn't even touch myself, but in my fantasy I had two hot men making love to me, doing things I've never done in real life. It felt real."

And it had. She could still feel the burn of that one guy entering her backside. Felt the pressure and the hot slide of his cock, the way he slid over Morgan's erection deep inside her. Shaking herself, Rodie realized her heart was pounding and she was getting wet between her legs—again. Raising her eyes, her breathing stuttering in her lungs as if she were back in the dream, as if her body was filled again by two amazingly beautiful men, she gazed blindly at Kiera. "I really can't explain it, but it was so much more than just a fantasy."

So much more that she was still a little lost in the memory.

Rodie shook her head, physically shaking herself out of the dream, and shrugged again. "When I came?" She fanned herself with her fingers. "Wow. So hard. It was pretty amazing. I mean, it's one thing to use a vibrator or even your hand to bring yourself off, but it was just my imagination—my fantasy." She snorted and slapped a hand over her mouth. "And it wasn't just any old climax—this sucker was off-the-charts hot."

She giggled, relaxing more as she woke up, as she actually talked about what had happened. Somehow, talking about it made it seem less intense, more like an adventure. "I came so fucking hard I just about soaked through my jeans. I actually got out of the chair to make sure I didn't leave a wet spot. I swear, Kiera . . . I've never had sex that good."

"Oh, shit." Laughing, Kiera set her cup on the table between them and wrapped her arms around her knees. "Lizzie's in there now. I wonder how that little girl's doing? Believe me, she's got a wicked imagination. And I saw Finn a little while ago, but he looked sort of shell-shocked. Walked right by me without a word."

She giggled. "And he did leave a wet spot. At least on his jeans. I sure hope the dude brought some extra pants, or that he doesn't mind doing laundry."

"Finn? That reminds me. What did you and Lizzie do to him yesterday?"

Kiera stood. "I'll tell you while we're hiking."

"While we're what?" Rodie set her cup on the table, crawled off the couch, and stretched.

"Hiking. I don't have to be in the shack until noon, but I really need to stretch my legs. I'm not all that used to the elevation yet, so I don't plan to run this morning, but I thought I'd go for a hike. Why don't you come with me and I'll tell you all about

Lizzie and Kiera's truly amazing sex attack on Finnegan O'-Toole." She bent at the waist and touched her toes. Then she straightened and grabbed both empty coffee cups.

"Meet me in the lodge in fifteen minutes. There's plenty of food over there that you can carry with you. C'mon, girl. This is an adventure. You're sleeping through it!"

Grumbling, Rodie agreed. "Okay. Fifteen, but I'm gonna want all the details."

"You got it." Then Kiera totally surprised her. She leaned close and planted a warm kiss on Rodie's mouth.

Rodie hadn't expected it, but she didn't hesitate. She'd thought Kiera was hot when she'd watched her yesterday, and the kiss proved it. Rodie'd never kissed a woman before—at least not like this—but it felt right. More than just right.

Go figure. But Kiera's lips were full and soft, and when her hand found Rodie's breast, bare beneath her cotton tank, it felt too damned good to ignore. Rodie moved closer and wrapped her hand around the back of Kiera's neck, cupping her skull beneath the thick ponytail caught up in her ball cap.

She thought of the kiss she'd shared with Cameron just last night, and the way he'd held her. The same way she was holding Kiera.

A moment later, Kiera broke the kiss, but the broad smile she flashed at Rodie was pure invitation for more. Rodie actually recovered first. "Fifteen minutes. Now quit tempting me." She plucked Kiera's hand off her breast and kissed her fingers. "Go. Now." She made shooing motions with all ten fingers.

"Yes, ma'am." Kiera grinned and saluted. Rodie watched the girl's slim butt as she closed the door behind her. Then she headed into the bathroom. She'd get her shower later. Right now, she needed to go out and burn off some of the energy that seemed to be thrumming in her veins. And she couldn't wait to see how the others had fared with their time in the dream shack.

* * *

They'd decided to follow the fence line, and it turned out to be a harder hike than Rodie'd expected. It was all fairly flat on the plateau, but the ground was rough and brush that had been cleared away to build the fence had begun to grow back in some areas, making it almost impassable.

They still got back in plenty of time for Kiera's shift. Sweaty and feeling great, Rodie paused in front of Kiera's cabin and gave her a quick hug. "That was fun. Is your ankle okay?"

Kiera had twisted it going over a fallen tree. "It's fine. I'm going to take a quick shower and grab something to eat on my way to the dream shack."

"I'm hungry, too." Rodie glanced toward the lodge and wondered if that was where everyone had gone. It had been empty when she'd grabbed a couple of muffins and some bottled water to take along on their hike. "You've got plenty of time." She checked her wristwatch. "Almost half an hour before your shift."

Kiera unlocked her door. "Thanks for going with me. That really was fun. Mac said the loop is a little over four miles, so it's good exercise. Gotta tone this baby up." She slapped her butt for emphasis, waved, and slipped through the door.

Rodie's cabin was on the opposite side of the lodge. She headed around the back of the building, taking the shortest way to her cabin. Shower first, then food.

"Hey, Rodie."

"Morgan!" There was no controlling the flush that must have her cheeks turning deep red, but that fantasy last night had been so real, so *intimate*.

She took a deep breath and smiled. Moved closer and grinned. "Whatcha got?"

It was a squirrel, an adorable little squirrel perched on Morgan's knee, all fluffy and gray with a white tummy and sparkling eyes, sitting on its haunches with its little paws folded over its chest. Like it was waiting for something, or maybe just begging.

Rodie walked closer. "Oh god. That is so cute. And it's so tame." Moving slowly, she took the seat next to Morgan. The squirrel didn't even flinch. Rodie reached into her pocket, searching for any of the leftovers from her breakfast. She found the muffin wrapper, pulled it out, and picked some tiny bits of leftover whole-grain muffin off the paper.

The squirrel immediately hopped off Morgan's knee and perched on the flat arm of her wooden deck chair. Rodie held a tiny bit of muffin out on the end of her finger. The squirrel sniffed, gave Rodie a very appraising eye, and then daintily nibbled the tiny offering.

Morgan chuckled. "Well, she's certainly fickle."

Rodie couldn't take her eyes off the squirrel. She gave her another bit of muffin. "Why do you say that?"

"She was my best buddy as long as I had sunflower seeds left." He held up the empty bag. "Just like a woman. She can be bought."

Rodie laughed as the squirrel pried her fingers open with tiny little paws, looking for more. She scraped the last of the muffin off the wrapper and glanced at Morgan as she held out the final morsel to the little beast. "Be grateful she's not asking for diamonds."

The squirrel cocked her head and stared at Rodie. Her little muzzle was covered in crumbs, and Rodie had the oddest feeling it understood her. One day at the array and she was already getting weird. She turned as Morgan stood. "You leaving?" Laughing, she waved him off. "Talk about fickle. Your new girlfriend spends a minute with someone else and you're gone."

He smiled at her, and for a moment the tough guy with all the attitude was gone. Rodie's breath caught in her throat, but Morgan merely nodded toward the door. "Going after more squirrel food," he said. "Now that I know her affections are for sale."

The squirrel chattered and sat on Rodie's knee, but Rodie

was watching the door. Watching as Morgan disappeared inside the lodge and took a little chunk of her heart with him.

How? She hardly knew him. Didn't totally like what she did know and wasn't at all ready to fall for anyone. Not when she was up here with more available man—and woman—flesh, than she'd ever had a chance to connect with in one place before.

This was nuts. Purely nuts, but she was still staring at the door a moment later when Morgan walked through. He had another whole grain muffin and a handful of peanuts. And he was still smiling, but this time it was all for Rodie.

Morgan didn't know what it was about the little black—or almost black—chick, but he couldn't stay away from her, and whenever he was around her, he was either hard as stone or wanting to laugh at something. Anything, because he knew she liked to see him smile.

Had she totally forgotten that they had to block their minds so they wouldn't broadcast every thought? Hers were wide open to him, but since she wasn't reacting to any of the prurient ideas currently filtering through his head, he had to assume he was blocking his own just fine.

"Hold out your hand."

She did. He dumped some peanuts into her palm. The squirrel hopped up on the arm of the chair, reached out with a little paw, and dragged Rodie's hand down so she could get to the nuts.

Rodie's face lit up and she looked about twelve, though after the dream he'd had last night, Morgan could never see her as a kid. Not ever.

He'd gone to bed early—no point in staying awake since he didn't have his first shift until late afternoon—but he'd barely fallen asleep when the dream started. Only he wasn't sure if he'd been dreaming or maybe picking up on Rodie's fantasies.

She was in the dream shack and his cabin was really close to it, so he could have been catching her thoughts, couldn't he? If so, that made the whole thing even hotter, if he'd actually been sharing something she was fantasizing, but he'd fallen into a fantasy that still teased him today.

He'd been with Rodie, but there'd been another guy there as well. He was big and dark, his chest smooth and well muscled, and the two of them had taken Rodie at the same time.

Sitting here now, watching her laugh and hand peanuts to a cute little squirrel—hell, who'd ever think of her taking on two guys, even if it was only in her fantasies? She looked so sweet and innocent, but that dream had been pure passion.

He'd imagined a threesome before, though he'd never done it. One man or one woman at a time had been the extent of his sexual experience, but he'd been inside Rodie at the same time the other guy had entered her from behind, and he could still feel the smooth, hot slide of another man's dick against his own. The tight, rhythmic clenching of Rodie's muscles, holding both of them inside her.

His fantasy? Or hers? He didn't think it had been his. For one thing, he'd always gone for guys who were slighter of build or smaller than him, for some reason—guys like O'Toole, who were just out for a good fuck, or even Cam, with his little-boy look and a body that was all tight, sculpted muscles just made for screwing—but the guy last night had been tall and muscular—lean, hard angles—and dark all over. Bronzed skin, dark hair, dark eyes. Mysterious, but still very hot.

Had to be Rodie's fantasy guy, but Morgan figured he'd hang on to the image himself for a while. He glanced at Rodie. She'd put a small pile of peanuts on the arm of the chair and the squirrel was happily munching away.

"I don't want to give her too many. Wonder why she's so tame?" Rodie ran a finger over the squirrel's head. She flicked an ear as if Rodie's gentle touch tickled, but she stayed put.

"There've been a lot of workmen up here. I imagine they've

been feeding the wildlife." Morgan ran a finger along the squirrel's tail. "Fluffy little thing, isn't she?"

Rodie nodded. "Wonder if it means we'll have a really cold winter. Isn't that some kind of sign?" Then she sort of shook herself. "I'm losing track of time." She stood and brushed the crumbs off her lap. "I need to get a shower and then some lunch. Kiera and I walked around the entire plateau this morning. Mac told her it's about four miles, but it was fun."

"Will you have lunch with me?" He wasn't sure where that came from, but as soon as he made the invitation, Morgan thought it felt right.

Rodie blinked, like she was really surprised by his request, but before he could backpedal his way out of it she smiled at him and nodded. "Twenty minutes?"

"I'll meet you inside. Lizzie should be in by then. I want to find out all I can about your time in the dream shack."

Laughing, Rodie spun away. "And maybe I'll fill you in on some of what Kiera told me she and Lizzie pulled on Finn on the way up. I want to get Lizzie's side of the story."

Then she really surprised him. Rodie leaned close and planted a kiss on him. Her soft lips slid easily over his with just enough pressure to leave a promise lingering. Before he had time to respond, she spun away, ran down the steps, and across the open area to her cabin.

He rubbed a fingertip over his lips, and his mind went back to the fantasy, back to a different side of Rodie Bishop. Was she the kind of woman who would welcome something that earthy, that raw? Sex with two men—men who enjoyed each other as much as they enjoyed her?

Well, there was bound to be a chance to find out. Morgan cracked another peanut and fed it to the squirrel, but his thoughts were all tied up in Rodie.

8

Mac shut off the computer and glanced at the clock. It was already 12:30, and he hadn't been out of his room since a quick run downstairs to snag a cinnamon bagel and a cup of coffee sometime before six this morning. But he'd promised to stay in touch with his CEO at Beyond Global Ventures while he was at the site, and that meant logging on early and putting in a good five or six hours before everyone got too busy to respond.

None of the BGV employees, including the guys at the top, had any idea at all what this project of his entailed. All they really knew was that it was Mac's baby, and now that it was up and running, it was his number-one priority. He paid his top people a lot of money to run his company and make more money, something they did quite well. He'd pulled in the finest research and development team in the world, had excellent people in management, and he'd quickly discovered that R and D worked best when left on their own to do their thing—and management managed quite well without him.

That didn't mean he wasn't involved in just about every aspect of the company. That single-minded concentration and involvement—and the need to maintain total control—was why he'd been so successful, and why he'd never gone public. He'd been good enough early enough that he'd made a shitload of money before competition got so stiff, but it gave him the control he demanded.

No one, not even the closest members of his management team, realized the ultimate focus of all BGV's technical advances had gone toward the creation of this array, that MacArthur Dugan had spent the last twenty years specifically developing the software and hardware he'd need to rescue Zianne and her people.

The fact that he'd changed the direction of the modern world—including modern warfare—with his innovative inventions along the way hadn't mattered to him as much as the fact that he'd been able to make more than enough money to pay for the project.

And he'd built it purely to find Zianne. To save her, and hopefully rescue her people. Oh, yeah. And save Earth from the evil aliens while he was at it. Crap. When he actually thought about his goals, he sounded like an absolute nutcase.

No wonder the generals at the Pentagon had walked away from his warnings. Mac pushed his chair back from the desk and stood. Glancing around the quiet room, at the sunlight slanting through the blinds and the sparkling dust motes in the air, it was hard to remember how discouraged he'd felt last night.

This morning for some reason he felt more hopeful. Like things were going to be okay if he'd just have patience.

Hell, he'd been patient for twenty fucking years. What was another day or two?

Closing the door behind him, Mac stepped out on to the landing in front of his room. The sound of laughter caught his attention, and he headed down the stairs in search of the source.

Rodie, Morgan, and Lizzie sat at one of the smaller tables

talking and laughing like they'd been friends for years. He couldn't get over the way everyone seemed to have bonded so quickly. He'd had so few friends throughout his life. Dink was the closest, but their lives had taken them in such different directions that they rarely got together anymore. He had a feeling the kids from his team were going to be friends forever.

There was a tray loaded with sandwiches in front of them. It appeared Meg had been busy in the kitchen. Mac walked over to the table and stood to one side. "Mind if I join you?"

"Hey, Mac. Have a seat." Rodie cleared a spot on the table next to her plate.

Mac grabbed the empty chair and sat between her and Lizzie. "Thanks. I got busy and didn't realize it was already lunchtime." He glanced at the three of them and then focused on Lizzie, since she was the one he knew best. "How'd it go? You just finished your slot, didn't you?"

"I did. Kiera's in there now." Lizzie grinned, but her thoughts were locked down tight. So were Morgan's, for that matter, but he could read Rodie like an open book.

An X-rated open book. He shifted his focus to Rodie. "You need to work on your mental blocks. Your shields." He grinned at her as he said it and grabbed half a sandwich off the plate.

"Me?"

Her voice squeaked and she shot a quick glance at Morgan. It looked like he struggled for a moment not to laugh, but then he apparently lost the battle. Laughing, he nodded vigorously. "Yep. You."

Rodie glared at him. Then she spun around and sent the same glare at Mac. He raised his hands in mock surrender. "Hey, I'm just trying to help, but, sweetheart, I can read you like an open book. You need a visual to shut off the flow of information when you don't want any of us seeing what you're thinking."

Rodie groaned and dropped her head to the table. "I think I'll just die now."

"Don't you dare," Morgan said, patting her on the shoulder. "I wouldn't want to miss any of your fantasies."

Her head popped up. "You didn't. Did you?"

Morgan shrugged and grinned. A blush spread over Rodie's cheeks. Mac tuned in and started laughing when he realized Morgan was sharing Rodie's fantasy from the night before, recalling it and giving it back to her.

After a moment, she raised her head and glared at Morgan. "How in the hell did you get that? Were you sneaking around the dream shack while I was in there last night?"

"Nope." Morgan shook his head. "I went to bed early and thought I'd dreamed it. Then I picked up your thoughts this morning while we were feeding the squirrel and I realized you were broadcasting on a pretty wide channel."

"And you didn't think to tell me?" She practically growled as she questioned him.

Morgan leaned over and kissed the end of her nose. She blinked, obviously shocked. Mac sat back and enjoyed the interplay between the two.

"And totally screw up the best entertainment I've had in ages?" Morgan shook his head again. "Rodie, that was the hottest fantasy I've ever been part of, and believe me, I've got an excellent imagination."

She only looked slightly mollified as she spun around and focused on Mac. "Okay. So how do I block? I am not sharing my fantasies with this jerk anymore."

"Jerk? Since when did I become a jerk?" Morgan flashed an innocent look at Mac. "Last night, I did everything she wanted me to do in that devilish mind of hers. I know for a fact I left her totally satisfied and looking forward to her next shift in the dream shack."

"That was then. This is now. Mac?" She raised one eyebrow.

Chuckling, Mac swallowed his bite of ham and cheese. "As I said, you need a visual. I've found thinking of my brain as a one-way mirror works if I want to pick up random thoughts without sharing my own. Think of a mirror only you can see out of so you can watch people on the other side, but they can't see in. The dark side, the side you're on, blocks your thoughts. That visual should do the trick. If you want to block other people's thoughts as well as your own, think of a door you can close, or even a solid wall of some kind or a soundproof window shade coming down. With practice, you'll be able to block what you're thinking from just about everyone."

Rodie's eyes narrowed to dark slits. "Why didn't you tell us how to do this yesterday?"

Fighting his grin, Mac put both hands on the table and stared at the sandwich between them. It took him a minute to get his humor—and his burgeoning laughter—under control. Only then did he raise his head, and while he focused on Rodie, his words were for all of them.

"I had no idea any of you would catch on so quickly. That was something I intended to teach you this week." He looked at the three of them and shook his head, but he gave up on trying to control his smile. This was just too damned cool. "You guys are amazing. All of you. I never expected the level of intelligence, the openness to new things, the . . ." He spread his hands wide. "The honest acceptance of this project. Of me."

Rodie and Morgan exchanged a quick look, but it was Morgan who spoke. "It goes both ways, Mac. I think we've all seen ourselves as the 'odd man out' in one way or another. The same attributes that most people see as odd or unusual . . ."

"Or just plain weird." Rodie glanced at Morgan again and shrugged. "Those things that have made all of us feel sort of like outcasts in the rest of the world are exactly the traits you seem to want."

She glanced at Lizzie and then again at Morgan, and Mac

had the distinct impression she was fighting tears. "I've never felt as if I fit anywhere. But I fit here, with these guys. With all of them. Finn and Cameron, too."

"What about Finn and Cam?"

They all glanced toward the door as the two in question walked into the lodge. Mac waved them over and dragged an extra chair up to the table. Morgan did the same. "Rodie's just saying that she feels like she fits in with this group."

Finn spun his chair around and straddled it with his arms folded across the back. "Yeah. I could say the same thing." He winked at Lizzie. "I imagine you've all heard the details of the heartfelt welcome I got from Lizzie and Kiera."

Mac glanced at Morgan and Rodie. Both of them, grinning broadly, nodded. "I haven't," he said, chuckling, "but it appears these two have, so I imagine I'll get the details later."

Finn laughed. "I'm sure you will. But yeah." He glanced at the others around the table. "We're all sort of odd ducks in our own way, but for whatever reason, we seem to click."

Cameron watched them, nodding. He was quieter than the rest, but Mac sensed a lot going on behind that enigmatic expression. "Cam? How'd your shift go last night?"

He turned and seemed to focus everything in him directly on Mac. "It went well. Painting afterward went even better."

It was a little disconcerting, to have that kind of perusal, but Mac maintained eye contact until, frowning, Cam turned away and stared off into space for a moment.

Then he swung around and once again focused intently on Mac. "I always have pretty explicit dreams. Fantasies, if you will. Last night was beyond anything I've ever experienced. The dials on the console didn't change much, so I'm not sure if the images were coming out of my own subconscious or if someone was giving the visuals to me."

Cam's words sent an inexplicable shiver racing along Mac's spine. He tried to shake it off, but the sensation persisted. He gazed at Cam and asked, "Would you be willing to share what you painted?"

Cam seemed to pull back into himself. Then he took a deep breath and nodded. "Back in a minute."

Mac watched him leave, aware of the lingering chill. He turned back to the others, ignoring it as best he could. "Did any of you have a similar feeling? That maybe what you were imagining wasn't all coming from your own mind?"

Morgan and Rodie shared a quick glance. Rodie shoved both her hands through her curly hair and growled in what could only be total frustration. "I don't know, Mac. It was so weird. I had a really explicit fantasy of sex with two men. I don't know if you're aware of my illicit past . . ." She blushed. Then she appeared to shake it off and looked directly at Mac. "A few weeks ago, I caught my longtime boyfriend in bed—my bed, to be specific—with another guy and a woman. To put it bluntly, I didn't handle it well, and the ensuing incident ended up going viral on the Internet. Everyone saw it."

"How and what got online?" Mac just watched her, giving her time to think about whether or not to answer him.

She laughed, obviously embarrassed. "Neighbor with a smartphone took a video of me chasing three naked people out of my apartment with a Taser. He posted it on YouTube."

"Ouch."

"Big ouch. Point is, catching the boyfriend playing the salami in a three-person sandwich really did a number on me. Yet my fantasy was just that—a ménage with me between two men. Not something I would choose on my own, but the fantasy was really explicit and it seemed to come out of nowhere."

"Did you know the men?" Mac already knew the answer. He had, after all, been listening in on Rodie's thoughts, though she'd started blocking them better over the past few minutes since he'd given her some ideas about how it was done. He wanted to see if she'd admit that Morgan was part of the dream.

"I knew one of them," she said. She glanced at Morgan and blushed. "Morgan was there, along with some guy I've never seen before."

Obviously, admitting it wasn't too great an issue. Mac grinned at both of them. "I'll be curious to hear what Morgan's first shot at the dream shack's like."

"Well, for what it's worth, I shared Rodie's fantasy last night." Morgan poked her with his elbow and she blushed. "It was so hot, I might just borrow it for myself tonight."

"No fair. You have to come up with your own."

Rodie stuck out her tongue, while Morgan grumbled like a sleepy toddler and slid down in his seat. "You're no fun."

She pouted and gave him a sultry look. "You didn't seem to think that last night."

Morgan shot her a surprised look, but just then Cameron stepped into the room and everyone's attention went to the large canvas he held in both hands. "This is the one I did last night," he said. Then he leaned the thing against the wall where the overhead light caught the painting perfectly.

Mac didn't remember standing up. He was only vaguely aware of the others beside him. He couldn't recall walking across the room, but he stopped a few feet from Cam's painting with Rodie, Morgan, Lizzie, and Finn in a half circle on either side and stared, totally blown away by the vision he'd seen only once before. "Did you see this? Last night, in the dream shack?"

Cam nodded. "I started out just coming up with my own fantasy, but I must have fallen asleep." He glanced at Mac and then turned once again to study the painting. "That's when I get my visions, the scenes that I paint. They're from dreams when I sleep, not stuff I imagine when I'm awake. When I finally woke up, about an hour had passed, but this was so clear in my head I actually sketched it out on a pad I'd taken with me."

"The colors? Those flickers of light and the structures that seem to grow right out of the ground? The rivers that are ribbons of color all flowing together? You saw this in your dream?" Mac realized his hands were shaking. He shoved them into his pockets to keep from touching the fresh paint.

"Yeah." Cam shrugged like it was no big deal. "This is exactly what I saw." He frowned at Mac. "Why? Have you seen this place? Do you know what it is?"

Nodding slowly, Mac finally dragged his gaze away from the painting so he could look at Cameron. "It's Zianne's world. You've painted Nyria, the world the Gar destroyed. She showed it to me, shared her memories the night she came out to me and told me she was an alien." He swallowed, so close to breaking down and weeping that it took him a couple of deep breaths to regain his composure.

Hell, he'd been on the edge since that damned dream or whatever it was that had him smelling Zianne's scent last night. Definitely on the edge, but this was even worse. This was something Zianne had shared with him, something Cam shouldn't have been able to paint.

Not unless he had actually witnessed the world himself, through either Zianne's eyes or one of her fellow Nyrians. Oh, shit. He sucked in another deep, controlling breath. It wouldn't do, to start bawling like a damned baby in front of the kids, but he'd never forgotten this image.

Just as he'd never forgotten Zianne. "I want to buy this from you, Cam. Name your price. I have to have it." He glanced at the painting again, but then he had to look away. Later. When it was his, when he could study it privately. Not now, with his emotions running riot and his heart thudding in his chest.

"It's yours, Mac."

Cam reached out and touched his shoulder. The comfort he offered Mac was unexpected, as reserved as Cam had been so far, but he rested his hand on Mac's shoulder and squeezed lightly.

Mac shuddered, still fighting tears.

"I paint in oil," Cam said. His voice was soft, a comforting whisper drifting through Mac's convoluted memories. "It's going to take a while to dry. Then it's going to need a couple of coats of varnish, to set the paint, but you can have it now. Hang it wherever you want and when it's dry I'll do the final coat."

"You're just giving this to me?" Mac shook himself out of the world within the painting, out of his memories of sharing this same vision with Zianne so long ago. "Shit, Cam. Your paintings sell for thousands. I can afford thousands." He smiled, relaxed now that he knew the painting was his. "Don't pass up a good deal when you've got me at a weak point."

Cam laughed. "I can afford thousands, too, Mac. I may look the part of a starving artist, but I'm good, and I've got a great financial advisor. Besides, you're giving me an experience that I imagine will keep me in ideas for the rest of my life. Consider it a gift, and we're not even close to even."

Mac let out a deep breath. "Thank you. You know what this means, don't you?"

Cam nodded slowly. "It means we've made contact, doesn't it? I got this from one of them, from a Nyrian, while I was in the dream shack."

"You did." Mac glanced at Rodie. "That second guy in your fantasy? I imagine he was a Nyrian as well. They need the energy from our sexual fantasies to give them form and shape, but they're free-thinking, intelligent creatures. All you did was give him the body." Mac wrapped his arm around Rodie's shoulders and gave her a quick hug. "He gave you the fantasy once he showed up. For what it's worth, and probably TMI, Zianne loved to take over in bed, once she had substance. A real woman's body."

Rodie chuckled. "Never too much information, Mac. Not when I know my fantasies were open to the masses."

Mac gave her another squeeze and then focused on Finn. "What about you, Finn? Any visitors last night?"

"Actually, yes." Finn shot a quick glance at Lizzie. "And no, this was not one of Lizzie and Kiera's creations, but I thought it was just my mind wandering the way it always does." He shrugged and looked almost sheepish. "I sort of dozed off . . . hell, it was a long day and I couldn't sleep last night before my shift. Anyway, a brilliant blue light woke me and when I opened my eyes, there was an absolutely gorgeous redhead in the shack."

Lizzie laughed. "Of course she was gorgeous."

"And a redhead," added Rodie.

"Hey, cut me some slack. It's my fantasy. Or not." Finn shot Mac a sheepish look. "So there's a gorgeous redhead in front of me, and then I look to my right and there's a guy standing there. And no, I don't do guys, so this is where I wondered if I was still dreaming or they were really there. After hearing your experiences, I'm beginning to think they were actually there with me. Anyway, the guy's good-looking, has fair skin, dark hair, and I'm thinking that if I had to do him to get her, I'm okay with that, so I asked them—in my dream, of course—if they wanted to come back to my cabin with me when my shift was over."

Mac laughed. "And here I thought you were the sexual predator. You're saying you put the job first?"

"Of course I did. It was my first night, my very first shift. Too soon to screw up." Finn folded his arms across his chest and focused on Mac. "That comes later. Besides, at this point, I was still thinking I was either dreaming or it was still a fantasy."

"What changed your mind?" Mac couldn't figure out why, but he got such a kick out of this guy. Finn could be such a jerk, but there was something terribly appealing about him as well.

Maybe the fact that he was totally honest about being a jerk.

"I told them I was on duty but said I'd be off at eight and asked if they wanted to join me in my room then." He shook his head. "They said no, that it took too much energy to maintain form during the daylight hours without their soulstones. Then . . . well, they said they'd come to my cabin tonight, before my shift. I guess I'll find out later if I was dreaming, or if they do show up, they were actually there in the shack with me, too."

"Lizzie." Mac spun around and stared at the youngest of the group. "You're the first to have a full daylight shift. Did you have any weird dreams? Did anyone come to you?"

Lizzie shook her head. "No, and I'm feeling really left out right now." She pouted, but then she couldn't hold it and giggled. "I did project my fantasies the way we were supposed to, and no, you do not get details."

"Aw, c'mon, Liz. Please?" Finn wrapped his arms around her from behind and kissed the top of her head. "Just a hint."

"Absolutely not." Still giggling, she twisted out of his loose embrace. "However, if—and that's a big if—I have any actual visitors when I'm in my cabin, I will be sure and let you know."

"You notice she said 'visitors,' plural, didn't you?" Finn grabbed her hand and tugged her close. This time Lizzie leaned against him and sighed.

"You noticed that, did you?" she said. "Believe me, Finn, when I fantasize, it's not going to be about one guy, and definitely not about you. Nothing personal, but if it's entirely up to me, I want my own harem of sexy, gorgeous, and willing men."

"That's the spirit." Rodie gave her a high five and the two women slapped palms.

Mac realized he was staring once again at the painting, though he was fully aware of the teasing going on around him. It was all good. Even better than he'd hoped. It sounded as if Rodie, Finn, and Cam had all been visited. He figured Liz might have visitors once she went to bed tonight, and he was almost certain Morgan would connect as well.

But for Mac, the proof was here, in front of him. In the bold brush strokes Cameron had left across the large canvas. In the tiny details that only became visible after studying the painting more deeply. The man was truly a brilliant artist, but it also appeared he'd shared the vision of a Nyrian who had lived on this world.

Now where in the hell was Zianne? Obviously, her people were beginning to connect to his team, but why not Zianne? Hell, he guessed he'd see her when she wanted him to. Or not. He spun away from the painting, effectively spinning away from thoughts of Zianne as well. For now. "I think we'll hang this here in the lodge. Is that okay with you, Cam?"

The kid gave him a big grin. "I'd be honored. Where?"

"Over the fireplace? It's a non-polluting wood burner. The glass doors keep the temperature even and the smoke is all filtered, so I don't think the painting will be damaged there. I want it where everyone can enjoy it."

Mac really wanted it in his room where he could see it as the last thing when he went to sleep and the first thing when he awoke, but it was too beautiful to hide away.

"That's perfect." Cameron's smile lit up his entire face. "Thank you."

Mac nodded. "Good. I'll have Ralph hang it as soon as he gets a chance. It really is an amazing piece of art, Cam. I will treasure this. Even more, Zianne will love it. It's a beautiful image of the world she and her people have lost. Thank you."

The others moved away, back to the table and the plate of sandwiches. Mac stood in front of the painting, staring at the lush colors, the vivid landscape, thinking of Zianne. Obviously, they'd already made contact, but why not him? Why hadn't Zianne come to him?

He spun around and caught all five of them staring his way. The words spilled out of him without Mac even thinking of how much of himself he was giving away. "I have a favor to ask. When you're in the dream shack, if you happen to have a chance to engage in any conversation with anyone in your fantasies, will you please ask what's happened to Zianne? I haven't heard from her, and I'm worried something's wrong. More so, now that I know some of you have already been contacted. I need to know if she's okay. If she's been imprisoned or something worse."

Shit. If they'd had any question of his relationship with Zianne before, they didn't now. But did it matter? He hoped not.

"I will, Mac." Rodie glanced at the others. "We all will."

"Thank you." He turned away before he made a bigger fool of himself and walked quickly to the door. Went outside and stared across the unforgiving landscape.

"Where the hell are you, Zianne?"

There was no answer. A squirrel chattered from the branch of a big Jeffrey pine growing near the lodge, but he ignored it and headed across the open area to check the array. He had to keep busy. Had to do something, anything, or he wouldn't be of any use to anyone.

Ralph met him halfway across the open area between the lodge and the shack. "Ralph. I was hoping to run into you." Mac paused and wiped the sweat off his forehead. It was damned hot, but August at seven thousand feet could be miserably cold, too.

"I've been looking for you, too, Boss."

"What's up?"

"Those damned protestors are at the front gate again. Gave Meg a bad time when she left to go into town for supplies."

"Bad time? How so?"

Ralph removed his ever-present ball cap, wiped his bald head with a clean handkerchief, then stuck the hat back on his head. "They blocked the road and tried to hold the gate closed when she opened it. Called her a lot of bad names. She got through, but she was pretty upset about it. I plan to meet her with a couple of guys from security when she's due home."

"Crap. You definitely need to be there, but whatever you

do, don't start anything. Use one of the bigger cameras on the entry, one that covers the entire area where they're demonstrating. Make sure we're able to record whatever it sees." He sighed and stared down the long driveway. "I wish I knew what their problem was."

"I'm hoping they're just a bunch of good old boys that don't like to see change, though I'm wondering if they're as harmless as the sheriff has led us to believe."

"Why do you say that?" Mac folded his arms across his chest. "Because of the way they acted with your wife?"

Ralph shrugged. "Yes and no. They had no right to harass Meg, but the security guys walking the perimeter last night thought they heard someone on the downhill side of the fence. That's all open country and could have been a bear or coyote, but the two I talked to didn't seem to think so. Said they thought they heard voices."

"What the hell would anyone be doing down there?" The area surrounding the array was nothing but rugged volcanic cliffs and a dense cover of sagebrush and stunted pines. "The entire area is fenced. There's no way in unless they want to tangle with the wire across the top."

"Exactly. Which begs the question—why was anyone down there at three in the morning?"

"Three?" Mac shook his head. "Guess I'd better call the sheriff and let him know we might have another problem." He nodded to Ralph. "And I'll let him know about the hassle they gave Meg. There's no excuse for that."

"Thanks, Mac. Why were you looking for me?"

"Sorry. Got sidetracked." He rubbed the back of his neck, well aware of the tightness in his muscles, the sense of strain that continued to grow. "There's a painting I want you to hang. One of our guys is a well-known artist. He painted it last night. I'd like to see it hanging over the fireplace, but be careful. It's oil and the paint's still wet."

Ralph tipped his hat. "Gotcha. I'll get to it now."

Mac watched him walk away. Then he turned and stared at the array, at the white dishes glistening in the sunlight. Kiera was in the dream shack right now. He wondered how she was doing, what she was seeing.

Then he turned away and grabbed one of the four-wheelers Ralph and the security guys used to get around the property. Maybe it was time to check out the protestors.

9

Kiera glanced at the clock. It was almost one, which meant she'd been trying to get this blasted daydream stuff working right for almost an hour. Frustrated, she stared at the patch of blue sky through the skylight overhead and tried, once again, to lose herself in fantasy. Usually, it was no big deal—hell, she could fantasize during court proceedings and still win her cases.

So why not here? She was comfortable, she'd worn her super-soft yoga pants and the loose, cropped tee that showed her flat belly. No bra, no underwear. Even her feet were bare so she'd be totally in touch with her body.

She'd thought about going naked until visions of one of the guys walking in and catching her had nixed that idea in a hurry, but she was as comfortable, as relaxed as a girl could be, and it still wasn't working.

She'd settled in, pulled up explicit mental images of Liz and Rodie—because face it, the sisters were hot—but some big, dark guy kept butting in.

No way. She was so done with men.

Three serious relationships with guys, and every single one

of them had tried to rearrange her face. What was it about the males of the species and their testosterone-fueled power trips? Three losers out of three were pretty sucky odds, especially when it had taken a restraining order to keep number three, the ex-husband, off her back. No more. She was done with men. Stupid Neanderthals, every last one, ruled by their balls not their brains.

As if they even had brains. She was really beginning to wonder. Hell, she didn't want a man in real life, and she definitely didn't want them screwing with her fantasies.

Especially didn't want them in her fantasies, though she had to admit, pulling that gig on Finn had been worth sticking his imaginary cock down her throat. The guy was hot to look at, but he was still a guy. The best part about that whole thing had been showing him what a fool he was. Watching him shoot his load in his pants had been great payback. Idiot. Forget it. She was done with men. Forever.

So who the fuck was the guy barging in on her fantasy?

No one. She'd never seen him before, wasn't interested, and refused to waste time thinking about him.

She stared at the blue sky and tried once again to let her mind float. Okay. Not floating. She'd try visualization.

I am a cloud, light as air and, oh, yeah.

There was Lizzie beside her, nuzzling her breast, and yeah, okay. This was working. Rodie sprawled between her legs with her mouth against Kiera's inner thigh, leaving little love bites on the tender skin.

Kiera moaned. She did love the teasing.

Sighing, settling back in the comfortable recliner, she closed her eyes as her fantasy took shape. Then her eyes opened and she glanced at the dials on the readout. Had to be the lawyer mentality, but she needed to know that her thoughts were headed skyward.

The little needle was right where it was supposed to be. She let her lids droop once again. Just in time. Lips encircled her right nipple, sucking and licking, even nipping with sharp teeth. A different warm mouth worked her left nipple just as carefully, flicking over the taut peak with the tip of a very mobile tongue.

Teeth scraping one side, a tongue flicking the other, and thick . . . thick? Whose fingers were those, tracing her labia, slipping into her warm, wet pussy, trailing back over her perineum? Hell, they were even teasing the taut little ring of muscle on her ass. Damn. Whomever they belonged to, either Rodie or Lizzie, they were way talented. Kiera sighed, entirely surrounded in warm, wet mouths, in stroking fingers, soft lips.

She wondered if either Lizzie or Rodie had ever been with a woman before, and decided that maybe she'd teach them what they needed to know, so she incorporated their innocence into her fantasy.

Lizzie was lying on her back, and Kiera slowly worked her way up the girl's slim legs, licking and kissing her way to the dark thatch of curls at the sweet juncture of her thighs.

Rodie was there, too, her lips wet from sucking on Lizzie's breast, her fingers just as wet from slipping inside Kiera's pussy. This was good. This was how it should be, the three of them, all together, knowing exactly what it took to please a woman, using gentleness and love to find the perfect touch, the perfect pressure, the . . .

A hand slowly swept over Kiera's shoulder, cupped her breast, gently pinched her nipple. The palm was broad and rough, a bit callused, the fingers thick and strong. Definitely not Lizzie. Not Rodie, either, but it felt so good, that rolling, pinching, tugging pressure on first one nipple and then the other that she just let it slide.

When fantasy was working, it beat the real thing altogether. She sighed and sprawled in the recliner, forgetting all about

Rodie and Lizzie as a new set of warm, full lips coasted over her rib cage, paused for a quick lick of her belly button, and then went lower. She felt the warmth of a very mobile tongue slipping between her sensitive pussy lips, flicking her clit just the way she liked it, then slipping so deep inside she wouldn't have thought it possible.

But this was, after all, a fantasy, right? A thick fingertip teased the sensitive ring around her anus. Damn. She was so sensitive there. At one time, she'd thought she would love sex that way, but her ex-husband had sure screwed that up.

Anal sex might sound great in theory, but when it was forced on a girl, when it was done to you against your will, it hurt like hell. She'd screamed when he'd taken her. She'd fought him and tried to get away, but he was so big and so much stronger, he'd held her down and done it anyway. When he was through, she'd been torn and bloody, and that's when she'd gotten the fucking restraining order.

And that had marked the end of men for Kiera Pearce, but why the hell was she thinking of that jackass now? Crap. Slowly, she made a conscious effort to relax muscles gone all tense, to even out her breathing again. To calm down and go with the program.

Then she had to consciously crawl back into her fantasy with Rodie and Lizzie.

But where the hell had they gone? She couldn't bring up their images at all for some reason. Invisible lovers? That might work, though hadn't Mac said they needed to project explicit visual fantasies to give the Nyrians form? Didn't that mean they had to actually imagine a particular face?

Maybe they didn't need to be that specific.

Whatever. She wasn't going to worry about it now, not when her fantasy lover was back, doing some serious licking between her legs. Oh heavens . . . Kiera arched her hips and the tongue scored with a circling motion around her anus, then a slow lick up to her clit that left her legs quivering and all her inner muscles clenching.

Now this was where a cock would come in handy, but a dildo would work, so she pictured one, only it was big and hard and hot—hot like a real guy—and so real in shape and size and texture that when it entered her she was sure she felt the soft press of a guy's testicles against her ass, certain she could feel his heart beating against hers, his lips pressing along her hairline, dropping little kisses on her forehead.

Damn, if a guy could make love to her like this, with this much care and gentleness, she might even be willing to look at a man again. In fantasy, of course.

Never in real life.

She felt her climax building as the cock—whether dildo or fantasy guy didn't matter at all right now—filled her all the way on each downward thrust and then dragged perfectly across her clit each time it withdrew.

She was rising and falling with each thrust and retreat, so lost in the fantasy that when she reached for broad shoulders, she wasn't at all surprised to find them above her, but she kept her eyes closed. Kept the reality of her own traitorous imagination at bay.

He thrust harder and it was so perfect, so exactly the way she'd imagined sex could be but never had been that she wanted to weep as orgasm claimed her. She wrapped her legs around slim male hips, locked her heels against a truly fine butt, forgetting how much she hated and feared men, forgetting that this was merely a dildo between her legs and an imaginary one at that.

Her heels slid higher and rested at the small of his back and she clung to his broad shoulders as he took her over the edge. Her inner muscles tightened and released, then tightened again, holding him deep inside. She felt the steady jerking spurts as he joined her, his hot seed filling her, bathing her sensitive vaginal walls.

And when she opened her eyes, he was smiling back at her.

Her breath caught as he filled her vision. Perfect. He was an absolutely, perfectly beautiful man. Beautiful, big, and so very male. The real shock came when she realized she wasn't even surprised to see that her fantasy was a man. Wasn't surprised at the solid feel to him, the details she'd not consciously added to the dream. The tightly curled pubic hair against her mons was scratchy and coarse, as was the hair on his thighs, so much so that it abraded her sensitive skin.

His eyes were dark with tiny flecks of gold, and his skin was a deep, rich, bittersweet chocolate. That surprised her, because two of the three men in her life had been white while the one she'd married—the one she'd gotten the restraining order against—had been Asian.

She was proud of her African-American heritage, but for some reason, she'd never dated a man like herself. Maybe that was her problem. For whatever reason, she'd fantasized a lover who was even darker than she was, but damn, he was absolutely perfect—even if he was male.

The final stirrings of her climax faded, and Kiera climbed out of her fantasy long enough to wonder how much longer her shift would last, because now that she'd gotten the hang of it, she wondered if four-hour shifts would be enough time.

She blinked as reality intruded, fully expecting the fantasy to disappear, but the man of her dreams merely lifted himself away from her and she actually heard the wet, sucking sound as he pulled his heavily engorged penis from her wet vagina with her nether lips still swollen with arousal.

She was blinking like an idiot when he leaned close and kissed her. His lips were full and soft; the smile he gave her enough to melt bones—or even the most dedicated man-hater around.

He touched the side of her face, his fingers gently caressing her cheek. "I must go," he said. He kissed her mouth and she groaned softly. His lips were so sweet, so soft and warm that she could have kissed him forever. "It's difficult during daylight, but I was incapable of ignoring your passionate summons. Be ready for me. I will come to you in darkness."

Then he stepped away without another word and began to glow. His body dissolved into a mass of sparkling lights, swirling faster and faster until he was a dazzling blue flame that blazed brilliantly and, as if he'd never existed at all, disappeared.

Kiera fell back against the recliner. Her heart thudded painfully in her chest and she was afraid she was going to hyperventilate and pass out, but her mind was spinning so fast she couldn't seem to make sense of any of this. "What the fuck just happened?"

She glanced down at her yoga pants. "Holy shit." They lay partially on the floor, hanging from her left foot by the waistband. She was practically naked, but she couldn't remember anyone taking her pants off. They'd just disappeared in her fantasy—they weren't there at all.

Hands shaking, she leaned over and grabbed the waistband, untangled the legs, and tugged her pants up. Just before she pulled them over her hips, she noticed the creamy drops of fluid between her legs.

Semen? Impossible. She grabbed a tissue out of a box on the console and quickly cleaned herself, fully aware that she was hyperventilating again. That might have been an imaginary lover, but this was not imaginary sperm. Thank goodness for the birth-control implants Mac had insisted upon, but what about STDs?

Oh shit. This was so not happening. Who the hell was that guy? Didn't Mac say they had to picture someone in their fantasies to give those aliens a body? She had most definitely not pictured a big, sexy, black god between her thighs. No. Not even close, so who or what the fuck just screwed her silly?

She wadded up the tissue and threw it into the wastebasket. Then she wondered if Mac had a lab here. Was he set up to do DNA testing? Good lord, the dream shack smelled of sex and man and what the hell time was it, anyway?

She stared at the clock built into the console. Closed her eyes and looked again. "That can't be right." It was almost four. How could that be? She'd looked just a few minutes ago and it hadn't even been one o'clock, but according to the time, her shift was almost over. Morgan should be here to relieve her in about ten minutes, but where had the past three hours gone?

Kiera flopped back against the soft recliner and stared at the patch of sky overhead. There was no avoiding the truth. She'd just had the best sex in her life with an alien. A male alien.

A creature from another planet. "No way. Absolutely no frickin' way."

She was still staring at the patch of blue sky when Morgan tapped lightly on the door and walked into the dream shack. Kiera took a deep breath and forced herself to relax. She carefully slipped the cap with the sensors off her head and put it away. Should she tell Morgan what had happened? She had to tell Mac, but was she ready to tell another guy about such a personal, intimate encounter?

No. Not yet. Let him find out on his own. Right now she needed to find Rodie for some very important girl talk, like what the fuck had just happened? But she also needed a cold alcoholic drink—or three or four. Not necessarily in that order.

"How'd it go?" Morgan stepped aside so Kiera could get out of the chair.

"It was . . ." She paused and shrugged. Tried to swallow, but her mouth was too dry. "Interesting. Definitely interesting."

Morgan stared at her for what felt like a very long time. She managed to hold her smile and keep her thoughts blocked. At least she thought her shields were up. She sure as hell hoped so.

"Why does that leave me with more questions than answers?"

Kiera just laughed and then stepped back while he settled himself into the recliner. He carefully stretched the cap with the sensors over his dark hair. "I think it's something we all have to experience for ourselves," she said. Then she winked.

Morgan gave her an enigmatic smile that left her rattled. "For what it's worth," he said, adjusting the chair to fit his long legs, "Rodie and Cam both connected with Nyrians last night. You probably heard about Rodie, but I don't know if you were aware that Cam made contact, too. Lizzie wasn't so sure, and Finn's visit was questionable." He smiled at her, as if she could tell him anything. Anything at all.

No way. Not yet. She was still too rattled, still feeling tiny contractions deep inside her pussy from that amazing sex.

Morgan shrugged. "I was just wondering if you'd seen anything, had any kind of contact. Just so I'd know what to expect." He raised one dark eyebrow.

Kiera swallowed. "You might say that," she said, fully aware she was edging toward the door. "I think I can say it was more along the definitely contacted than the questionable. I, uh, need to go talk to Mac."

Morgan laughed. "You're not going to tell me anything at all, are you?"

She flashed him a big grin. "My lips are sealed. For now. Enjoy!" Then she spun away and slipped out the door before Morgan could ask her anything else.

Oh shit. She wasn't the only one. She knew about Rodie, but not Finn or Cameron. She really wanted to talk to Rodie, to compare notes, but she probably needed to talk to Mac first.

"No. What I really need is a drink." She glanced overhead, at the blue sky and the few wisps of cloud. They were up there. Aliens. In a spaceship, high above the earth.

And she'd just had sex with one of them.

Amazing sex. Only she wasn't sure what was most shocking—the fact that her lover had been an alien, or that the sex was the best she'd ever had, or that her lover had been male.

Kiera headed straight for the lodge in search of that drink. She'd feel more like talking after she'd knocked back a couple of whatever the bar offered.

Morgan stared at the door long after Kiera had shut it behind her. He'd not been able to glean a thing from her thoughts, which meant she'd figured out how to shield her mind.

Finally, he settled into the recliner and checked the fit of his cap with the sensors. Felt like everything was okay.

So what now? He was the last of the six to take up a position here in the dream shack, and as much as he shouldn't have been surprised, the first thing he'd noticed when he walked into the place was the rich, ripe smell of sex.

He chuckled, wondering if he was about to add to it. At least it should be pretty dark by the time he left the dream shack, so if he did "pull a Finn," as he and Cam were already calling Finn's little episode, at least the wet spot shouldn't be all that noticeable.

"Okay. Enough time wasted." He'd checked his cap with the sensors, gotten the chair adjusted so that he was entirely comfortable, stared out the skylight, and then stared at the control console. Fantasize. Sure. He could do that, except he'd never had to do it on command.

Shit. It wasn't as easy as he'd thought. He scrunched his butt down in the chair and tried closing his eyes.

Rodie immediately came to mind.

What was it about that chick? She was just an average girl. Nice smile, straight teeth, lots of curly dark hair and a wicked sense of humor, but he couldn't get her out of his mind.

Okay. He'd keep her in his head and use Rodie as his fantasy subject, but then he wondered if that meant that whatever Nyrian might check in with him would end up looking like Rodie.

Now that could be confusing.

Easing back into the chair, he started at the beginning, slowly peeling her clothes away, exposing the hot little body he knew was hiding under the sloppy sweats and old jeans she seemed to favor. She had a solid build, but he liked that. A lot. He'd never been into the really skinny, anorexic types.

He pictured long legs, but muscular. He was sure she'd be well muscled, and he liked that in a woman. Solid thighs, a firm butt, and a flat stomach with a bit of a washboard look. She struck him as a woman who took care of herself, who liked being physically strong. He could work with that.

Mentally, he helped her take off her sweatshirt and, sure enough, she was wearing a sports bra underneath. Those damned things looked more like torture devices, but they kept everything in place. It wasn't easy to get it off her, but that was part of the fun.

He decided to go the macho route and pictured a sharp knife, more like a dagger, that he slipped beneath the tight band under her boobs. He cut through the stretchy fabric like he was cutting through butter, running the blade slowly up between her breasts.

The stretchy cups gaped to each side, so he set the knife down and pushed the material away from her breasts. Her tits weren't real big, but they were perfectly shaped and the same sun-kissed color as the rest of her. Barely a handful. He wondered why she even bothered with the bra in the first place.

Then he realized he hadn't fantasized Rodie saying a word during the entire procedure, and there was no way in hell that would ever happen. He could just imagine her outrage if he were to cut a bra off her.

Maybe keeping her quiet was a good thing. Chuckling at the convoluted directions his mind kept taking, he went back to her breasts. Her skin was darker than he'd expected, not really black or brown, not olive, either. More as if she'd gotten a really good tan, though he didn't picture Rodie spending time topless in the sun, or hanging out in a tanning booth.

Then he pulled out of the fantasy and wondered if this was really the color of her skin, if he'd gotten close to the real thing at all in his imagination. And as soon as he thought of that, he realized he wanted to find out. As soon as possible.

So he went back to the fantasy, peeling the bra entirely off her shoulders, then unbuttoning her jeans and shoving them down her hips. She kicked off her sandals and lifted her legs, one at a time, so he could slip the pants off her.

He sat back and studied her, enjoying the sleek strength of her body, the sexy line of her black bikini underwear. They curved up high on her thighs and the waistband sat just below her navel. He hadn't really thought of what kind of underwear she'd have on, but he hadn't pictured her as a thong kind of girl.

Another thing he wanted to check in real life.

She didn't seem to mind being naked in front of him, which was a good thing. He liked to be dressed with his women naked, at least for a while. He figured it had to be some sort of dominance thing, like a control issue, but he liked the sense of being in charge, whether he was with a man or a woman.

He'd been with more men than women, maybe because guys were just easier. Girls wanted the romance and the promises. Guys just wanted to fuck. No complications there, as long as you were careful, and in a way, he thought it was a cool thing that Mac had tested all of them to make sure they were clean.

Made it easier to fantasize. He didn't have to add a rubber to the storyline, if you could call this a story. He raised his head and looked into Rodie's eyes. He knew they were brown like his, except he'd never really looked this closely before. There was nothing *brown* about them. No, they seemed to be filled with flecks of gold and green, with darkest chocolate and swirls of amber. Not like his eyes at all.

"Well," she said, leaning close. "You've got me naked. Now what are you going to do with me."

Oh, shit. He never should have considered her talking to him, but she sounded just like Rodie and he knew exactly what he wanted. He reached for her and pulled her into his lap. She snuggled close for a moment, and then she wiggled free and slid down between his legs.

The next thing he knew, she was unsnapping and unzipping his pants, lowering the damned zipper one set of teeth at a time. He swallowed and it felt like he had a frickin' tennis ball lodged in his throat by the time she slipped her fingers in through his open fly and lifted his dick out of his pants.

It didn't come easy, and he was glad he'd dressed with the thing pointed up and to the side, because if it'd been down the leg of his pants she might have snapped the sucker in two. He couldn't remember ever being this hard, this big, this turned on.

Rodie glanced up at him with her eyes twinkling. Then she lowered her head and wrapped her lips around the sensitive crown.

"Oh, shit." His breath came in deep pants, and he clutched the arms of the chair so he wouldn't grab her head and hold her in place. He didn't want to force her, to hurt her in any way.

She kept taking him deeper and deeper and he felt the muscles of her throat rippling around his length, felt a little hitch in her tongue and mouth when he must have passed by her gag reflex. He held perfectly still, aware she was working at relaxing her throat, and he realized she intended to take him all the way, to swallow him down.

Shit. Oh, shit, but she was doing it, and he had to close his eyes because he'd come if he watched anymore. It was so damned hot, watching her throat ripple around his shaft, but he couldn't look. His muscles quivered and trembled with the effort to hold still, to let her take control, but it wasn't easy.

She was killing him.

Dear god, but she was going to kill him with just her mouth.

He opened his eyes and damned if she didn't grin at him, her lips managing to tilt up around the thick base of his cock. Her eyes were twinkling and her lips were stretched wide, but he could tell she was loving the power, loving the fact she had him, that she'd taken all control away from him.

Everything went still. Rodie took a couple of deep breaths through her nose, and then she pulled back, slipping him from her throat and almost entirely free of her mouth. Then down again, and it was smooth this time. Her throat was relaxed and open for him, though still tight.

He felt the smooth glide as his cock moved over the sides of her teeth, their silky slide along his shaft. Her front teeth had sharp edges scraping him top and bottom as he slid past and everything else was warm and wet. The back of her throat was all soft silk and ridges as she swallowed him down, and he almost wept with the overwhelming pleasure, the pure eroticism of the act.

He'd seen this on porn flicks, heard about it from guys who'd been lucky, but he'd never felt it himself. Never expected to experience anything remotely this unreal.

She slipped her right hand up beneath his sac, cupping his balls beneath her chin, and it was like a bunch of little electric shocks wherever she touched him. Sensation inside and out, until his entire being existed in his cock and balls, all of him controlled by Rodie's mouth and hands.

Down again, and back, and then again, and he knew he couldn't last. Knew he was going to come but he didn't know how she felt about that, about swallowing his stuff. He could barely catch his breath, much less talk. Then he remembered— she could read his mind if he projected what he was thinking.

Rodie. Sweetie, it's too good. I'm going to come.

Good.

Shit, Rodie. Unless you want a mouthful of spunk, you might want to stop.

Do you want me to stop?

Hell, no. C'mon. I'm trying to be a gentleman here.

You'll get your chance.

She squeezed his balls and sucked hard. Then she let him slide almost entirely free and her tongue found the little eye at the tip. She swirled around it, stretching the skin, and he lost it. Lost it entirely.

His hips arched up, and as much as he fought it, he knew he'd shoved his dick all the way down her throat. She took him deep and sucked even harder, until he felt the hard ridges on the roof of her mouth and the rough curl of her tongue pressing the thick vein on the underside of his cock. The muscles in her throat rippled as she swallowed, and her fingers were all over the place, squeezing his sac, pressing against his ass. He was coming like he'd never come before, shooting so much that she couldn't take it all and his seed was spilling from the corners of her mouth.

Everything went dark except for the sparkling lights behind his eyes. He felt her tongue on him, licking his shaft and his balls, almost as if she wanted to get every last drop, but he couldn't open his eyes. Could barely catch his breath.

It was too real. Too intense. Just too *everything*.

Long minutes later, Morgan blinked. The sky overhead was no longer blue, though not entirely dark, either, and he knew the sun had probably just set.

"How the hell . . . ?" He'd still been getting settled in when he'd started fantasizing a little after four. He glanced at the clock. Eight minutes after seven. Impossible.

There was no sign of Rodie. For a moment he would have sworn she was really here, really sucking him deep. She'd been so real—the heat in her mouth, her tongue stroking over his skin, her hands on his balls.

A cool breeze brushed over his junk. He glanced down and actually blushed so hard he felt the flush spreading over his face and neck. His damned prick was soft but lying outside his pants. So were his balls, just resting on the open fly like he was on display like some perv.

Had he been in here, jacking off while he fantasized? Crap. What if someone had come in to check on him? How embarrassing would that be? He tucked himself inside his jeans, stuffing his junk through the fly of his boxers. His balls ached like he'd had one hell of an orgasm. He remembered the fantasy, the visual of Rodie's mouth on him, of her hands on his balls and then her lips and tongue.

He reached inside his pants and touched the smooth skin over his shaft. The skin was still damp. Not sweat. Not sticky from spunk. Almost as if he'd been licked clean, but that was impossible, right? Rodie'd been nothing more than a fantasy, hadn't she?

Shit. Talk about one very weird experience.

He took off his sensor cap and got out of the recliner, walked to the back, and found a cold beer in the refrigerator. IPA, from a little boutique brewery Morgan liked. Leave it to Mac to think of everything. He used the opener lying on top of the fridge and popped the cap, took a long swallow, and then carried the bottle back to the recliner. He set it on the console and got himself hooked up again.

The fantasy really had him rattled. He needed to talk to Rodie, see if she'd been aware of what he'd been thinking, though that might get a little awkward, too. What if she wasn't the type of chick to go down on a guy? Would she think he was pressuring her? He took another swallow of beer and settled back in the chair. Let his mind roam as twilight turned to night and stars slowly filled the skylight above his head. He didn't doubt the Nyrians were out there, didn't doubt they were somehow making contact, but there'd been no one but Rodie in his fantasy.

At least, as far as he knew. He finished the beer in a couple more swallows and set the empty bottle in the little recycling basket beside the chair. He had less than an hour left, so he closed his eyes and let his mind wander.

It seemed like mere seconds passed before Rodie was back, only this time she wasn't alone. She had that guy with her—the same guy from last night. Tall, lean but muscular, his skin smooth and bronzed. He didn't have any body hair on his chest, belly, or groin, though the hair on his head was thick and long, brushing the firm line of his chin, curling against his neck.

His cock was engorged, thick and so heavy it hung down between his legs. His foreskin stretched back beyond the smooth, dark surface of his broad crown. His balls hung heavy in their sac and the skin over his testicles was as hairless as the rest of him. He gazed steadily at Morgan. Then he turned to Rodie and smiled. "I want him. He's mine. Will you share?"

She grinned at the guy, totally ignoring Morgan. "Only if I can watch," she said.

Morgan choked back his surprise, but even though he wasn't sure anymore if this was his fantasy—because it certainly wasn't something he'd normally come up with—he didn't refuse. As soon as he'd mentally acquiesced, he realized he was no longer in his chair. There'd been no sense of movement, but he was back in his cabin, leaning over the bed with his ass bare and his fingers clutching the spread.

A shiver ran along his spine. He could have blamed the cool night air and the fact that he was buck naked, but he knew it was more than that. He didn't bottom. Never had, but it seemed right to lie here passively and wait, shivers of apprehension and all.

Even with Rodie watching. He raised his head and she was there, sitting cross-legged in the middle of the bed, naked but for those sexy black bikini panties, watching him with bright eyes and flushed cheeks. She had her fingers between her legs, stroking herself through the black nylon. Morgan thought of trying to go down on her while he got fucked, but he wasn't sure his imagination and/or coordination were that good.

Then all thoughts of pleasing Rodie fled. Warm fingers parted his cheeks and spread something slick and creamy inside the crease. It was cool against his hot skin; once again shivers raced along his spine. Then there was a sense of pressure as the guy behind him pressed forward without any warning or prep at all beyond the lube he'd slopped on Morgan's ass.

No, he just slapped one hand down on Morgan's butt, pushed forward with that damned monster cock of his, and slipped neatly through Morgan's virgin hole as if he'd been fucking him in the ass for years.

It was all a fantasy, right? But how does a guy imagine something he's never done? Where'd he get the details? Morgan felt his anal ring stretch and give, and the thick slide as that big cock went through, went deep, but other than the sharp burn of stretching skin, it didn't hurt. He'd heard how painful this could be, had expected the worst.

Instead, he groaned with unexpected pleasure.

The guy behind him didn't miss a beat—right away he was pumping in and out, thrusting hard enough to slide Morgan forward on the thick bedspread. He kept one hand on Morgan's butt, the other on his back, holding him in place though not entirely still. The gentle abrasion against his cock, trapped as it was between his belly and the blankets, was enough to get him hard again, but it wasn't what took him close to climax.

No, what really took him over the edge was the steady, deep penetration of his ass by a guy who didn't exist. This was one for the books, this amazing sense of arousal, the sparks of pleasure from a pressure he'd never experienced in his life. The deep thrust and retreat was more arousing than he'd imagined. He tried to concentrate on the mechanics, the pure physicality of the act, but there wasn't enough time.

The guy was coming and so was Morgan. Even Rodie writhed with her own climax. Her fingers were jammed down inside the waistband of her panties, deep between her legs. Her eyes closed and her lips twisted in a rictus of pleasure.

Her moans and the soft hitch in her breath as she went right along with Morgan took him again. He felt another small spasm as he came a second time—no, a third if he counted the first fantasy, when Rodie'd sucked him off.

His body shuddered. He closed his eyes, lost in sensation.

When he opened his eyes again, Morgan was alone in the dream shack. He glanced at the clock. Almost eight. Once again he'd lost track of time, though this fantasy had taken barely an hour. At least he was dressed, his pants were zipped and his junk under cover, not hanging out for all the world to see.

And no wet spot. But how? He knew he'd come. Somewhere.

Rodie was due any minute. He'd been here for four hours— four hours that seemed to have disappeared in minutes.

And somehow, he was fully aware his entire life had changed in that short span of time. "Holy shit." He flopped back against the padded chair. "And this is just the first fucking day."

10

Sucking air, Mac climbed out of the lap pool, wrapped a towel around his waist, and finger-combed his wet hair back from his face. His eyes burned from the chlorine; his shoulders ached. He shook out his arms, but the burn from pushing the last ten laps with the butterfly stroke radiated to the tips of his fingers.

Damn, but getting old sucked. Twenty years ago he could've done two hundred laps and still felt great. Still gasping air from the effort of a mere hundred, he headed upstairs, hoping he could get through the main floor of the lodge without running into anyone—or passing out. He sucked in another deep breath.

The basement was the only place where they'd been able to install an indoor pool. If he'd been thinking, he would have added direct access to his rooms on the top floor.

Right now an elevator sounded particularly practical.

He'd always intended on building a fully equipped gym in the basement beneath the lodge, but the lap pool had been more of an afterthought. Of course, once he'd decided on installing one, he'd wanted it Olympic sized.

He'd had to settle for a short course—twenty-five meters

instead of fifty—but a hundred laps put him at a little over four and a half miles. The crappy shape he was in, it felt like one hell of a workout.

For now, it was the one thing keeping him sane. He'd discovered that swimming was as close as he could get to sensory deprivation. For some reason, as long as he was pushing himself really hard, he didn't seem to pick up on the random thoughts of the others on the site—the sound of the water churning by his ears with each hard stroke seemed to block everything else, and the gut-wrenching effort of finishing the full hundred laps left him too tired to care.

And, for the last three hours, it had kept him from thinking about the blasted protestors, too. There was no excuse for those idiots blocking his front gate. It really pissed him off that they'd harassed Meg earlier in the day. He didn't want to lose her and Ralph because she was afraid to leave the place. The sheriff was doing what he could, but it wasn't enough.

The fact that Ralph had heard men outside the perimeter last night didn't set well, either. It was enough to make him crazy. Crazier.

Day two and he was already worried about his sanity? This did not bode well for the coming months. Mac stepped through the double doors from the staircase and headed through the main floor of the lodge. Thank goodness it was empty.

Or was it? The top of a dark head showed over the back of one of the big overstuffed chairs by the front window. Cam? He hoped so—he wondered what the artist thought of his painting now hanging over the big fireplace. Ralph had gotten the thing hung in record time, and Mac had quickly discovered he couldn't walk through the lodge without stopping to stare at a world long gone.

It wasn't Cameron, but Kiera sitting alone, staring out at the array marching across the plateau.

It appeared she'd discovered the supplies for gin and tonic, if the fresh lime and ice cubes in her tall but otherwise almost empty glass meant anything. Mac stopped beside her chair and checked to make sure the towel around his waist hadn't slipped. "Got enough to make one of those for me?"

"Mac?"

She jerked around so quickly he apologized. "Sorry. Didn't mean to startle you." He tightened the towel around his waist and parked his butt on the coffee table. "How'd your shift go?"

She held up the drink and then took a swallow. "I plan to tell you all about it, as soon as I have at least two more of these."

He raised one eyebrow. "How many have you had?"

She laughed. "Not nearly enough, and this one's empty. Stay here. I'll make one for you."

"You don't have to . . ."

She held up a hand to stop him and shoved herself out of the chair. "Yeah, I do. It'll be a lot easier to talk to you if I know you're half lit, too." She glanced at the white towel around his hips. "Especially knowing you're probably buck naked under that towel. Oh. My." Grinning, waving her hand in front of her face as if to cool the heat, she stood, swayed, and then blinked rapidly when Mac grabbed her arm to steady her. "I'm okay. I think it's more a reaction to the dream shack than the alcohol."

With that enigmatic comment hanging in the air, she turned smoothly and headed across the large room to the kitchen. Mac waited impatiently, curious to know what had caused this kind of reaction in a woman he thought of as both totally pragmatic and entirely unflappable.

"Here ya go." She handed Mac a cold gin and tonic and sat down with a fresh one for herself.

Mac took the drink and tapped her glass in salute when she held it out. After a couple of swallows he smiled at Kiera, more curious than he could imagine. Something pretty extreme must have happened to her, that she'd be in here drinking alone. Her shift had ended barely an hour ago.

"You gonna tell me?"

She nodded. "One more swallow." She smiled back at him, took a couple of huge gulps of her drink, and then set the glass on the coffee table beside Mac.

And then she told him everything, or at least, Mac decided, as much as she was comfortable discussing. She didn't appear to have many inhibitions, though, and he figured he got the whole story. "Do you have a problem with what happened? With the fact that the guy might have been real?"

She let out a deep breath and shook her head. "Not that so much. I think what bothers me is the fact that he might know me better than I know myself. I keep wondering—how could that be?"

"What do you mean?" Mac tightened the towel around his waist. Rules for the pool were clothing optional, and he'd been the only one down there this afternoon, but he didn't want to shock her any more than she'd been shocked already. The last thing he needed to do was lose the towel.

He watched her face as she so obviously thought about his question. Always thoughtful and practical by nature, Kiera was a striking woman. Tall and lean with beautiful nut-brown skin and mesmerizing almond-shaped dark eyes. Right now there was a definite frown wrinkle between those eyes.

She picked up her drink. This time she merely sipped, as if the act helped her think. Holding the glass in both hands, she stared at the contents for a minute. She was still frowning.

Mac bit the inside of his cheek when the image of a gypsy staring at her crystal ball popped into his head.

Kiera raised her head and studied him. "It's difficult to put into words." She laughed. "I know. Dumb thing for an attorney to say, but I'd always considered myself bisexual, at least until a really ugly breakup with my ex-husband." She shrugged and rolled her eyes. "You know, the kind that requires calling the cops, a trip to the emergency room, and a subsequent re-straining order?"

"I'm sorry," he said. "I knew you were divorced. I had no idea it was that bad a situation."

She shook her head. "Water under the bridge, but yeah, that kind. Anyway, since we split, I've only been with women. I'd convinced myself that maybe the marriage and the other het re-lationships didn't work because I wasn't bi at all. Maybe I was a hundred-percent into girls, ya know?"

He nodded and resisted putting his arms around her for a hug. That probably wasn't what she wanted right now, at least from him, but she certainly looked lost. It was more than obvi-ous something had shaken her foundations.

"The only one I've talked to about their experience in the dream shack is Rodie, and she said something to me while we were hiking around the plateau today that really stuck. I know she's already told you about her fantasy, or I wouldn't say any-thing." Kiera rolled her eyes. "I think she wanted to crawl in a hole when she realized everyone could see what she was think-ing, but she told me how she'd fantasized about sex with two guys, that one of them was Morgan but the other guy was a complete stranger. He, just like the guy in my fantasy, showed up without a conscious invitation. In fact, she was totally sur-prised because she said she'd hated the idea of a ménage, espe-cially after what happened with her old boyfriend."

Mac chuckled. "I've heard about that episode."

Kiera flashed him a bright grin. "I think anyone who's con-nected to the Internet has heard about it. Poor Rodie." She took another sip of her drink before setting it on the table. "What she said, though, was that her fantasy was such an amaz-ing sexual experience, so unbelievably good, that she couldn't help but wonder if maybe that was a secret desire she was hid-ing even from herself. If maybe she's wanted to try sex with two guys but couldn't admit it. Makes you wonder, ya know?"

"Why? What about your experience makes you think that?"

She looked him in the eye, and he knew it took a lot for her to face her own demons as well as a relatively strange man. She hardly knew him, and yet she was spilling some pretty personal stuff. It couldn't be easy for her.

"Because as soon as that guy showed up in my fantasy, not in the beginning, because he'd just sort of barged in the first time, but the second time he came on with a lot more finesse, as if he'd thought about it and decided the subtle approach was better. Anyway, he came on so gently, with so much tenderness, that I didn't even care when the imaginary visuals of Rodie and Liz disappeared. I only wanted him. Everything about him, from the way he smelled to the way the calluses on his hands felt against my skin."

She paused and took a deep breath, then slowly let it out. Her eyes sparkled with unshed tears. "Mac, you want to know what convinced me it wasn't a fantasy, that the guy was real? That he was an alien? It's because it's impossible for me to imagine what he did to me. I wouldn't know how to dream a gentle male lover, because every man I've ever been with has been a jerk. They've done nothing but take. This guy just gave, and it made me wonder if that's what lovemaking is supposed to be like. Is it supposed to be gentle like that, so sweet it makes your body sing? Because if that's the way it's supposed to be, I've been cheated my whole life. Until today."

Silence hung between them, and Mac made sure his thoughts were totally shielded from Kiera, because he was afraid that what he was thinking could destroy her. She was so damaged by the bastards she'd known. So open to love and yet afraid to believe that any man could actually be gentle and loving toward her.

He'd like to take every single guy out of her past and beat the crap out of them, if only to prove to her that she was worth gentleness. That she deserved kindness and love.

And maybe she deserved a Nyrian who knew how to treat a woman like a queen.

Kiera laughed and grabbed her drink again. Took a big swallow and crunched on an ice cube, effectively ending the moment. "Anyway, it's got me wondering now if I've been totally wrong. That I was right when I thought of myself as bi, because as much as I like women, that guy left me feeling way too good."

"I take it your first day on the job was okay, then?" Mac had to bite his lip to keep the stupid grin off his face as he stood up and grabbed his drink.

"Oh. My. Mac, I am so glad you picked me for this. And I'm so glad the lawsuit those idiots were trying to lodge against you didn't fly, though if they hadn't tried, I never would have heard about this. I swear it's gonna change my life—for the good."

"Well, you know how it is—we want our employees satisfied."

She took his double entendre for what it was worth and doubled over laughing. He could still hear her chuckling as he headed up the stairs to his room to dress. Damn. They were all making contact, sooner and more intimately than he'd expected.

He wondered how Morgan's shift was going. Wondered if the guy who seemed to have a permanent chip on his shoulder could open up enough to contact Zianne's people.

Zianne. Damn it all, where the hell was she? He hadn't felt her presence at all today. Hadn't had any contact at all. What if she hadn't made it? How would he feel about rescuing everyone but the woman he loved?

Sighing, he set his drink on the bathroom counter, dropped his towel on the floor, and stepped into the shower to wash off the chlorine. He stood beneath the warm spray, thinking of all that had happened to get him to this point. Of what he still had to do, and he realized it didn't change anything.

Not in the long run. He'd made a promise to Zianne, and he always kept his promises. He'd do everything in his power to save her people, even if she was no longer among them. Except she had to be out there, somewhere. She had to be alive.

He refused to accept an alternative.

Morgan's head felt muzzy, as if he'd had too much to drink, and his body still throbbed with the remnants of that last climax, but he turned and managed a smile when Rodie walked in. She made eye contact, and there was nothing in her appearance that made him suspect she'd been aware of his fantasies.

Nothing at all. She seemed perfectly relaxed, not at all nervous or uncomfortable seeing him. As open as Rodie was, she wouldn't be able to hide it if she'd been there with him.

It took everything he had to see her up close and personal without getting hard. He couldn't get that look on her face as she'd climaxed out of his head. Even so, what he was feeling, what was making him hard all over again, wasn't all Rodie. No, damn it. It was remembering that guy's dick shoved up his ass.

Fuck.

He couldn't let himself think of that. Not and make it out of here without Rodie guessing something was up.

Like him.

He got out of the chair and put his sensor cap back in the drawer. Rodie dropped her tote bag on the floor beside the chair and took her seat. Morgan leaned over and gave her a quick kiss. "Sweet dreams and good luck." He turned to leave.

"Did anything happen?" Her voice sounded a little gravely, like she might be coming down with a cold. He hoped not, but she smiled at him. Open. Honest. Cute as ever.

He gazed at her smile and his mind's eye saw the stretch of her lips around his cock, the bright twinkle in her eyes as she relaxed her throat muscles and took him deep. He looked closer, and her eyes were indeed a swirl of gold and green and darkest brown, with amber highlights glistening.

He wondered if she wore black bikini panties. Almost asked. But then he took a deep breath. "Not really," he said. "Hope your night goes well." Then he gave her a quick wave and closed the door behind him.

He hoped she didn't realize he'd been lying, but he wasn't quite ready to tell her what he'd experienced.

And there was absolutely no way in hell he could explain the fact that his ass burned like blazes, just as if some guy hung like a bull had buggered him really good and hard.

Rodie didn't let out her breath until Morgan had shut the door behind him. How the hell could she explain the past four hours? She'd grabbed some lasagna Meg had left for them before she went to town, took it back to her cabin, and nuked it in the microwave. Kiera was just getting off and Morgan had reported in, and no one else had been around.

She'd needed time to think.

She hadn't intended to fall asleep after eating and she certainly hadn't expected the dreams that took over her mind—and her body. Maybe she could blame it on the lasagna, but she was almost positive Morgan had drawn her directly into his fantasies.

And if he was anything in real life the way he was in his imagination, she wanted him. Now. Laughing softly, Rodie settled the cap over her head and sat back in the chair, but there was no way she'd get Morgan or those images out of her mind.

She really wanted to ask him if his butt hurt. Oh god. No way could she find the nerve to do that! But he'd pictured her so perfectly with her black bikinis. And the other guy, the one who'd fucked Morgan, was the same guy who'd been in her fantasy.

So how did it all play out? Had she really managed to suck Morgan's cock all the way down her throat? It was a frickin' fantasy, damn it, but why did her throat hurt? Hell, even her voice sounded scratchy, as if she'd stretched something deep inside. She didn't feel like she was sick or anything, but she wondered if this was how a woman felt after deep-throating a guy.

And if she'd actually done it, how? Where? Had she been in his cabin, on Morgan's bed? If so, there should be a damp stain on his bedspread, because she knew he'd come all over it.

So had she. Figuring out the difference between fantasy and reality was so confusing it made her head hurt. She settled back in the chair and tried to relax. Tried to let her thoughts flow.

What the hell was that noise?

She glanced at the door. It almost sounded like something scratching at the bottom of the door. More curious than concerned, Rodie got up and opened the door. It was dark outside and the stars glistened overhead, but she didn't see anyone.

She stepped outside and looked around. There were lights on at the lodge. She saw Morgan's cabin to the right and Kiera's to the left. Kiera's was dark, but lights were on in Morgan's.

Chuckling softly, she wondered again if there'd been a spot on his bedspread. Just the thought of it was so sexy. Sitting there in front of him with her hand down her panties playing with herself while Morgan was bent over the bed, right there in front of her. Naked. Hot and gorgeous with those wide, muscular shoulders, his dark hair tangled with sweat and a totally hot guy behind him.

Remembering the rhythm, the pure lust on Morgan's face, knowing another man was fucking him and that Morgan was getting off on it made her mouth go dry. Made her pussy wet.

She'd never watched two guys screwing before, at least in real life. She'd seen some online porn, but it was nothing like the real thing—if that was the real thing. The expression on

Morgan's face, like he wasn't really sure he wanted to do it when that big guy held him down and rubbed lube on his butt, the look in the guy's eyes as he slowly pressed forward.

And then watching Morgan's expression change. Realizing he was getting turned on by what was happening. Knowing he loved it.

She hadn't known whom to concentrate on first—Morgan or the guy—because both of them were so into it, so damned hot that it just blew her mind.

She wondered if she could pull up the same guy again. If he'd be able to come back so quickly after spending time with Morgan. Or if he even was the same guy. Here she'd only been at the site for a night and a day, and already she was totally confused. At least it was a good confused. Kind of.

She really needed to get back inside, but the sky was absolutely brilliant with so many stars out tonight. There was the faintest smudge of twilight on the western horizon and the moon wasn't up yet, but darkness out here, in spite of the lights from the lodge, was a whole lot darker than she was used to.

Surprisingly, Rodie found it unbelievably peaceful. It was a wonderful reminder that places still existed where you could almost reach out and touch the stars.

You couldn't see them like this at home. Too many lights in the Bay Area. But up here in the high mountains, the diamonds glowing across the sky reminded her of scattered treasure.

Reluctantly, she turned to go back inside, but something chattered near her feet. Rodie glanced down. "What are you doing here, little girl? Squirrels don't go out after dark." She certainly hadn't expected to see the little gray squirrel on her proverbial doorstep, but she reached down and held out her hands.

The squirrel didn't hesitate to crawl into her grasp.

Rodie picked up the adorable little thing and carried her inside. "You shouldn't be out at night. Don't you have a nest in a tree somewhere? If you're not careful, an owl or a coyote might get you."

Settling back in the recliner, she put the squirrel on her lap and stretched the mesh cap over her hair to connect with the array. The squirrel watched everything she did, but didn't appear to be the least bit nervous.

"You're lucky. I brought a muffin with me." Rodie reached over the arm of the chair and grabbed her tote bag off the floor. She dug around inside and pulled out the wrapped muffin she'd snatched from the kitchen. The squirrel reached for it with tiny paws. Rodie broke off a few pieces and set them on the arm of the chair. "You can have those, but you're going to have to let me work. Tonight Mac wants us to try and talk with any of the Nyrians we might connect with."

The squirrel stopped eating and stared at Rodie. She was such a cute little thing—so fluffy with dark, sparkling eyes, but what was totally weird is that she looked as if she paid attention to every word Rodie said.

Rodie ran her finger over the squirrel's furry head. "Mac hasn't said too much, but we know he's searching for a woman he's loved for twenty years. That's just about the most romantic thing ever, but for some reason, she hasn't contacted him. I think he's really worried she can't, because all of us appear to be making contact with her people. All except for Mac."

Sighing, Rodie stared at the squirrel. "I know he's afraid she's dead or that she's been captured. He doesn't talk about her too much, but we know he's done all of this—the array and the search to bring us together—just so he can get her back."

The squirrel scratched at Rodie's hand.

"I should have known—you're more interested in eating my muffin than hearing about lost love, you little piglet." She put a couple more pieces of muffin in front of the squirrel's nose, but the animal merely sat back on her haunches with her tail waving over her back like a flag and stared at Rodie. Then she hopped down on the floor.

What the heck did the critter want? Rodie glanced at the immobile dials. Was she ever going to get down to business tonight? "Do you want out? I'm afraid you'll get eaten if you . . ."

The squirrel began to waver, to stretch and change until she flashed into a glowing tower of blue flame. Rodie couldn't take her eyes off the brilliant light, but it lasted merely seconds and then flashed again, blinding her for a moment.

"Shit." Rubbing her eyes, Rodie consciously shut her mouth. Standing in front of her was an absolutely beautiful woman with long black hair curling all the way to her hips. Her eyes were violet, her lips a deep red. She wore a simple white gown that attached at one shoulder and had sort of a Grecian style to it.

It all happened in the space of a heartbeat—the squirrel, the flame, and the woman who smiled so sadly at Rodie and slowly collapsed to the floor.

Rodie had her cap off and was out of the chair in a heartbeat, but where the woman had been standing lay the limp body of the squirrel.

She couldn't tell whether it was dead or alive, but she'd heard something as the woman collapsed. She was positive she'd heard Zianne's voice in her head.

Rodie spun around and slammed her palm down on the red button on the console as she scooped up the little creature. If this wasn't a reason to call Mac, then nothing was.

She held the tiny creature gently in her palms, relieved to feel the rapid thud of its little heart beating. Once she was sure it lived, Rodie sat back in the chair with the squirrel cradled in her lap. She tried to make sense of Zianne's frantic message while she waited impatiently for Mac.

Mac had expected to see Morgan this evening, but it appeared he'd bypassed the lodge altogether and must have gone straight to his cabin. The light was on there, which meant Rodie had to be settled into her shift in the dream shack by now.

Curiosity, wondering what Morgan might have experienced, had Mac down the stairs and standing on Morgan's front step within moments. He knocked on the door and waited.

A minute later, Morgan answered the door. He was wrapped in a towel and using another to dry his hair. "C'mon in." He held the door and stepped back.

"I'm sorry. I didn't even think you might be busy when I saw your light on." That didn't keep him from entering the cabin at Morgan's invitation.

"Not a problem. Let me get some clothes on. There's a cold beer in the refrigerator if you want." Morgan nodded toward the small kitchen and headed back to his bedroom. Mac found the beer and opened one. He was waiting by the front window, staring into the darkness when Morgan returned.

He'd slipped on a pair of ratty-looking sweats and an old T-shirt with the sleeves ripped out. Mac watched as Morgan detoured to the kitchen for a beer of his own, used the bottle opener to lift the top, and carried the bottle into the front room.

He took a swallow and then said, "I wondered if you might stop by. I was going to go over to the lodge and find you after I cleaned up, but I'm glad you're here."

Mac glanced over his shoulder. Morgan stood just behind him and to one side, and while his clothing screamed relaxation, the man was obviously tense about something.

"Want to tell me what happened?"

"That obvious, eh?" Morgan took a swallow of his beer. "I never had a chance to call you, not while it was going on."

He looked away, not meeting Mac's eyes. Then he shook his head. "No. That's not really true. I knew something was up, but I wasn't sure what it was. I knew if I called, you'd come running, and to be perfectly honest, I didn't want the interruption. I wanted to follow the . . . hell, I don't know what to call it. The event? It was way more than a fantasy, but I wanted to see it to completion. I didn't want it to stop."

"Can you tell me what happened?" Mac folded his arms across his chest, frustrated by the fact that just about everyone had made a connection now except him. What the hell was going on?

"I wish I knew. I started out with a fantasy and it was all about Rodie. Very explicit, but for some reason I noticed her eyes, the color of them, and I hadn't really paid attention before. When she came to relieve me, her eyes freaked me out—they were exactly as I'd seen in the fantasy."

Mac shrugged. "That could be explained by the fact that your subconscious remembered the details."

"True, but in my fantasy, she deep-throated me. I mean all the way down until her chin was resting on my balls." Morgan stopped and cleared his throat. "Not that I'm anything special, but I'm pretty big and no one's ever been able to do that for me, which would probably confirm that it was all fantasy, except that when Rodie showed up for her shift, her voice was rough. Really scratchy. At first I wondered if she was coming down with a cold. Then I had to wonder if deep-throating a guy with a big dick could injure a woman's throat. You know, leave it a little raw. Is that why her throat hurt?"

Mac frowned. Morgan wasn't bragging, wasn't making anything up. He seemed to have given this a lot of thought. "You're saying you think it actually happened? That it wasn't purely fantasy?"

"I'm saying she took me all the way down, sucked me off, and swallowed every drop. When I came out of the fantasy, I was alone but coming down from an orgasm. My junk was totally exposed, hanging out of my pants. No wet spot anywhere. Where'd it go?"

Mac chuckled. "Did you ask Rodie?"

"Are you kidding?" Laughing nervously, Morgan finished

off his beer and set the bottle aside. "How do you bring up a question like that? Besides, it gets better."

"How so?"

"I checked the clock. Almost three hours had passed since I'd started the fantasy, but it felt like minutes, not hours. I still had an hour left on my shift, so I leaned back and let my mind float. Next thing I know, Rodie's back, but with a guy this time. The same guy we both fantasized about last night. Only this time he says I'm all his and Rodie goes along with it, and then all of a sudden we're here in my cabin and he's got me naked and bent over the bed."

"Do you usually bottom?" Mac had pegged Morgan as the eternal top. There was nothing at all submissive about him, and he seemed to agree. He was shaking his head in absolute denial.

"Never. When I'm with a guy, he usually sucks me off, then I do him, usually with my hands. If we screw, I'm the top. Always." He took a deep breath. "Until tonight, and that's just one of the things about this that's weird."

"One of the things?"

"Rodie was with us. I need to ask her if she wears black bikini panties with high-cut legs. I don't know what she wears, but that's what she had on in my fantasy. And a couple of other things are hard to explain as fantasy only. Come with me."

He turned and headed to the bedroom. Curious, Mac followed. Morgan stopped beside the bed. "As far as I know, I never left the shack, but in my fantasy we had sex with me lying across the bed with my feet on the floor, and Rodie sitting on the covers in front of me with her hand in her panties. The guy fucked my ass and I came. Right here."

He pointed to a dark stain on the bedspread. It looked as if he'd tried to clean it up, but the fabric was still damp. Before Mac could say anything, Morgan smiled and looked away as if he were embarrassed. He was talking fast, almost in a monotone, as if he was reciting something from memory. Mac wondered how hard it must be for a man like Morgan to discuss things like this—acts of such a personal nature—but he was doing it in spite of his obvious discomfort.

One more reason to feel proud of his team. All of them had taken Mac's goal to heart. All of them not only believed— they'd thrown themselves into the project one hundred percent.

"Another thing." Morgan stared at the wet spot on the bed, but Mac was almost sure he caught a hint of laughter in the man's voice, as if he couldn't believe what he was saying. "And this really freaked me out. My ass hurts." He shot a quick look at Mac, and yes, he was grinning. A very self-deprecating grin.

"I feel just the way I imagine I'd feel if a guy who was hung like a horse decided to have his way with me. And see that?" he said, skipping away from something he probably wasn't ready to think through all that much.

He pointed to another smaller damp spot on the spread. "That's where Rodie was sitting, where she brought herself off with her fingers while I was getting my ass fucked. Explain that, Mac. Are we fantasizing, or are your Nyrians actually here, actually fucking with our heads along with our bodies?"

Mac didn't know, but his head was spinning. What the hell was going on? "I don't . . ." The beeper in his pocket went off. He grabbed the little alert, but he was already in motion and headed for the door before he even took the time to confirm the source of the signal.

Morgan was right behind him.

"C'mon, Morgan. It's Rodie. She just hit the panic button."

11

The dream shack door flew open and Mac rushed in. "Rodie? What's happened?"

Morgan was right behind him. "Rodie, are you okay?"

Mac was white as a ghost. Morgan didn't look much better. He also looked like he'd just gotten out of the shower—his hair was wet and tousled and Rodie could have sworn he looked better every time she saw him.

"Nothing bad," she said. "Still, I think it was worth the call." She glanced at the squirrel in her lap and grinned. "Mac? I think this is Zianne."

"What?" He dropped to a crouch beside her chair and stared at the squirrel lying unconscious in her lap. "I don't get it. Zianne? What's wrong with the squirrel?"

"Is she okay?" Morgan leaned over and ran his fingers gently over the squirrel's body. As if she were waking up from a nap, the little creature stretched, scratched her ear with a hind leg, and blinked at the men.

"She seems to be." Rodie couldn't stop smiling, though if she'd heard Zianne correctly, they definitely had a problem.

Mac stared at the squirrel. The squirrel focused on him just as intently. "Tell me everything," he said.

Rodie launched into the story. "So I brought her inside," she said, after explaining how she'd heard the scratching on the door. "I was afraid something would eat her. Anyway, I gave her a couple of pieces of muffin, but then she jumped to the floor and just..." Rodie took a deep breath. "It was just weird."

She coughed. "Sorry. My throat's sore, for some reason." It took a conscious effort not to glance at Morgan, but she felt him watching her and his gaze had substance, almost like a physical caress. "Anyway, she hit the floor and seemed to waver and stretch. Suddenly, I was staring into a column of blue light that hurt my eyes it was so bright. I glanced away. When I turned back, I was looking at a gorgeous woman."

She glanced at Mac. He'd been watching Rodie, but his gaze snapped back to the squirrel. "Describe her."

"Tall, slender, with really long black hair and gorgeous violet eyes. She smiled at me. Then she just sort of crumpled and collapsed. When she hit the floor, she was the squirrel again, but she was totally out of it."

Mac let out a long, soft breath. "Zianne? It's got to be you in there, sweetheart, but why the squirrel?"

"Mac, I think I know. She didn't speak, but I got a telepathic message from her. It came at me so fast that I've been trying to figure it out. She was only a woman for a fraction of a second, but she said something about her soulstone. She's here without it because the Gar found out she was leaving the ship and they kept it from her. She escaped to Earth so they wouldn't find her and kill her."

"How long has she been here?" Mac raised his head. His eyes were almost feverishly bright when he stared at Rodie. She glanced at Morgan.

He shrugged. "The squirrel showed up on the deck at the

lodge yesterday before lunch. I don't know if she'd been here before or not. That's the first time I saw her. She just ran across the deck and sat on the arm of my chair."

"Shit. I think this is her second night." Mac sat back on his butt on the floor and stared at the squirrel. He'd looked stunned at first, but now it was obvious his mind had kicked into gear and the need to act was overriding his emotions. Rodie wished she could read his mind. What was the man thinking right now, after so many years waiting for his lost love?

He let out a deep breath. Blinked rapidly as if he might be fighting tears, but the man's control was pretty amazing.

He glanced quickly at Morgan and Rodie. "Zianne had a really unique scent I will always associate with her. Honey and vanilla. I was sure I smelled it in my room last night, but I couldn't find her. Now I know why. Without her soulstone, she's weak, probably dying. The only way to keep her alive is to get her soulstone away from the Gar. I don't know how."

He pushed himself to his feet and paced the small confines of the dream shack. Stopped and spun around. "Wait a minute. Morgan? You're sure you made contact tonight, right?"

Morgan nodded. Rodie noticed he didn't look her way at all.

"Rodie, you think you did last night, right?"

"Yes. I'm positive I did." She glanced at Morgan. There was a definite flush to his cheeks. "Tonight, too, if Morgan had the same fantasy as I did."

"Crap. You were really there?"

She didn't even try to hold back her grin. "How's your butt?"

"Fine," he said. "How's your throat?"

"Touché." She rubbed her fingers over the front of her neck. "It's a bit sore, but worth it." She winked. Morgan glanced away so she couldn't see his expression.

Mac interrupted. "I hate to get in the middle of this . . ."

Rodie and Morgan both turned and focused on Mac.

"Thank you. Zianne told me one time that her people could share energy when they were separated from their soulstones. Rodie, the minute you think you've got a visitor, I want you to ask them to share energy with Zianne." He looked at the squirrel. "Will that work, with you in this form?"

"Holy shit." Rodie stared at the little squirrel as she nodded her head, chattering. "I didn't expect that."

Mac ran his fingers over the squirrel's fluffy tail. "I did. This is the same woman who went inside the electrical components of a computer back in 1992 to get some classified information on a crook. She turned into a stream of energy to do it." His fingers lingered over the tip of her tail. Then he drew back and folded his arms over his chest. "I'm guessing that she's able to draw enough energy from the squirrel to keep herself alive, but if she got caught coming back from my time in 1992, that means she's gone thirty-six to forty-eight hours, maybe more, without drawing from her soulstone. I don't think she can last much longer, even conserving energy as she is, without an influx from one of her people."

Rodie glanced from Mac to Morgan and back at Mac. "I don't know if I'm uninhibited enough to fantasize with you guys here."

"I've got an idea." Morgan focused on Rodie. "Only if Rodie's willing. What if both of us were hooked up to the array and broadcasting while actually having sex? That should make it a pretty potent call for help."

"Oh? And this is a totally altruistic offer on your part?" Crap. She wasn't ready for real sex with Morgan. Not yet. Fantasy was working just fine, thank you.

"Actually, it is," Morgan said. "As proof, I'm just as willing to do the deed with Mac. We need to generate enough energy to get a Nyrian down here in a solid enough form that we can actually talk with them."

"I think I can do just fine on my own." She glared at both men. "Give me an hour. If I can't connect, then we'll talk."

A cell phone rang. Rodie'd left hers in her cabin. Morgan shrugged. "Not mine," he said, but Mac pulled his out of his pocket.

He frowned at the screen and answered. "Dugan here." A moment later he shot a quick glance at the squirrel. "Okay. When did you notice them?" He let out a frustrated breath. "I can. Give me ten minutes, but call the sheriff. Now."

Then he ended the call. "That was my head of security. Someone's trying to break through the fence on the eastern end of the array. Morgan, I want you to stay with Rodie and Zianne. I'll be back as soon as I can. Rodie . . ." He let out a frustrated breath. "Get someone here, someone who can share energy with Zianne. I can feel her growing weaker."

Rodie nodded. "I will." She glanced at Morgan. "I think I'll do better by myself, though."

"You two work it out, though it might not be a good idea for you to be alone here with these jerks trying to break into the site. I have to go. Morgan? If anything happens, if you need weapons, check with Ralph or Meg. They know where everything's stored."

"Go. We'll be fine. I'll tell the others what's going on. That'll give Rodie time by herself."

"Good." Mac started to leave, turned back, and ran his fingers over the squirrel's head. "Damn it all, Zianne." He stared at the squirrel. Then he spun around and left.

Mac's eyes had sparkled with tears. Rodie felt like crying herself. The man had been through too damned much. As the door shut, she looked up at Morgan. "What next?"

"If you think you'll be okay, I'll find the rest of the team and tell them what's happening. It'll take me a while to talk to everyone, so keep the door locked until I come back. Try and get a Nyrian here and communicate as best you can."

Rodie nodded. "Do it," she said. "We'll be fine."

He leaned close and kissed her, and Rodie thought of the amazing dreams she'd had during his shift. She returned the kiss, almost losing herself in the soft slide of his lips over hers, in his scent and the warmth of his breath, the comfort of his big hand cupping the side of her face.

Then he was gone, and she was alone with a squirrel and her little mesh cap connecting her to the array. Rodie cuddled the squirrel snug against her chest, closed her eyes, and thought of the same guy who'd made such amazing things happen last night. She searched her memories, found the fantasy.

Or was it fantasy at all? She was so confused by everything that had happened, but the memories were so fresh, so real, that she had to believe the man was real as well.

She pictured him as she'd seen him earlier in Morgan's cabin, standing between Morgan's parted thighs with one hand planted firmly in the middle of his back, the other on his butt. His entire body had rippled with each powerful thrust of his hips. Morgan's soft grunts, the steady slap of the Nyrian's hard thighs against Morgan's.

This time, though, Rodie wanted to be part of it. She needed to connect, but how? She wasn't in the room with them as she'd been last night, wearing only her black panties. No, this time she placed herself beside the Nyrian, still holding Zianne and standing next to the man as he slowly fucked Morgan.

How the hell did she know how this would look—the thick, slow slide of the man's huge cock going in and out of Morgan's butt. This was too close, too intimate, but it was so hard to look away. Finally, she managed to raise her head and focus on the Nyrian's face. His eyes were closed, his perfect countenance suffused with pleasure—lips slightly parted as he breathed deeply, steadily, in time with each rock and sway of his body.

Where before she'd watched Morgan, this time she concentrated on the alien. Her heart rate sped up and she felt the flush covering her skin. It took an actual physical act of will to re-member why she was here, why he was here.

In her mind, she forced him to acknowledge her presence.

Finally, after what felt like forever, he raised his head and opened his eyes—eyes of deepest turquoise blue. She stared at him a moment longer and her concentration began to waver.

He smiled and winked. Startled, she jerked back, blinking in surprise, but thank goodness he'd pulled her back to the job. Perfect! She moved close, holding the squirrel in the crook of her left arm, stroking Morgan's shoulder with her right hand, but focusing on the one who was bringing him close to climax.

"We need your help." She spoke the words aloud.

This was no longer fantasy. This was for Zianne. The man tilted his head, but he never missed a stroke.

"Zianne is trapped here without her soulstone. Can you help her?" Rodie held up the squirrel. "This is her. She's barely hanging on to this form, and she can't communicate like this, at least not with us. Maybe you can hear her, but we can't. She's growing weak. We're trying to figure out how to rescue all of you, but right now we need your help. Your energy. For Zianne."

He didn't speak, but he smiled at Rodie. Reached out of her dream, took the tiny squirrel in his hand, and held her close against his chest. Then he began to glow, brighter and brighter until his entire body and Morgan's were surrounded in a bril-liant blue aura, a pulsing, living field of energy.

Still holding the squirrel in one big hand, he began thrusting once again. The glow flowed with him as he reached beneath Morgan with his other hand and grasped his erect cock in his fist.

It only took a couple of quick strokes and Morgan's climax exploded out of him. The Nyrian followed almost immediately, and somehow the force of their orgasm strengthened the blue aura. Brighter and brighter it glowed, until Rodie had to look away.

Morgan cried out. The Nyrian gave a harsh shout, and the aura exploded in a swirling mass of crackling blue energy. Around and around, spinning faster and faster, screaming with the sound of a jet airplane ready for takeoff. The visual of Morgan's room was gone. The dream shack disappeared, and they were surrounded in an endless night sky filled with glittering stars.

Rodie's hair stood on end, crackling with sparks, blowing in an unseen wind, and still the sense of power grew. Spreading, pulsing within an endless universe—a universe that was somehow in and of Rodie's mind.

The squirrel stood on her hind legs and reached for the whirling power. As if she'd called it to her, the mass of seething blue energy arrowed down and disappeared inside the tiny beast. She sat back down, blinking, and words slipped into Rodie's head.

It worked. I wasn't sure if this tiny creature could control the energy, but it can. Can you hear me? My mind is clear, at least for now.

I can. We need to get you to Mac, but he's dealing with some kind of crisis. How long will this last for you?

I'm not sure. At least until tomorrow. Bolt? Can you or one of the others share energy with me again?

If not me, one of us will be here for you. But, Zianne, be warned. Escape is paramount. The Gar are becoming restless. We fear they are planning to move on this world, stripping its resources sooner rather than later.

Rodie glanced around and realized there was no sign of Morgan or his bedroom and all the stars inside the shack had disappeared. The fantasy had ended, but her body still throbbed with need. Bolt, if that was his name, looked exhausted. He'd obviously given all he could to Zianne.

Will you be able to make it back to your ship?

With the aid of your amazing mind. He smiled and cupped Rodie's cheek beneath his palm. *I like your man. Give me another fantasy with him.*

I will, if you'll promise to tell the others about Zianne, that she needs your help.

Of course I will.

Rodie stroked the tiny squirrel in her lap, who appeared to have fallen asleep. Then she brought up Morgan's image once again, only this time she had him kneeling in front of Bolt. Both men were naked and she added a shower with water beating down on Morgan's back and coursing over Bolt's muscular chest.

Morgan cupped the Nyrian's heavy sac in one hand and firmly stroked his thick cock with the other. Fascinated, she watched the skin stretch as blood filled the organ. His soft foreskin slid back over his glans, exposing the broad, glistening crown.

The Morgan in her mind didn't hesitate. He leaned close and licked the firm tip, then slowly slid his mouth around the entire end of Bolt's erect cock. Bolt's eyes closed and he leaned back against the wall as Morgan licked and sucked, drawing him deep inside his mouth, though not, as Rodie noticed, nearly as deep as she'd sucked Morgan.

She still wasn't sure how that worked, how she'd been drawn into his fantasy, and she wondered if he was here in hers, or was he talking to Cam or Finn, or maybe with Kiera or Lizzie? And how would that work, if he was there and here at the same time?

When things were settled, when the Nyrians were free and the Gar gone for good, she fully intended to ask a lot of questions. But not now. Now she needed to help Bolt find the strength to get back to his ship before anyone discovered he was missing.

Her Nyrian was enjoying himself. She heard his soft groans and shivered with the arousal he shared. The tiny shack throbbed with desire, with the scents and sounds and even the tastes of sex. Morgan grabbed Bolt's buttocks in both hands and his long fingers disappeared into the dark crease between his cheeks.

She imagined him teasing that sensitive pucker, the way he'd teased her in her fantasy last night, imagined the way it would feel for Bolt to have Morgan barely penetrate the nerve-rich ring of muscle.

Bolt jerked, cried out, and cupped Morgan's head in his hands. Morgan drew the alien's penis even deeper inside his mouth, sucking and swallowing as Bolt climaxed once again. And as he came, his aura glowed brilliantly, but this time he drew the blue fire close around his body. The light sparked, enveloped the man in a crackling tower of energy.

The sparkling light blinked out, and Bolt was gone.

Rodie leaned back in her chair. Morgan had disappeared, too. Zianne was asleep, and Rodie's shift was almost over. It felt as if she'd just arrived, but obviously fantasy took more time than she realized.

She wondered what had happened along the fence line, where Morgan was, and why he hadn't returned. Was Cam going to be here to relieve her? Where was Mac? And what about Zianne?

She glanced around the small room and finally decided her tote would make a perfect bed. She took out her wallet and stuck it in her pocket, wadded up her sweater, and made a nest in the bottom of the tote. Then she lifted the sleeping squirrel into the bag and settled her in the soft sweater.

She found a dish in the kitchen area and filled it with water, and set it on the floor out of the way. Put the tote bag next to it with the top folded down so the squirrel could get out. Then she went to the door, to see if she could get an idea of what was going on.

Cam was walking across the open area from the lodge. He waved when he saw her at the doorway. "Everything okay?"

"Yeah. Did Morgan tell you what happened? That we've got Mac's Zianne?"

"He did. He's gone down to the fence line to see if Mac needs any help. I told him I'd come and relieve you. Finn's awake and watching the front gate, and Kiera's in Lizzie's cabin for the night. You can join them if you want. Kiera said the bed's big enough for three."

Yawning, Rodie covered her mouth with her hand. "Thanks, Cam. I think I'm just going to go back to my cabin. It's been a long day. Zianne's here." She showed him the tote bag on the floor. "She got enough energy from Bolt—he's the Nyrian I've connected with—that she can communicate a little. The minute Mac returns, let him know so he can talk to her directly. I know he'll want to do that while he can. The other Nyrians can keep her alive for a while by sharing energy, but they can't do it indefinitely."

"They need their soulstones." Cam stood over the tote and watched the little squirrel. "Can you believe this?" He chuckled softly. "All these years I've painted the worlds I see in my dreams, and now I find that some of them, at least, really existed. I've always wondered about life on other worlds, and here we are, already communicating with aliens from another planet. It's really beyond bizarre."

Rodie glanced at Cam. "I know. I hope it all works, though. When we first got here, I honestly didn't think we'd really make contact, but Mac was so sincere. I figured I was open to just about anything. Not this, though. Not the understanding that an entire race of people are slaves, that we're their only chance. That's a terrifying responsibility."

Cam nodded. "Even worse is knowing the ones holding them prisoner have the power to destroy Earth. That's scary stuff."

"I know. Bolt said they're worried the Gar might do something sooner rather than later." Rodie shook her head. "I'm really tired. It's like all of this is too far beyond my ability to comprehend right now. I think I've used up all my adrenaline and every one of my brain cells tonight. If Morgan comes by, tell him I'm in my cabin. I don't want him to worry."

"G'night, Rodie." Cam leaned over and kissed her, and she felt her body responding in spite of her exhaustion.

What was it about this place? Laughing, she broke the kiss. "I hope you have a good night. If you get a Nyrian to show up, see if they'll share energy with Zianne."

She left as Cam was settling into the recliner. It was quiet outside. The moon was finally up, though not nearly as full as it had been last night. It was so weird, knowing the Nyrians were in a spaceship on the far side. Between the moon and the lights from the lodge, there was enough light for Rodie to walk to her cabin without a flashlight, which was a good thing, since she'd left hers in the pocket of her tote.

She was exhausted but buzzing. There was just too much going on tonight, and how in the hell were they going to get the Nyrians off the Gar's ship, with all their soulstones, including Zianne's?

Yawning, she reached her cabin and went inside. Sometimes there was just too much to worry about for her head to handle. Especially when it was all totally unbelievable shit that she knew for a fact was true.

Scary stuff. Very scary stuff.

Cam stared at the door after it closed behind Rodie, then got himself situated in the recliner. He put the cap on and checked the dials. All the readouts looked normal, and yet there was an alien in the room with him right now. The consciousness of a woman who had actually lived on the world he'd painted last night. *Head trip* didn't even come close to describing the feelings coursing through him right now.

Did Rodie—did anyone—understand the danger they were in? Everyone seemed so concerned about the Nyrians and their plight, when the gravest risk was from their captors. An alien race responsible for the destruction of untold planets and their inhabitants, capable of sucking the world dry, of taking all its resources, from precious metals to every drop of water on the planet—that was the threat they should be worried about.

He glanced at the tote bag and its sleeping occupant. Then he stretched out in the recliner and stared through the skylight overhead. This time, instead of fantasizing something sexual or imagining the worlds he loved to paint, Cam thought of the ship hiding behind Earth's moon—close yet so far away. And instead of projecting a sexual fantasy, he decided to try something else.

He thought of the Nyrians as a race of intelligent, thinking beings. Then he called on them for help.

Mac drove one of the four-wheelers back to the lodge with Morgan as his passenger. They'd left a few members of the security team on watch for the night, but he thought the immediate threat—whatever the hell it was—had passed. They'd finally flushed the trespassers out with the helicopter, but then they'd lost them in the heavy scrub. The sheriff and his team had eventually arrived and searched the area, but the night was dark, the mountainside extremely rugged, and the ones they hunted were dressed in dark gear with night goggles.

Whatever their goal, they'd come prepared. That didn't sound like the evangelical protestors who'd been hanging around the front gate, though Mac had the sneaking suspicion the two groups were somehow connected.

"What the hell do you think they want?" Mac stopped in front of Morgan's cabin.

Morgan shook his head. "No idea, but they're definitely not kids out screwing around. Did you see the weapons they were carrying?"

Mac nodded. Assault rifles with night-vision scopes. The kind of stuff his guys weren't prepared to fight. Hell, he had a regular security force—a few ex-military but not all trained soldiers. Whoever was trying to come through the fence tonight was geared up and appeared trained for an all-out assault.

Mac stared out across the plateau, at the symmetrical pattern of huge satellite dishes aligned in perfect order across the barren landscape. There was no longer a question as to whether or not they'd make contact. Now it was a matter of how they were going to use the connection to save the Nyrians. As dangerous as the situation with the Gar appeared, actual contact felt almost anticlimactic.

He thought about calling Dink. Maybe his resources could discover who was behind the assault attempt tonight, possibly dig up something on the pseudo-fundamentalist group picketing the front gate, see if they were connected to the ones who'd tried to file a lawsuit with Kiera. He didn't think there was any kind of religious issue behind them at all. It was something more, and he'd bet good money it was connected to tonight's activities.

"I'm going back to the dream shack," he said. "I need to see if Rodie was able to get help for Zianne."

Morgan already had one foot on the ground. He pulled it back inside and sat. "Drop me off at Rodie's cabin, okay? I should check on her. Crap, but I really screwed up. I told her I'd stay and keep an eye on things, and then after I went to tell the others what was going on, I never got back to the shack."

Morgan looked totally disgusted with himself. Mac rubbed his fingers across his chin and mouth to cover the amusement he couldn't contain. This was a relationship he hadn't seen coming, but it was obvious there was something going on between the two. "Well, for what it's worth," he said, "I'm glad you came down to help us out. I had no idea there were so many potential intruders."

"I know. That was just nuts. And freaky, when you think about it. Hell, you can't get much farther out in the boonies than you are here. What the fuck do they want?"

"I wish I knew." Morgan was right, and it was driving Mac nuts, trying to figure out what the hell was going on. He turned the wheel, spun the vehicle around in front of Morgan's cabin, and pulled up in front of Rodie's. "See you in the morning."

"You, too." Morgan climbed out and headed up the steps. Mac drove to the dream shack and parked out in front. He stared at the little building, much too aware of all the things that could go wrong. He'd not allowed himself to even think of Zianne—not while they were busy dealing with the idiots trying to break through the back fence.

Now, though, she was all he could think of. He didn't know whether to laugh or cry—the woman he loved, trapped in the body of a little gray squirrel.

He was almost afraid of what he'd find once he stepped inside the shack.

Cam had to physically shake himself out of the visual he was caught in as Mac walked through the door. It was after two in the morning. Cam felt as if he'd only been here a couple of minutes, but his head was filled with images.

"I'm sorry to disturb you." Mac paused by the door and glanced around the shack, frowning.

"You must be looking for a particularly tame squirrel." Cam pointed to the tote bag on the floor in the corner. The squirrel had slept almost the entire time he'd been here. Right now she was curled in a tight ball and had her tail wrapped around her body, covering her nose. "She got a full load of energy from the guy Rodie's been channeling, or whatever you want to call it."

Mac knelt by the bag. Cam couldn't see his face, but the line of his body spoke of a sorrow too obvious to ignore.

"Have you been able to get any more for her?" Mac turned and glanced his way, then focused once more on the sleeping squirrel.

"She can't handle any more now. Rodie said Bolt, the guy she brought in, was going to tell the others. They'll take turns sharing with her for as long as they can. One thing he told Rodie, though. He's worried about the Gar. He thinks they might want to move on the earth sooner rather than later. He doesn't think we have much time."

Mac stood up. He had Rodie's tote bag with the squirrel in his arms. "Thanks, Cam. I'm going to take her with me. Tell Finn I'll probably bring her back during his shift."

"Sure, Mac. Later." Cam turned back to the console, staring blindly at the dials. What a mess. Mac was so focused on Zianne, had he even heard what Cam had said about the Gar? Of course, Cam couldn't blame him. Mac had spent his entire adult life designing and building the array so he could save the woman he loved, and she'd come back as a fucking squirrel. If it wasn't such a horrible tragedy, he'd laugh, except there was nothing funny about it.

He glanced at the sketches he'd made after connecting with the Nyrians. The one who'd come had taken shape here in the shack, not because of sex or any kind of prurient fantasy on Cam's part. No, he'd come in response to Cam's request for help.

Instead of a hot chick, he'd gotten one of the elders, a quiet, soft-spoken man with an amazing mind. He'd offered energy to Zianne and she'd declined, but then he'd given Cam everything he needed, more than he'd asked for.

There were a few details to fill in, but the older Nyrian was going to find out what he could, and he'd added something else that Cam figured was in their favor. The Nyrians had abilities the Gar were totally unaware of. Things they could do that might help ensure their escape.

They'd just never had any place to escape to, before. Now they did—they had Earth as a refuge and a group of humans willing to help them.

It was an opportunity the Nyrians couldn't ignore.

Cam settled back in the recliner. He still had two hours to go on his shift. He let his mind flow freely this time, not into the realms of other worlds but into his own sexual fantasies, though it felt so weird, trying to imagine a fantasy lover.

His dreams had always been places, not people. He really had no idea what kind of lover he wanted. Didn't even know what sex he preferred in fantasy, and that was strange. He'd always thought of himself as heterosexual but open-minded.

Maybe that was the way to dream. Just open his mind and think of sensations. Of what felt good, not necessarily who was making him feel that way.

Smiling, he settled back and merely thought of the Nyrians, of an entire race of intelligent people held captive, desperate for freedom. He sent his thoughts into space, his hopes for their freedom, for their future, and left the fantasy up to whomever caught his dreams.

12

This couldn't be real. None of it—his life was so screwed up right now, his head so full of questions, he found it difficult to do more than put one foot in front of the other. Mac left the four-wheeler in front of the dream shack and walked back to the lodge, carefully carrying the tote bag and Zianne.

She'd awakened as soon as he'd picked up the bag, but she sat calmly in her little nest and watched him. He felt like sobbing with frustration. To wait so long, to come so close, and not to have the woman he loved in his arms was killing him.

He carried her up to his room and shut the door, set the tote bag on his bed, and stripped off his shirt. Got a whiff of himself and decided he was a bit too funky to go to bed like this, so he shucked his shoes and pants.

Zianne watched him. Her dark little eyes practically sparkled. He glared at her—the woman he'd loved his entire adult life, stuck in the body of a fucking squirrel—and he was frustrated, angry, and scared half to death. "Stay there," he growled. "I need a shower."

Damn, he was giving orders to a squirrel. He wouldn't be

surprised if the men in white coats showed up, except he knew this squirrel could understand him. He turned on the water, waited for it to heat, and stepped under the spray.

They needed a plan. Somehow, they had to figure out how to get the Nyrians' soulstones so they could bring them all to Earth, but how the hell they were going to manage that was beyond him right now. In the meantime, they'd have to hope that the energy Zianne's people were able to share was enough to keep her alive. At least it shouldn't be too taxing for her to maintain her life force within the squirrel's body.

If only she didn't have to do it for too long.

Crap. And if Bolt's fears were correct, that the Gar were considering moving against the earth anytime soon, the entire thing was a moot point. He'd tried to convince his contacts in the government of the danger, but not a single person would take him seriously. The military men he'd spoken to at the Pentagon thought he was a complete nutcase, in spite of the fact that their soldiers were armed with weapons Mac and BGV had developed.

Hell if he didn't wonder the same thing himself. He scrubbed himself from head to foot, lathering up and rinsing away the stink of the long day. He needed sleep and he needed to eat. He hadn't had a thing since lunch with the kids hours ago, but there hadn't been time.

He'd never expected them to make contact so quickly. Hadn't imagined something like Zianne's situation or the horrible sense of pressure with time of the essence if he wanted even a chance of saving her, but it seemed that since they'd arrived at the site, there was never any time.

No time, and so many things to worry about with Zianne and the Nyrians. And now he had a bunch of nuts trying to break into his site for whatever reason. He'd call Dink first thing in the morning. His buddy had resources for ferreting out information superior to anything even the military had.

One more thing to worry about. "Just put it on the list. Crap. Damned list is as long as my arm."

Mac leaned his head against the wall. Steamy water beat down on his back and shoulders, and he let his exhausted mind drift for a brief moment, a respite amid all the hassles. He thought of that night so many years ago when he'd come home after too much beer at Dink's. He'd taken a shower that had marked the beginning of the long and winding road leading to tonight.

He almost wished he was as drunk now as he'd been then. At least the Jack was still in his room. Along with the tote bag and the squirrel.

Shit. This was so not what he'd expected.

"What did you expect, Mac?"

His eyes flew open. Zianne knelt in front of him, as breathtakingly beautiful as she'd been so many years ago. Water sluiced through her long dark hair, and her violet eyes sparkled. Water beaded on her lashes, coursed over her cheeks like tears. Her lips were parted. She held her hand out to him.

He was almost sure his heart stopped beating, but then the damned thing tripped into overtime. He wanted to say her name, but he couldn't form the sound. Instead of taking the hand she offered and pulling her up, his legs gave out.

He knelt on the tile in front of her.

"Dear God. Zianne? How? My God, it's you. I can't believe you're here. Finally here, but you . . . oh, shit. I love you. I've missed you so much." He was babbling like an idiot and choking on sobs that felt ripped from his gut. And Zianne was reaching for him, wrapping her arms around him, and holding on so tight, and thank goodness for that because he was sure he'd fly apart without the warm band of her arms.

Her lips moved almost frantically against his throat. He heard her soft words of love but he still couldn't speak. Couldn't say a thing through the lump in his throat, through the thick, wracking sobs that had him doubled over her body, clinging to her with such frantic need.

Twenty years of grief, of pain and frustration and the worry of not knowing if she lived or died. Twenty years condensed into this one moment in time when he held her in his arms and once again felt a sense of hope, a chance that maybe they could succeed, that possibly all was not lost.

Zianne held him close, hugged him to her breast and soothed him with tiny kisses and meaningless words. She was the one who helped him to his feet, who shut off the tap, who handed him a towel. He dried himself, unable to take his eyes off her, afraid she'd disappear. He helped dry her off as well, but he quickly dropped the towel to run his hands over her smooth skin, to feel the body that he'd once known so well.

She was exactly the same as the last time he'd held her. He was twenty years older. Twenty unbelievably hard years.

Right now, though, that didn't matter. All that mattered was the fact that she was here, in his room, in his arms, and he couldn't stop touching her. Couldn't stop staring at her, as if she were nothing more than a fantasy. His fantasy, come to life.

Finally, he cupped her face in his palms and held her, leaned close and kissed her, tasted the flavors he'd never forgotten and feared he'd never taste again. Sighing, he inhaled the sweet scent of honey and vanilla. "How? How can you be here?"

She smiled and ran her fingers over his cheek. "Bolt gave me enough energy. I can't stay in this form, not for long, but I had to be with you. I need you, Mac."

"God, how I've needed you. Need you now. There are no words to describe how much I've missed you, Zianne. Twenty long years without you. I thought I'd go insane, missing you." He kissed her hard and long and only pulled away to take a deep breath. "But we did it. Your ideas and the money they brought in paid for this entire site. I built the array exactly the way we planned, and it's working. It's calling your people. I've got a team that can communicate with the Nyrians, and we're doing our best to figure out how to get the soulstones and free everyone at once. Dear God, I was so afraid I'd never see you again."

"I didn't know if you'd be able to get it built, if you had enough information to produce the technology we need, but it's perfect. I know that some of my people doubted, but I never did. I've met some of your team." She laughed. "At least my little furry alter ego has met some of your team, and they're wonderful. The one named Rodie shares muffins with me. She's my favorite."

"I'll have to tell her. That's her tote bag you were sleeping in." He touched his forehead to hers and sighed. His tears were under control, but his heart still ached. So many things could still go wrong. "What happened? Why didn't you come back? I've worried all these years that you might have been dead. That I'd never see you again."

"And for me, it's been only a couple of days. I'm so sorry, Mac." She leaned back and cupped his face in her palms, and he couldn't stop from turning his head, from kissing her hand, her fingers. Inhaling the scent he'd missed so much.

She tugged his face back to hers and kissed him, but once again she held his face in her hands and made him listen. "The Gar discovered I was leaving the ship to be with you. They have no idea I passed through time. I don't think they even know which planet I was visiting, though Earth is the only habitable one in your solar system, so we have to assume they're aware that I was coming here. Luckily, one of my people heard them talking. That's how we discovered they planned to capture and kill me, to set an example. I didn't expect them to go that far because they need every one of us to power the ship."

"They're not going to have any of you much longer. Not if I have anything to say about it. I love you, Zianne. I've never stopped loving you, but if I don't make love to you right now, I think I'm going to go insane." He wrapped his fingers around hers and tugged her toward the bed.

Smiling, she followed him. When they reached the edge of the mattress, she gave him a gentle push and he tumbled backward, but he caught her slim waist and pulled her down with him.

He'd dreamed of this for so long. Dreamed of Zianne in his arms, in his bed. In his life. She rose up over him, holding her weight on her forearms. Her breasts rested against his chest, her long legs twined with his, and tangling both of them together was her long dark hair.

She was so perfect, so absolutely perfect, and it was as if they'd never been apart. When she leaned close and kissed him, he was surrounded by the sweet scent of honey and vanilla.

Surrounded by Zianne. By her delicious scent, her soft breasts, the strength of her arms holding him tight. Her body draped across his, her perfect lips pressed kisses to his chest, to his throat, across his jaw. She crawled up his body, straddled him, and lifted up on her knees. He was hard and pulsing with need, and it was such a simple thing to raise his hips, to find her warmth, her tight sheath swollen and wet. Ready just for him.

She came down on him, too slowly when he wanted her *now,* but he held on to his control as she lowered her body by fractions, taking his smooth crown first so that he felt just the heat and dampness on his very tip, then more until he couldn't take it like this, not this slow torture by fractions of inches. He arched up, plunging deep inside, filling her, pulling her down as he pushed up. She cried out, clutching his shoulders and tilting her hips to take him even deeper, and as she rocked her hips against his, he lay back, closed his eyes, and opened his senses.

Her sheath clutched at him, holding his erection in a tight, fiery grip. He felt the ripple of muscles along his length, and his head was filled with her scent, with the richness of honey, the sweet scent of vanilla, and he remembered that first night, when he'd wondered if she tasted as good as she smelled.

She had, and more, and he shared the memory with her. Her thighs tightened against his hips and he lifted, plunged deep, then retreated. She rolled forward, planted her hands on his shoulders, and began to move in a steady, flowing pattern. Rolling her hips back and forth, taking him deep, letting him slide almost to freedom, then once again taking him inside.

He knew he couldn't last. Not after wanting Zianne for so many years, but he tried to go slow, tried not to rush the sensations exploding deep inside. His heart pounded out a staccato rhythm, his lungs pumped air like a damned bellows, but he kept up the slow and steady rhythm that he knew she loved.

He felt her body tighten, knew her climax was close, until finally, he let himself go. The years melted away, until it was just Mac and Zianne. He almost expected Dink to show up in the room, crawl into bed with them, and make it a threesome, the way they'd done so many years ago.

But not tonight. Tonight it was Mac and Zianne and twenty years' worth of missing the only woman he'd ever love. She arched over him. Her fingers tangled in the mat of hair on his chest, and he almost laughed when he realized how much more there was now than when he'd been just a twenty-six-year-old kid.

Zianne hadn't changed, though he'd lived a lifetime since they'd last made love. But as she reached her peak, as she cried out and her muscles tightened around his cock, it was as if the years melted away. He groaned when his balls pulled up tight between his legs, when the surge of pressure told him he'd lost the battle to hang on.

"Mac! Mac, I love you. I love you." Her cry and her sighs blended with his deep, guttural groan. He wrapped his arms around her and pulled her close, held her against his heart while the damned organ thundered in his chest. This time Zianne's tears dampened his throat and her fingers clutched his shoulders, hanging on as if she'd never let him go.

But he knew she would. He was well aware she had to return to the form of the tiny squirrel in order to conserve energy.

"How long can you stay with me? Like this."

She shook her head and sniffed. "Not much longer. If I go back now and become the small creature, I'll retain enough energy to communicate. If I wait, I will have to remain mute until I can take more energy from one of my kind."

"I see." He brushed his hand over her hair, inhaled her scent, and wondered if he'd ever hold her again. He had no idea what the future would bring. Zianne could travel to the past, but she was unable to move forward in time.

It didn't exist. Everything they would do, every action, every word they might say, had yet to be written. "Sweetheart, I don't want to let you go, but we're going to have to talk, to plan. You'd better return to your other form." He glanced at the tote bag. Saw the squirrel sleeping and looked at Zianne. "I don't get it? How can you be both places?"

Smiling, she kissed his nose. "Because that's a real squirrel who is lending me her body. She's really quite friendly and doesn't seem to mind when I'm inside her. She has enough of her own natural life force that she helps me to preserve mine."

She kissed his lips this time. "I'll need to go back to that little room."

"The dream shack?" He chuckled. Then, without warning, he rolled over so that she was beneath him, but he held his weight off her body, propped on his elbows with his legs encasing hers. His cock was between her thighs, and he was still aroused and growing hard again.

He knew he'd never have enough of her. Not if they lived a

thousand years. This one night couldn't come close to sating a need that had grown since the day he'd met her.

Had only grown stronger since she'd disappeared.

She arched, raising her hips against him. Brushed his tangled hair back from his face and kissed him. Then she smiled. "Is that what they call it? The dream shack? Then yes. I need to go back there before the night is over. It's easier for my people to share energy with me at night. It doesn't take as much from them to travel here at night as it does in the daytime."

"I don't want to let you go. I'm afraid you won't come back."

"Mac, I will return. And we'll figure out how to retrieve the soulstones and save my people. Cameron is working on that."

"Cam? How do you know?"

"Trust me. And trust the amazing team you've brought here to help us. They're good, sincere men and women. They'll do whatever they can to make this work."

He shook his head. "I know. I need to quit thinking of them as kids. They're absolutely amazing."

"Not as amazing as you." She kissed him again, but this time her arms went around him, her legs locked at the small of his back, and she held him like that, kissing him, taking his kisses in return, unable to stop this physical connection long enough to speak aloud the words they wanted to say. Yet Mac knew her thoughts as Zianne knew his. Hearts and minds open, they shared the sense of loss he'd known, the fears she'd felt. Shared and absorbed the amazing love they'd so quickly rediscovered.

As Mac kissed her, Zianne moved against him. He tilted his hips forward and slipped inside her warm sheath. This time their loving was slow and sweet without that desperate rush, that frantic need to couple. Orgasm rippled over and through the two of them, pulling them together in a warm wave of passion that mentally and emotionally satisfied something deep inside Mac.

He felt Zianne's rhythmic contractions holding him close and linked to feel the surge of his seed spilling deep inside her body. Their connection was soul deep, heartfelt. Life affirming.

God, how he loved her. He'd dreamed of this night for so many years, yet his dreams hadn't come close to the reality of finally holding Zianne against him. She was so much a part of him, Mac realized he'd lived as an amputee for the past twenty years, suffering the pain of a lost part of his heart and soul. Right now, with Zianne in his arms, he was complete once again.

But she needed to return to her other form. He sensed it even as her body rippled around him, as her climax carried her over the edge and away. He felt a tingle of energy wherever they touched, a sense of current passing between them.

Between one breath and the next, Zianne was gone. Mac let out a deep breath and his head fell forward, heavy with despair. The beautiful woman beneath him was no more now than tangled sheets and a warm bed. He let out a long, soft sigh and closed his eyes against the burn of tears.

There was no time for that. No time at all now. He managed to roll to his side, swing his legs over the edge of the bed, and sit up. The squirrel sat in the tote bag, sparkling dark eyes staring at him.

But it was Zianne's sweet voice that rippled through his mind. *Good night, Mac. Sleep well, my love. Try not to worry.*

I promise. I love you. Good night, Zianne. Sleep well.

She watched him, dark eyes twinkling as he crawled slowly out of bed and pulled on his sweats and a warm shirt. He slipped his feet into a pair of old clogs, gathered up Rodie's tote, and carried Zianne back to the dream shack.

Try not to worry, she says. Now that's almost funny.

Finn glanced at the clock. Two more hours before his shift started. His brain wouldn't stop buzzing, so he knew he wasn't going to get any more sleep, but there was just too much going on. For a guy who never had enough to keep him busy, life here at the array was never dull.

He stared at his bed a minute, then turned away and went back to the front room, dragged his laptop out of the case, and booted up. First thing he did was check mail. Nothing but spam, so obviously no one missed him all that much. Then he hit the social networking pages. He'd given up on Twitter—it felt like too much of a commitment to stay on top of stuff—but Facebook was fun. He scrolled through the posts on his wall and chuckled.

All from women. Beautiful women, every last one of them. He stared at their pictures a moment and realized every single one on the page had been in his bed.

There were an awful lot of them.

So why did that make him feel depressed? Normally, he'd get a charge out of all those thumbnail photos of gorgeous women, knowing he'd fucked each of them at least a couple of times, and in a few rare cases, maybe more.

Not tonight. What really pissed him off was knowing why he felt so crappy. So much like a total loser.

It was all Mac's fault. He couldn't get the dude's story out of his head, the fact that he'd loved one woman for twenty years without even knowing if she was still alive. Mac had devoted his personal and professional life—and a fucking fortune—to the single-minded purpose of getting her back.

What would it be like, to feel that way about someone? To love that much? "Fucking terrifying, that's what it is. And stupid. Really stupid."

Angry for no particular reason, he slammed the laptop shut, stalked into his dark bedroom, and flopped down on the bed. His alarm was already set for three-thirty, which was a good thing. He didn't want to be late for his four o'clock shift. He punched the pillow. Flopped back down. Sat up and threw the pillow against the wall.

Then he stared at it lying on the floor across the room and cursed again. Fuck. Why was he feeling so pissed at everything? Finn O'Toole was a good-time guy. He didn't do angst.

He got out of bed and retrieved his pillow. Then he sat on the edge of the bed hugging the thing against his belly, wondering about his piss-poor mood.

It was his third night without getting laid, which had to be a record, though when he thought of sex, he couldn't think of a single woman in particular he wanted all that badly.

Which meant he had to be coming down with something. There was never a time when Finnegan O'Toole didn't want to have sex.

Except when he thought of all those women on his Facebook page, he realized he couldn't remember anything special about a single one of them.

Not even their names.

None of them mattered enough to recall the details.

Wait . . . what about Mary or Macy or whatever the fuck her name was? They'd actually dated for almost a week. She'd even stayed overnight once.

He tried to picture her and couldn't remember which one she was. He did remember that she got pissed because he wouldn't agree to take her to her sister's wedding. No way was he taking a woman to a wedding. Didn't they know that's how guys got trapped into relationships of their own? Shit.

That was the last thing he wanted—a relationship.

Just saying the word made him nauseous. Relationships led to marriage, which meant kids and responsibilities and a fucking house in the suburbs, and that entire scene was definitely out of the question. Maybe, when he was too old to screw around. Not now. He didn't want any part of a relationship.

What the hell did he want?

He rolled back and stretched out on the bed, still hugging the pillow to his chest. Did he really know what he wanted? He'd tried so many things, changing jobs as easily as he'd changed girlfriends. He'd had so many different positions, had studied in so many different fields over the years, he figured he could do just about anything short of brain surgery.

He'd actually completed all the required courses for pre-med, but that was as far as he'd gone, and then that really cool job on an oil platform in the Gulf opened up and . . .

Yeah. That was sort of how he rolled.

Why couldn't anything hold his attention? It seemed that once the thrill of discovery has passed, there was nothing left to hang on to. Was he destined to a life of one woman after the next, of one short-term job following another? When would something not only catch his interest but hold it?

The image of the woman who'd come to him in the dream shack popped into his head. Why would he think of her now? And where the hell was she? When she and her buddy showed up in his dreams last night, they'd promised to come to him during the night, before his next shift.

Well, fuck. It was officially before his next shift. It was still night. Was she just a dream? And what about the guy with her? He'd been quiet, but watching everything she and Finn had said—if they'd really said anything at all.

The guy was interesting. If it was supposed to be sexual fantasy that gave the Nyrians corporeal form, why the fuck had he gotten a guy? And why did he find himself thinking about the guy as much as he had the woman? Both of them were beautiful. Both sexy as hell, and he remembered seeing the two of them standing there in the shack and thinking they were equally hot. Which was weird, but in a good way. Maybe that's what he was missing—a fresh perspective. Something new and exciting.

He shoved the pillow under his head and thought of the things that three people could do in the sack. He'd actually been with two women on more than one occasion. That was cool except there was a lot of pressure to perform, which wasn't easy with one broad sucking your dick and the other offering her breasts or whatever else was close. He knew the right things to do, and he knew they'd talked because the gossip had come back to him.

His reputation as a stud had definitely been enhanced.

But with a guy in the mix . . . He closed his eyes, picturing the dark-haired man with the redhead. Tall, well built, and quietly attentive, but it appeared it was merely a fantasy, or they'd have shown up by now.

They'd promised to come to him tonight, but obviously that wasn't going to happen. Of course, if they were real, they probably didn't want to deal with his crappy mood.

He couldn't blame them.

"Actually, Finn, we're here."

His eyes flashed open. He spun around and sat up. "Shit." He took a deep breath. Swallowed back another curse. They were here.

The redhead stood not two feet away, wearing nothing but a short, pale green tunic that matched her eyes. Her long legs seemed to go forever. Finn shoved his hair back from his face, blinking. Crap. Was it really her? Here. In his room. "How?"

She smiled and held out her hand. "Feel. I am quite real."

He took hold of her hand, squeezing lightly. She felt warm and very much alive. Smiling, she wrapped her fingers around his and then sat beside him on the edge of the bed.

"You had to think about us first. We weren't sure which cabin was yours. The little building is directly wired to the big antennae that pull us here so quickly, but once we're here, we need to lock in on the person we want to find."

"And we wanted to find you."

Finn turned at the sound of a man's voice. It was the same guy who'd shown up during his first shift. He had on a pair of soft pants like silky sweats, the same color green as the woman's dress. He was every bit as handsome as Finn had remembered.

Dark hair, fair skin, blue eyes, ripped body. *Black Irish? Could be.*

"Why me?" he asked.

The woman shrugged. Such a typical human response it made his head swim. "You were the one strong enough to give us a conduit. Zianne has told us about humans, about your fascinating minds, your amazingly powerful thoughts, but each of us has to find someone to connect with. Duran and I—I'm called Tara—wanted to come together, and that meant we needed a very strong mind."

"Are you a couple? I mean, like married?" So many questions, but were these really the most important? *C'mon, Finn. Focus.*

Duran shook his head. "Nyrians don't marry, though when our world was still in existence, we took a mate when we wanted to extend our energy into offspring. Now, though, with Nyria destroyed and our freedom forfeit, we have those who are friends, special ones we enjoy. Tara is mine. I am hers."

He glanced lovingly toward Tara. His woman. Then he smiled at Finn. "We both want to be yours, if you'll have us."

13

Blinking stupidly, Finn slowly gazed from Duran to Tara and then back at Duran. This was so far beyond bizarre, and yet their simple request touched him in a way he never would have expected. "I thought you needed the power of a sexual fantasy to take on physical bodies. I wasn't fantasizing at all. How . . . ?"

And why was he sitting here asking such stupid questions when they supposedly really loved sex?

Because he wanted to know. He had to know more about them, to understand why they'd chosen him. If there was something more. Something important he might be missing. About them.

About him.

"Fantasy makes it easier for us to take on solid forms," Duran said. "But there is so much power here. The array magnifies all of your thoughts; even the simplest mental bursts are amazingly strong. We wanted our chance to see this world before the Gar decide to destroy it."

"Shit." He glanced at Tara and then at Duran. "They're really planning to do that?"

Duran nodded. "They are, but we are a democratic people. We have voted on this. We're taking a stand here and we will not let them rape this world. Even Zianne doesn't know, but our plan is simple. We will stop them by disincorporating. Unless, of course, you can somehow help free us as Zianne hoped."

That didn't sound good at all. "Disincorporating means?"

Tara smiled and squeezed his hand. "We will scatter our energy throughout space and then return to the heart of Nyria, our goddess. Even without our world, she exists."

"Sounds like mass suicide to me. Am I right?"

Tara sighed, and he wondered how it was that they knew the human movements, the patterns of speech, the way to behave that left no doubt they were human. "That's a crude way of putting it, but yes. If we die, the Gar's ship will die. Our energy is all that keeps it alive."

The idea made him physically ill, but it said a lot about their character, that they would choose to end their own species rather than take part in yet another world's destruction.

"Don't." He put as much feeling into his words as he could. "Please, not until there's nothing else left. We're trying to save all of you." He practically growled his frustration. "First we have to figure out some way to retrieve your soulstones."

"They're locked away from half of our people at any given time," Duran said. "We can't get to them. We've decided that unless all of us can be free, none will escape alive."

He said it like it was no big deal. Why such passive indifference to their fate? Yes, it made logical sense that a few should die rather than an entire world if there were no other choice, but until the very end there was always a chance.

Furious, Finn shook his head. "Don't even think of it. Look, we may be only human, but we're a resourceful bunch. We'll figure out a way. Can you trust us to do something to help?"

Tara sighed and smiled at him as if she were talking to a

child. "We are but few. You are an entire world. Maybe it's time for us to end our existence. We've aided evil far too long."

Finn dropped Tara's hand, lunged to his feet, and glared at the two of them. Then he took a quick step back, shocked by his own surging emotions.

Why did he feel so passionately about people he didn't know? He never felt passionate about anything. Not even about passion, to be perfectly honest. Not anymore, but his blood boiled, his heart thundered in his chest, and anger surged, hot and furious.

He cared. More than he could imagine, he cared.

Because he did know them, and they knew him. They'd come into his mind, into his room—had searched just for him.

Somehow, having these two people here in his bedroom made everything personal. They'd been in his head, they knew what he was really like, and yet they still seemed to like him.

Hell, he didn't even like himself most of the time.

Tara stood and cupped his face in her hands. Her eyes had darkened now to a brilliant emerald green. Her lips were red and full as if she'd been kissed for hours.

If this was her first time as a human, she'd probably never been kissed at all.

She smiled. "Show us, Finn. You have what we lack. We need your passion, your desire to fix things. Use your mind to give us strength, your dreams to give us time. We want to know what Zianne found so tempting, so addictive, that she would trade her very soul to come back to the man she loves."

Tara reached up and kissed him and Finn's head swam with the sweet scent of vanilla and honey. Wrapping his arms around her, he tasted her lips and thought of cookies fresh from the oven. Working on instinct alone, he turned her toward the bed and they were falling back against the blankets. She was warm and willing beneath him, filling his arms, teasing his senses, her body fitting to his as if made just for Finnegan O'Toole.

Cookies were the last thing on his mind, though he wondered if she tasted the same everywhere. If she were truly real, or merely a construct of his thoughts—if both of them were fantasy.

Though it almost hurt to pull away, Finn ended the kiss, trailing smaller ones along her throat, across her collarbone. He glanced up. Duran stood silently beside the bed, watching as Finn kissed Tara, but he didn't attempt to join them. It was as if he didn't know what to do next. Then Finn realized that maybe it was because he—Finn—didn't know what to do.

This was as new for him as for Duran.

"You're welcome to join us." He scooted over to make room. "I'm just as new at this as you are."

"New to sex?" Duran raised one dark eyebrow. Finn laughed. "New to sex with a man. I'm good to go with women."

A big man, equal in height, in strength, Duran nodded as he stretched out next to Finn. "We quickly discovered that her human form and mine are different. Zianne said as much." He shrugged. "I like this form."

"Good. I wonder where it came from." Finn studied him for some sense of recognition, well aware he was half lying on the man's partner. "I don't know anyone who looks like either of you."

Tara raised her head and kissed him, tangling her fingers in his hair. "But you do. Sort of. I'm a composite of those women you've loved, the ones you could not entice to your bed."

Chuckling, Finn pushed her thick hair back from her eyes. "There can't have been all that many."

"Ah, but there are." She had a beautiful smile. "You convince yourself you're not interested in the ones who deny you, but your heart knows differently."

That wasn't what he wanted to hear. It made him sound like a bigger flake than he was. He glanced at Duran. "Then what about him? Where does his body and face come from?"

Tara leaned across Finn's belly and kissed Duran. His eyes lit up and he kissed her back. Finn watched the two of them, all lips and tongue and teeth. Instead of feeling left out, he was more turned on than before.

Duran broke the kiss, leaned back, and stared at Finn. "That is amazing. We have nothing like it in our own form."

Rolling to one side and scooting back against the headboard, Finn crossed his arms over his bare chest and shot a glance from Tara to Duran. Then he focused on Tara. "You were going to tell me where he came from?"

She laughed, and he wondered how they knew laughter. Then she scooted around until she was sitting cross-legged between Finn's and Duran's legs, like she wanted to see both men at once. "Duran is all the men you've admired over the years. We took them from your memories. Duran's face and body are what we ended up with."

He didn't know quite how to feel. They had stolen his thoughts, though for the best of reasons. That was, after all, why he was here—to provide those visuals that would make them whole. Their bodies were constructed of his memories, and yet their minds, their personalities, were their own.

At least it explained why they seemed familiar.

Why he wanted to trust them both. It didn't really explain why he wanted so much more from them. He was growing more aroused by the second. He glanced at the clock. Almost two hours until his shift. So much he wanted to know, to experience.

Two men and a woman could do an awful lot in two hours. He turned his attention to Duran, but before he could make a suggestion, somewhere along the line of how much more comfortable they'd all be as soon as they got out of their clothes, he felt Tara's naked breasts against his chest, her lips on his shoulder, and the rest of her body lying along his.

By the time he caught his breath, Finn realized that Duran

had somehow lost those silky pants he'd been wearing, too. Curious, Finn imagined Tara's lips trailing across his groin and she moved lower, falling perfectly into his fantasy. But was it what she wanted, or was she merely trying to please him?

Whatever. It was beyond pleasing. But what of Duran? Finn knew what men did together—he wasn't an idiot—but what did he, personally, want to do with a man? And just as important, what did he want to do *for* Duran?

Something that would show the man what kinds of pleasure this body was capable of. Finn curled away from the headboard and planted his hand on Duran's broad chest. Gently he shoved him to his back and leaned over him. Tara moved to lie across Finn's legs, still using her mouth on him. Part of Finn's mind was tangled up in Tara's amazing touch, but he stared at Duran's groin for a minute, working himself up to the next step. Just as Tara sucked Finn deep, he cupped Duran's balls in his palm, wrapped his other hand around the base of Duran's flaccid cock, and gently squeezed.

He'd expected to feel awkward about touching a man, but with Tara's mouth taking him higher by the second, he discovered that watching the surprise in Duran's eyes, sensing his pleasure, was a turn-on all its own. Duran groaned and arched his hips, and his cock immediately filled Finn's grasp. Within mere seconds he was as thick and hard as Finn.

Duran rose up on his elbows, eyes wide open, and stared at his erection.

"Amazing how that works, eh?" Finn winked. Then he lowered his head and took Duran's broad crown into his mouth. He'd never sucked another man before, had never fondled any balls but his own, but with Tara's lips doing to him exactly what Finn was doing for Duran, it felt like the most natural thing in the world to take as much of that thick shaft as he could inside his mouth.

He felt Tara's lips and tongue on his own package, and she

moaned softly as she licked and sucked, but he was being self-ish, wasn't he? Finn wanted to please both Tara and Duran at the same time. There was something addictive about their taste, but even more arousing was the shared look of wonder. Their joy.

This was all new—not only for Finn, but for the Nyrians, too. He'd never felt like this. Never wanted or needed this much, this quickly. He moved away from Duran and tugged Tara around until she was lying with her head against the pillow. Then he lifted her hips and ran his tongue between her soft folds. At the same time, he used his imagination, showing Duran how he could kneel behind Finn and make use of the tube of hand cream beside the bed.

Finn had definitely not done this before, but there was a first time for everything, right? He wondered if he should move aside so Duran could make love to Tara, but both of them were in his head, so caught up in the here and now, and he felt their gentle denial and the focus on what they were learning now.

That could be the next lesson—showing Duran how to make love to Tara. Picturing the two of them together sent another spike of arousal coursing through his body, but a very focused Duran was already spreading the soft cream over Finn's ass. He shivered.

Then he glanced over his shoulder, at Duran kneeling behind him, and took a deep, calming breath. It appeared this was going to be a first time for all of them. Hoping he'd not just made the biggest mistake of his life, Finn focused on Tara, on making her first time feel truly special.

He hoped like hell he didn't make a fool of himself. Duran's fingers slid over his ass and he shuddered, as much from pleasure as from nerves. Damn. What if it really hurt? No, he couldn't go there. He had to look at this as a new experience. A learning experience, the same as for the Nyrians.

They still had over an hour. That should be enough time, at least for this first lesson, but in the back of his mind, Finn wondered—who was the teacher, and which of them the student?

Then he felt Duran's fingers pressing harder at his back door and figured he'd better concentrate on the woman beneath him. It was a lot easier than thinking about what was coming next.

As Mac pulled away in the four-wheeler, Morgan raised his fist to knock on Rodie's door.

She screamed.

He tried the handle. Locked. So he put his shoulder to the door and shoved hard. The door popped open. The floor plan was just like his, and he raced through the main room to Rodie's bedroom in back. Skidded into the room and flipped on the light.

Rodie huddled in the corner of the bed, surrounded back and side by wall and headboard. Her arms were wrapped around her pillow with just her nose and eyes and a tangle of dark curly hair showing over the top. Breathing like she'd just run a mile, she stared at the opposite wall where a glowing tower of gold and blue energy crackled between the floor and ceiling.

"Rodie? What happened?"

"Morgan!" She launched herself across the bed and into his arms. He stumbled back a step but caught her against his chest and held her tight. Her bare legs wrapped around his waist and her arms went around his neck tight enough to strangle.

"Okay, sweetie. You're okay. It looks like you've got a Nyrian in your room. Any idea if it's anyone we know?"

She shook her head against his shoulder but didn't look. "I don't know. I just got off my shift a while ago, and I was so tired I went straight to bed and must have fallen asleep right away. I woke up and there was a man in my bed. At first I thought it was you, and I rolled over to kiss you, and it wasn't."

She burst into tears. "Oh, shit. I feel like such an idiot. I know it's okay, but I woke up and he was naked and I could feel him against my belly, and . . ."

"It's okay, sweetie." Morgan tried to peel her arms from around his throat, but his heart was singing. She'd thought he was in her bed, and her reaction was to roll over and kiss him? Wow!

"Let loose, okay? I can't breathe."

"Oh. Oh, Morgan. I'm sorry. God, I feel like such an idiot. I'm so sorry, but I'm so glad you're here."

She turned her head and stared at the blue column. Took a slow, deep breath and let it out. "Who is it?"

Morgan grinned. His hands were linked beneath her bare butt, and he decided he liked having his arms filled with Rodie Bishop wearing nothing but an oversized T-shirt. "Why don't you ask?"

"I am so embarrassed." She ducked her head against his chest.

Morgan shifted her weight, but he didn't set her down. She really did feel awfully good in his arms. "It's okay," he said, addressing the living energy. "She was startled. Who are you?"

The crackling calmed, the swirling sparks slowly took form, and Bolt stepped out of the last of the sparkles. He was beautifully, perfectly naked. His big cock hung down, entirely flaccid, his head was bowed, and he looked like he was ready to cry. "It's just me. I'm sorry I frightened you, Rodie, but you dreamed me here. I wasn't planning to come back yet—my shift on board the ship is almost over. When I'm on duty is the only time I can escape—but you dreamed me so beautifully I had to come."

Morgan felt her sag against him, felt the jerky movements of her chest against his as she tried not to laugh, but it was such a palpable reaction to the adrenaline rush of her fear, it made perfect sense. After a moment, she managed to raise her head and look directly at Bolt without blushing. Morgan had to give her credit for that.

"I don't remember what I was dreaming, Bolt, but if it was about you, I imagine it was really good. I'm so sorry I screamed. Please forgive me. I think I scared you more than you scared me."

Morgan set her on the edge of the bed and looked closer at Bolt. There was nothing about him now that didn't look human. His form was solid, his eyes clear, and while he was definitely handsome, there was nothing so remarkable that he would stand out in a crowd. He shrugged and smiled at the Nyrian. "How long before you have to go back?"

Obviously fully aware of the thoughts racing through Morgan's mind, Bolt glanced at Rodie. A smile spread slowly across his face. "Not for about an hour of your time. But only if Rodie is willing."

It took merely seconds before Rodie realized what Morgan and Bolt were discussing. Wide-eyed, she glanced from one man to the other. *I've never really done this before, not in real life. Only in my fantasies.*

I imagine that between us, Bolt and I can make it even better than a fantasy.

Morgan glanced at Bolt. This would be their first time in real life, without the buffer of fantasy. The Nyrian crawled up on the bed beside Rodie. He carefully wrapped his fingers around the hem of her sleep shirt. "Okay?"

Rodie nodded and closed her eyes as Bolt tugged the big shirt over her head. She slipped her arms free and he tossed the shirt aside. Then he helped Rodie stretch out on the rumpled bed.

Morgan stared at her for a moment, remembering his fantasy. "Tell me, Rodie. What kind of panties do you usually wear?"

Her face flushed. "Black bikini high-cuts, usually. Why?" She glanced up almost frantically at the bright light overhead.

Grinning broadly, Morgan reached for the switch and dimmed the light, but he didn't turn it off. "No reason in particular," he said, lowering the light. The room filled with shadows, but all remained perfectly visible.

Rodie stared at him, and he expected her to tell him to shut it off entirely, but just then Bolt's tongue flicked out and touched her inner thigh. Sighing, Rodie lay back.

Morgan sat on his heels beside her, watching while Bolt made love to Rodie with his mouth. It was the strangest thing, to watch another man with this amazing woman he'd already begun thinking of as his and not want to punch the guy's lights out.

What was really weird was how turned on he was getting, sitting beside Rodie and Bolt, watching. Bolt's tongue swept across her mons and he nuzzled the dark hair between her legs. Then he lifted her hips and concentrated on the fleshy lips of her sex, suckling first one side and then the other into his mouth. His tongue swept from her ass to her clit.

Rodie cried out as he concentrated on her pleasure, licking and sucking. He lifted her hips a bit higher until her legs sprawled, displaying her sex. He licked deep between her folds.

Rodie moaned and whispered soft curses like a prayer. Twisting and bucking her hips, she squirmed against Bolt's gentle assault in an obvious attempt to bring herself closer to his mouth. Her fingers curved into claws and she clutched the blankets.

Morgan found himself watching Bolt, the play of smooth, bronzed skin over powerful muscle and the way sweat dampened his sleek back and reflected the dim overhead light. The Nyrian adjusted his stance, kneeling between Rodie's legs with his weight resting on his forearms. Morgan's gaze was drawn to the smooth line of his flank and the taut curve of his raised butt.

He felt Bolt's blatant invitation and glanced at the bedside table. A small tube of hand cream sat next to Rodie's glass of water and a book.

The cream would have to do—it was better than nothing.

Morgan slid around behind Bolt and ran his hands over the man's flanks, down the front of his thighs, and back up to his heavy sac. Wrapping his fingers around the Nyrian's testicles, squeezing the solid orbs inside and then gently cupping them in his palm inexplicably sent a shock directly to Morgan's balls.

Bolt moaned and spread his knees, but he kept licking and sucking Rodie, using his fingers now as well as his mouth. The scent of her arousal filled Morgan's senses, but it was Bolt's beautiful body that held his gaze. He grabbed the hand cream and filled his palm with a fair amount. It smelled like honey and vanilla, much like the Nyrian's natural scent. He dribbled some along the crevice between Bolt's taut cheeks and ran his finger through the cool cream.

Morgan wrapped his fist around his own shaft and slowly rubbed the sensitive head of his cock along the crease. Bolt shuddered as he leaned back against Morgan, but he kept licking and teasing Rodie. Morgan shivered with an overload of sensation both visual and physical—and pressed forward.

"Relax," he said. Bolt let out a shuddering breath and pushed back. The soft tip of Morgan's penis slipped through Bolt's sphincter and both of them groaned. Carefully, pushing slowly, Morgan reached around the Nyrian's slim hips and wrapped his cream-filled palm around the man's thick erection.

Bolt's muscles tensed. Breath hissed between his lips.

Morgan slid his hand from base to tip as he drove deep, then dragged his hand back as he pulled almost out of the tight channel. In again, and then out, until they found a rhythm that worked for the three of them. Rodie's soft whimpers made a sweet counterpoint to Bolt's deep groans of pleasure, to Morgan's soft litany of curses.

It was so damned good, so amazingly fulfilling to be with both of them, to feel their thoughts and sense the myriad bits and pieces of arousal, of Rodie's and Bolt's profoundly strong desire, all spilled freely and shared.

Spilling out, spilling over, and linking the three as one.

Rodie was the first to go. She cried out, arching her hips for Bolt's busy tongue and lips and thrusting fingers. Then Morgan, caught in the loop of Rodie's climax, came apart.

"Holy fuck." It felt more like a prayer than a curse as pressure flashed from his balls to his cock. His body jerked, his cock spasmed, and before he could withdraw, he'd flooded Bolt's dark channel with his seed.

He was still shuddering with the strength of his climax when Bolt arched his back, words in an unfamiliar tongue spilling from his lips. Morgan continued stroking Bolt's cock with one hand, but he reached around the Nyrian's lean hip with the other, clasped his sac in his palm, and held him close. Massaging his balls, stroking his shaft.

A thick stream of Bolt's seed spilled into and over his hand. Morgan rubbed Bolt's ejaculate along the Nyrian's spasming shaft, but it was over much too soon. Morgan slipped out of Bolt and rolled to one side, sticky with sweat and semen, while Bolt moved to Rodie's other side. The three of them lay there, sucking in huge breaths as their bodies recovered from orgasm.

Rodie lost it first. Giggling, she flattened her palm over her mouth, but that only made things worse. Morgan turned his head, caught the twinkle in her eyes, realized they were tears of laughter, and the whole situation took him right over the top.

Bolt rose up on one elbow and watched the two of them as they laughed hysterically. Morgan felt the gentle contact of his mind as the Nyrian searched for understanding of this strange behavior. Morgan opened to him. Tried to show him how utterly bizarre this was—that he and Rodie, strangers until a couple of days ago, had just joined an alien from another world for some of the best, most meaningful sex in their lives.

It just didn't get any odder than that. Or better.

But the best part was the sudden light in Bolt's eyes as everything made sense and one more bit of his humanity clicked into place. His laughter sounded a bit rusty at first, but within a few seconds the three of them lay there giggling like children.

Finally, Bolt rolled to one side. He leaned over and kissed Rodie, and then he reached for Morgan and kissed him as well. "I must return. I will talk to the others, see if there is some way to retrieve the soulstones." He sighed and shook his head.

Such a natural reaction. Again, so very human. "We have pondered this question for eons, but there was no place for us to go should we escape. This is the first world that could give us a refuge. You may be the incentive we need for success."

He stood, but Rodie lunged to her knees and threw her arms around him. "Be careful. Don't take any risks, at least not yet. Don't let the Gar catch you coming and going. Somehow, we're going to get all of you out of there. We have to." She kissed him. "Now go. Hurry. I don't want you to be late."

He frowned and studied her for a moment. "Why is that? Why would that matter to you?"

She laughed. "Idiot! Because you matter to me. I want you to come back to stay." She glanced at Morgan. "So does he. Take care, Bolt. Please?"

He was smiling and then he was merely a burst of crackling blue and gold energy, spinning for the breadth of a second.

And then he was gone.

Rodie flopped back on the bed beside Morgan. She rolled to one side and smiled at him. "Will you stay?"

He nodded. "If you want me to. After I go clean up a bit." He leaned close and kissed her. "I don't want to disappoint you, but I'm totally exhausted."

Her smile lit up the room. "Me, too. I just want to sleep, but I don't want to sleep alone."

"Works for me." He crawled out of bed and headed toward the bathroom, surprised at just how true that was. He wanted to be with Rodie. Wanted to keep her safe, feel her beside him as he slept. Wanted to wake up with her.

That was something new. Something unexpected. Something he definitely wanted to explore.

Rodie was still sleeping when Morgan awoke. Sunlight streamed through the window, but it was early. He felt surprisingly rested, considering how little sleep he'd had the night before, but he pulled on his sweats and wandered out to the kitchen. Rodie's laptop was on the counter. He grabbed it and carried it to the kitchen table to check his mail.

But then he got to wondering about the group of men they'd routed last night, the ones attempting to break in through the eastern fence. Mac thought the religious aspects behind the protest were a ruse, that there was something else going on.

But what the hell was it?

He ran the name of the lead protestor, Bartholomew Roberts. It wasn't that common, and at first when he searched, all he came up with was stuff about a dead pirate.

He was still searching for information when Rodie finally crawled out of bed, but by the time he'd retrieved clothes from his cabin and Rodie'd gotten dressed, Morgan had a few bits and pieces of info certain to interest Mac.

14

Mac shut off his cell phone and stared out across the plateau. Sunlight shimmered off the large satellite dishes and a hawk circled lazily over the array. It was barely nine here at the site, but he'd caught Dink packing to catch a red-eye flight tonight to Germany to cover an important European Union financial summit scheduled for tomorrow.

When Mac explained the situation, Dink had done exactly as he'd hoped—the nationally famous reporter had changed his plans and would be arriving here at the site later tonight. Things were moving so incredibly fast, Mac figured that if Dink wanted a story, he'd damned well better get here soon.

He glanced up as Rodie and Morgan stepped out of Rodie's cabin. Looked like Morgan had probably spent the night, which had Mac biting back a grin. Ya just never knew. He pocketed his phone and waved. "G'morning." He fell into step with them, as they walked to the lodge. "I was just going to call you guys. I want everyone together for a meeting. You two okay with that?"

"Sure thing." Morgan winked and tightened his hold on Rodie.

They went in together. Kiera sat at a table, sipping a cup of coffee. Finn dozed in the overstuffed chair by the window. Mac had already called Cam, surprised when the artist answered on the first ring after his late shift. He'd be arriving soon.

The only one missing was Lizzie, but she was on duty in the dream shack. Mac went straight for the coffee and poured cups for both Rodie and Morgan as well as a refill for himself. "Breakfast rolls are over there." He waved in the general direction of the overflowing tray. "I'm going to get Lizzie."

Morgan grabbed a cinnamon roll and glanced at Mac. "Any new problems we're not aware of?"

"No, but things are moving much faster than I expected. A lot has happened over the past couple of days. I think we need to compare notes. I'll be right back."

As he walked from the lodge to the dream shack, Mac felt as if his head were ready to explode. Talk about an understatement. So much had happened in the past two days, he needed a spreadsheet to keep track.

Even worse, the sense of impending danger was growing, and Zianne was running out of time. He paused at the door and knocked, then stuck his head inside the shack. "G'morning, Liz."

She glanced up from her chair with a dreamy smile on her face. Her eyes went wide and then focused. "Mac!" Laughing, she slipped the mesh cap off her hair. "Sorry. I didn't hear you come in. What's up?"

"I want you to come over to the lodge. We're having a meeting this morning, and I'd like to have everyone there." He leaned over and scooped up the bag with Zianne. The squirrel slept soundly and barely stirred when he slipped the strap over his shoulder. "Did you have a chance to connect with anyone?"

"I did, though they're quick to tell me it's harder during

daylight. I don't know the guy's name, but he came . . ." She chuckled as she shoved herself out of the chair. "In more ways than one, I might add. At least he was able to load Zianne up with energy. I think they get it from us and share it with her."

"Good. Now let's hope she'll wake up." He held the door open for Lizzie. She stopped and stared at the squirrel.

"Finn told me that's Zianne, that she's in the squirrel." Lizzie glanced in the tote as she walked past Mac. "As hard as it is to believe, it makes sense. I was positive she was totally aware of what I said to her. Now I know why."

"You'll know a lot more in a few minutes, I hope."

When they stepped inside the main room at the lodge, Cam was at the table with a cup of coffee, already looking wired. Finn was awake and filling a cup for himself. Mac poured coffee for Lizzie and topped his off. Everyone took a seat.

He set the tote bag on the table and sat there, just staring at the sleeping squirrel inside. His heart was so full, his mind spinning, and he couldn't stop thinking of last night, of Zianne in his arms. Had that been their last night together?

He couldn't think that way. Refused to be that pessimistic. A pessimist wouldn't have spent twenty years and millions of dollars building the array. That wasn't the way he worked, so he carefully stroked the squirrel awake and then plucked her out of the bag. When he set her on the table in front of him, she stretched and yawned, stared at Mac and chattered.

It was hard to feel depressed with a cute little squirrel chattering in your face. Raising his head, Mac glanced around him at the now familiar faces, at men and women he saw as closer friends than people he'd known for years. They watched him, some more alert than others. He could certainly excuse Cam and Finn, though they actually seemed pretty alert, considering they'd gone without sleep for much of the night.

Morgan and Rodie, too, if the satisfaction they wore like a cloak of contentment was any indication. Smiling to himself,

Mac ran his fingers over the squirrel's head and back. She closed her eyes and shivered with pleasure.

He knew exactly how she felt. Damn, how he wished Zianne was touching him right now. He'd waited so long, and last night had barely been enough to tease him. He would always want more of her. Always. *Zianne? Sweetheart, do you have the energy to shift?*

The squirrel turned and faced him. It was so weird, to see Zianne's intelligence in the creature's eyes. *For a brief time. If they see me, this project might feel more personal, more real to them, but I cannot hold the form for long. I'm afraid. I grow weaker, Mac. Soon my people's energy will not be enough to keep me alive, no matter how much they share.*

Stay with me, Zianne. We'll make this work. Every one of my team has a stake in your survival.

I hope so. Ankar shared power with me this morning. He said the Gar are definitely making plans to move against this world. Right now they're testing Earth's defenses. We both know they'll discover there are none that can stop them. We may not have much time.

Nodding, Mac took one more swallow of coffee before setting the cup aside and addressing his team members. "Good morning, and thanks for coming on such short notice. I know it may be a bit hard to believe, but this is only our third day here. Everyone's had at least a couple of shifts. I know all of you have made contact with Nyrians in one form or another."

"Or multiple forms," Finn added drily.

The rest of them laughed, but Mac nodded in agreement. "Multiple partners, at least." He chuckled softly. "That confirms my info on each of you, that you're sexually adventurous. Remember everything that happens begins with your imagination."

Kiera took a sip of her coffee and stared at him over the top of her cup. He couldn't tell if she was smiling or not when she added, "Adventurous or at least willing to be surprised. In my case, my imagination was not talking to my conscious brain. I'll swear to that."

Obviously, Kiera was still coming to terms with her fantasy. "Too true. Okay. Here's what I've got. After talking with all of you following your extraterrestrial visits, we're learning more." He held up a finger to make each point. "Nyrians need your initial fantasy to give them a strong visual. That, coupled with your mental strength, gives them something to lock onto and a form to take. The powerful signal coming through the satellite array is their actual conduit to the site."

He held up a second finger. "Once they have that visual and the corporeal form they can create from it, they're able to tweak as they wish by using your memories. Finn explained that to me this morning, that his visitors told him they were composites of people he remembered. That's why they don't look like anyone you actually know. They're combining multiple faces and bodies and creating their own unique looks."

A third finger. "They only need that visual once to give them shape. Once they have it, they're able to take that particular form whenever they wish. It is, in essence, the person they've become, though the actual personality you see is all theirs— who they are in their natural state."

Lizzie frowned and raised her hand. "Does that mean that once they've created a body, they don't need us anymore?"

"Not to take on that form, no. It's theirs. But without their soulstones, they can't come here without our energy calling them from the ship. Once here, they can't stay indefinitely, because they need the stones to stay alive."

"But if they had their soulstones?"

Cam had been really quiet since he'd arrived, but now, when Mac turned in response to his question, he noticed the excitement in Cam's eyes, the almost zealous fervor that had the young artist leaning forward, focusing all his attention not on Mac but on the squirrel.

On Zianne.

"If they are here, on this planet, in human form with their soulstones in place, theoretically they could stay forever. That's what I'm hoping will happen, though I haven't asked Zianne if Nyrians lose their immortality once they take on human form. I do know that they could live among us as humans and no one would be able to tell they were anything but what they appeared. Zianne told me they even replicate human DNA."

"Do we know how many Nyrians there are?" Rodie was watching the squirrel as she asked, but she was smiling. Mac needed to tell her, privately, that so far she was Zianne's favorite. Sharing muffins had gone a long way with his woman.

"Rodie, I think I'll defer to the expert on that. Zianne? Are you sure you have enough energy to shift?"

The squirrel nodded and then began to waver, to stretch and glow, as Zianne pulled herself free of the tiny beast. As a column of energy rose glowing and crackling above the table and moved to a spot next to Mac's chair, the squirrel yawned, crawled back into Rodie's tote bag, curled up, and closed her eyes.

Zianne took form, standing beside Mac. Her scent enveloped him, and a wave of longing almost left him gasping in pain. He steeled himself, wrapped his emotions deep inside, and casually looped an arm around her waist. He could do this. He had to.

The room had grown absolutely silent, all eyes on Zianne.

"I have not met all of you." Zianne's soft voice with the sexy accent sent shivers along his spine. Mac tightened his arm around her. She glanced down at him, nodded briefly, and focused once more on his dream team.

"But I feel as if I know each of you. My fellow Nyrians and

I are your greatest fans. Though we are creatures of energy, the energy you so freely share is unlike anything my people have ever experienced."

She glanced at Mac and grinned. "From the time I spent with Mac in California, I've learned a few nuances of your language. I would compare your energy to fine wine, when what we usually find to empower us is more like really cheap beer."

She got the laugh, but then she sighed. "To answer your question, Rodie, there are very few Nyrians left. Before the Gar destroyed our world, there were many millions of us, but it was a relatively small delegation that went aboard the Gar ship—a couple hundred of us. After witnessing the death of our world, facing eternity as slaves, most chose disincorporation, or death. They elected not go on, knowing our world was gone.

"Right now there are only twenty-seven Nyrians aboard the ship. I am the twenty-eighth, but without access to my soulstone, I will not live much longer. I may not be among those who are saved, if you are successful, but now there are but twenty-eight left of a once proud and numerous race of Nyrians."

A long silence met her comment. Mac saw shock, dismay, and even tears as Zianne's words registered. So few of them survived!

Finally, Finn broke in. "How many does it take to power the Gar ship at any given time? What's the minimum number that can run everything? And what, exactly, do you control?" Finn seemed to be running figures in that convoluted mind of his.

"We run everything—the engines, life support, and all onboard technology—with fewer than a quarter of our number, about five providing power at any one time, though we now work two shifts of fourteen to confuse the Gar. That's how I was able to sneak away from the ship to meet with Mac, and how those you've met have been able to come here. We avoid appearing as individuals so the Gar can't tell how many of us exist."

"Are you ever all in the same place at the same time?"

She sighed. "Yes, but only without our soulstones. All of us are required to power the planet-stripping mechanisms that steal resources from other worlds—it takes a lot of energy to strip the water and minerals, even the atmosphere."

There was a long, uncomfortable silence as they considered the implications of an alien force stripping Earth of everything.

Lizzie let out a deep breath. Mac noticed her hands were clenched into fists, and her focus was one hundred percent on Zianne. "What will happen if all of you suddenly leave the ship at once?" Lizzie glanced at the others. "Do they have a backup system in the event you escape?"

Zianne shook her head. "Not now. They must have, before we were enslaved, but we've powered their ship for millennia, through many generations of Gar. They are not as long-lived as Nyrians, so the population we now serve has never known anything beyond life on a ship powered by slaves. Our hope was that they had grown lax in their security."

She sighed. "Unfortunately, their discovery that I'd been leaving the ship during my shift was a wake-up call to them. Those I've talked to say the Gar have tightened their hold on us and watch us much closer than before. They have no idea how many Nyrians there are, and don't realize that they've reached the minimum number needed to run the ship. They know we can't be replaced. We have never found others like us."

"Shouldn't they be able to tell by the number of soulstones they keep locked up?" Finn glanced at the others. "I'm picturing a tray of diamonds that would be easy to count."

"The soulstones shimmer with angry energy when they're stored. The Gar can't look directly at them. The stones don't like to be parted from us, so the Gar see nothing but a fiery glow they can't touch. The energy would kill them."

"How is the exchange made?"

"The ones recharging deposit their stones and go to the engine room to relieve the Nyrians on duty, who then retrieve their soulstones. There is a time when all are without the stones. Never a time when we all have them."

"Damn." Finn tapped his fingers on the table in a frustrated staccato. "I was hoping we could make the rescue during a shift change. So, how do they take them from you?"

Zianne bowed her head. "We give them up. Freely. It was done in the beginning when we feared for the lives of our people. We thought that by giving up our souls and promising to serve the Gar, they would spare our world."

"But they didn't, did they?"

Cam's soft question seemed to rob Zianne of speech. Silently, she shook her head.

"Zianne, I think I know a way that we can free your people, with their soulstones." Cam stood and walked around to the end of the long trestle table. He held up a canvas, but this wasn't one of his fantastic paintings of other worlds.

Mac stared at the drawing, mostly done in charcoal and what looked like colored pens or even watercolor. Not Cam's usual medium or subject. "What is that?" He got up and stood in front of the art with Zianne close beside him.

"It's a schematic, drawn to scale, of the lower level of the ship." Zianne studied it and then raised her head to stare, wide-eyed, at Cam. "Cameron! This is perfect. How did you do this?"

"While the rest of these twerps were indulging in fantasy sex with Nyrians, I was talking to one of the elders." He grinned at Zianne. "He's fascinating. Told me so much about your people and your world."

"You must have met Nattoch. He's our leader, and the eldest among us all."

"That's the guy. I like him." Cam nodded as he tugged a

long-handled paintbrush from his back pocket to use as a pointer. "So here's what I've got. This is the engine room where the Nyrians work. They send power to the entire ship—all the life-support systems as well as the engines that keep everything going, even the barracks where the Nyrians not on duty spend time recharging. Everything we're interested in is on this level."

He swept the brush across most of the lower level. "Their energy also runs the force field that keeps the Nyrians trapped in their barracks. Over here, in a locked room under guard is where the soulstones are kept. When the shift changes, the energy field guarding the barracks lowers and that group of Nyrians drop off their soulstones and relieve the prior shift, while those who've been powering the ship go off duty, retrieve their stones, and return to the barracks to recharge."

He glanced at Zianne. "Please correct me if I screw up."

Vehemently, she shook her head. "No. You're good. Continue."

"I propose on the next shift change, or as soon as we can get word to your people, all but five from the engine room—the absolute minimum number of Nyrians needed to power the ship—collect their soulstones and come here, to Earth, instead of returning to their barracks. Five with their stones do return to the barracks to recharge. Only five from the charged Nyrians in the barracks go to the engine room. The rest keep their stones and come straight to Earth. That gives us seventeen Nyrians with their soulstones intact, free on Earth following that first shift. Ten-hour shifts, right?"

Zianne nodded. "Yes. Our schedule is set to that of the Gar planetary rotation. The planet is dead, but their time reference hasn't changed."

"Okay. Next shift, the five from the barracks leave their stones and relieve the five left in the engine room. If there's any way to run the ship for a short time with fewer than five Nyrians, then only the minimum report to the engine room. The ones coming off duty retrieve their soulstones, and all of them come to Earth. At the same time, a couple of us will go aboard the ship, and no, it's not impossible. Nattoch said it can be done. The Gar can't know they're losing Nyrians, so once we get to the bare minimum, we have to move quickly to overpower the guards and grab all the soulstones. Nattoch said the stones will know we're trying to help and won't harm us. And then," he said with a bow, "we get the hell out of Dodge."

Shocked, Mac stared at Cameron, the guy he'd thought of as the flakiest of the bunch, the artistic one. "You're talking about an armed attack on an alien ship, led by a couple of us?"

"Yep." Cam grinned. "Nattoch said the Gar aren't physically large or very strong, but they'll be well armed. One thing I can tell you, though, is that they've probably been to Earth before."

"How do you know?" Kiera's coffee sat forgotten. For a woman who hadn't been at all interested in aliens, she was certainly focused on Cam.

"Ya know the cartoon drawings of aliens and the rumors about Area 51? Well, Nattoch gave me a visual. This is what he showed me." Cam flipped the canvas around to show them a drawing he'd made on the back. His sketch of the alien had a bald, domed head, large eyes, and slits for nostrils.

Totally recognizable to everyone in the room. "Wow. Now that's scary." Kiera shot a glance at Mac, but immediately turned back to the drawing. "Very, very scary."

"They were probably scouts who crashed years ago, maybe came here checking to see what they could use. But for the ones who go on board, it should help you to know what you're up against."

"I see you're not saying 'I' when you talk about boarding the ship." Morgan laughed at Cam. "Count me in. I definitely want to volunteer for the boarding party—if anyone goes, one of them better be me."

"Good. You can take my place." Cam flipped the canvas back to the drawing of the ship. "The thing is, Morgan, I don't mind the idea of actually being on a ship in outer space; it's the going and coming back that has me worried. No offense, Zianne, but the idea of having to reduce myself down to the molecular level makes me very uncomfortable."

"I think Cam's worried that he'd get put back together wrong," Lizzie teased. "You know, with his dick between his eyes and balls hanging under his chin?"

"Exactly. It wouldn't fit my artist image, ya know?"

"Didn't hurt Salvador Dalí any." Morgan's dry comment was lost in laughter as everyone took a minute to blow off steam.

Mac glanced at Zianne. *It's a good plan. I think we can make this work.*

Oh, Mac. I hope so. Not just for me, but for my people. And for you. You've invested so much of your life in me, in this. I want you to win. I've been blessed by Nyria to have my time with you, to see a world outside our prison. My people have been imprisoned since our first foolish steps aboard the Gar ship. They've not had a chance at freedom for millennia. I believe this is their chance.

The laughter ended and Cam picked up where he'd left off. "So, if all goes according to plan, we should end up with up to six or seven Nyrians and two humans on board. Can we evacuate that many at once? If we have all the dishes aimed at the ship and everyone plugged in at the dream shack, could we generate enough power to get them all off the ship and back here at the same time?"

Mac nodded. "It might shut down all of Modoc County, but yeah. I think we can do that."

Finn had been unusually quiet during the discussion, but now he focused on Zianne. "It's going to take a lot of planning to get it right. Zianne, what do you think? We're sitting here making decisions for an entire race of people—and you're their de facto rep. Do you think we can do this?"

"I don't know. It will be difficult convincing some of my people to leave without the others, but Nattoch should be able to handle that. We all trust his judgment and follow his leadership. And yes, we do have the ability to get a couple of you on board the ship. It would require a complete subjugation of self, and I know humans have issues with personal space—the ones who go would have to allow Nyrians to enter them and then turn their bodies into energy particles able to cross the vast distance between Earth and the ship. You'll have to practice doing it here first, but even with practice, a lot will depend on luck, on overpowering the Gar, on retrieving the rest of the stones, and getting off the ship before it implodes."

Frowning, Finn said, "We're going to blow it up?"

"No," Zianne said. "You won't have to. When the final group of power slaves leaves, the ship will fail. We've always been instructed to make the switch between shifts quickly. Without us, there's nothing to power life support or maintain atmosphere. The emergency battery system only lasts a few minutes. The ship and its demands have grown as our numbers have decreased. It will begin to lose pressure immediately after power is cut, quickly become unstable, and eventually implode without explosives."

"Clarify 'immediately' and 'eventually,' if you can." Finn glanced from one to another. "How long after power is cut before the ship goes ka-boom?"

Zianne shook her head. "The star cruiser is massive, many times larger than your largest structures. I tried to describe it one day to Mac—we figured out that ten of your football fields would fit on one level. It has twelve levels with the engine room, slave barracks, and our soulstones on the lowest. The ship houses all of the Gar still in existence."

Rodie glanced at the others and asked, "What happened to their world?"

"They destroyed it. As slaves, we were never told the details. We have learned that their home world was rendered uninhabitable and their atmosphere poisoned by pollution. Weakened by their own excesses, the Gar suffered a series of plagues that wiped out most of them. A select few built their ship, abandoning their planet and the remaining citizens to their fate. They returned many, many years later in the hope of once again living on their world, but they found a dead planet without life of any kind. Not even an atmosphere."

"Holy shit." Morgan wrapped his hand around Rodie's, but Mac knew what they were thinking—that Earth and this civilization were on much the same course.

Finn watched Zianne. "You didn't answer me. How long from the time power is cut until the ship implodes?"

She glanced at Mac, took a deep breath, and faced Finn. "My people and any of you who are there to aid them would have, at most, thirty minutes to evacuate before implosion."

Finn nodded. Glanced at the schematic and then faced Mac. "I'm in. I want to volunteer to board the ship." He glanced at Morgan and grinned. "Hell, I've done every other kind of job. Raiding a Gar star cruiser would definitely be unique."

Mac listened to the chatter around the table as the team discussed boarding the ship, rescuing Zianne's people, and yes, acknowledging the fact that all the Gar on board would die—and questioning the morality of dooming one race to save another.

Mac wondered about his own sense of morality. Could he justify the death of an entire race to save the few remaining Nyrians? Zianne was a good and loving woman. Her people were peaceful. They weren't the ones traveling through space, raping planets, wiping out entire races and worlds.

There was no doubt in his mind. He could authorize a move like this without guilt, the sooner the better—before he had time to rationalize the morality of sending Morgan and Finn into such terrible danger. He glanced up and caught Lizzie watching him and realized time was growing short. "Lizzie, do you mind going back and taking your shift? If you connect with anyone, and I know it's not as easy during daylight, let them know that all the Nyrians have to make the jump here long enough to focus on a physical body, and it has to happen sooner rather than later. They'll all need someone to link to who can give them corporeal form if we're going to have any chance at all of rescuing everyone."

He glanced at Zianne. "And if any of them have energy to share, Zianne needs as much as they can give."

Zianne kissed him quickly and disappeared in a crackle of energy. The squirrel stirred, then lay down again with her tail over her nose. Mac fought the need to curse long and loud.

Each time she disappeared, he wondered if he'd ever hold her again, if he'd ever have his Zianne back. Right now, he had to rely on faith that they would succeed. He couldn't allow himself to think of any other outcome.

Lizzie filled her coffee cup as if it was no big deal that a woman was now a squirrel. She grabbed a cinnamon roll and looked up at him. "I'll do my best, Mac. Fill me in on anything I miss."

"I'll come with you," Rodie said. "Mac? I'll make sure Zianne's settled. Then I'll be right back."

"Thank you. And Liz? You have my promise. I'll catch you up on everything." He watched as they left, already missing Zianne, but feeling proud of how well all of them functioned as a team. They were going to need that to pull off this rescue, and even then, they were all taking a huge risk. And doing it willingly.

Focusing on the rescue once again, he turned his attention to the four remaining at the table, but he was painfully aware Zianne no longer stood beside him.

* * *

Rodie walked across the open area to the dream shack beside Lizzie, carrying the tote bag with Zianne. The squirrel was sound asleep, and it was obvious Zianne's strength was failing, that her time was growing short.

Rodie settled the tote on the floor in the corner while Lizzie got herself hooked to the array, then she turned to Rodie with a speculative glance. "So, you and Morgan, eh?"

Rodie's head snapped up. "Uh, is it that obvious?" She wondered if that was a problem, the fact that the two of them had spent the night together. "Does that bother you?"

"Oh, lordy, no. Not at all. He's just so scary." Lizzie smiled. "Well, not really scary, but he's kind of intimidating. I guess I go for guys who are a little easier to control."

Rodie relaxed. "I haven't tried to control him, that's for sure. And to be honest, I don't know why he's attracted to me. I mean, I'm just me." She shrugged. "I'm not generally the one the guys are all over. It's usually the girls like you they go for."

Lizzie just laughed at that. "Nah. That's your inner wimp talking. I'm nothing special, and you never know what's going to light some guy's fire, but when I was watching Morgan watch you . . ." Her smile turned tender, as if she was looking at something far away. "It's almost the same way Mac looks at Zianne. That's really special, Rodie. I'm envious."

"Really? He looks at me like that? Wow . . . thank you. That's really nice of you to tell me." She laughed. "I never would have noticed anything like that. Is there anyone in your life?"

Liz glanced away, but she had a huge smile on her face. "There wasn't, but I'm getting to know quite a few really hot Nyrian hunks."

She'd not said a word about her visitors at all, as far as Rodie knew. "What are they like?"

"Special." Lizzie focused on the dials on the console. "They came to me as fantasy here, but they showed up in my cabin last night, before that mess with the guys trying to break in. They took off, then, and I spent the night at Kiera's."

Rodie looked closer at Lizzie. "Are you blushing?"

"Yep." She giggled. "Because it didn't really end at her place. Kiera had more guys show up. One she knew but the other ones were new to her. And me. We, uh . . . had a really great night."

"Amazing, isn't it? They use the array to travel back and forth, but once they're here . . ." Rodie laughed. "If Mac had tried to tell me what I was in for, I would have thought he was nuts."

"What do you think of him?"

Lizzie had settled back into the recliner, and Rodie knew it was time to get back to the lodge, but she thought about Lizzie's question. "I think there's a lot more to Mac Dugan than I ever gave him credit for. I mean, I knew he was brilliant and had to be terribly focused to be as successful as he is, but there's so much more. He has an amazing strength of will, and he loves Zianne so much you can feel it. I guess it makes him seem a lot more human to me than before."

Lizzie waved as Rodie turned to go. "Funny thing, isn't it? I find myself thinking of the Nyrians as more human than a lot of the people I know. They're certainly nicer than some."

Rodie laughed as she closed the door behind her, but Lizzie's comment about Morgan stayed with her. That and what she had to say about the Nyrians.

It was true. Bolt was one of the nicest men she'd ever met. And he wasn't even close to human.

15

As soon as Rodie got back, Morgan spread a bunch of papers covered in handwritten notes across the table in front of him. "Mac, I want to run a few things by you about the protestors at the front gate."

Mac nodded. "Go on."

"The one leading them is named Bart Roberts. You said you have no idea who he is or why he might have it in for you. Does the name Patrick Randle mean anything to you?"

"Randle?" Mac rubbed his fingers over his chin, realized he needed a shave, and frowned. "Yeah. It does. Years ago a couple of guys broke into my apartment. Almost killed a friend of mine, but we fought them off. Actually, Zianne took care of them, but I managed to keep her out of the police report. One of the guys who died was named Randle. His first name might have been Pat. I'd have to check."

"Don't worry. I already did. Patrick Randle was Bart Roberts's brother. Bart legally changed his name to Roberts shortly after Pat's death. The original Bartholomew Roberts was a famous Welsh pirate in the seventeen hundreds—no idea if there's a link there or not. Anyway, Bart Roberts bought the property on the hillside below you the same year you bought yours."

That didn't make sense. Mac leaned back in his chair. "We checked into the ownership years ago. Are you sure Roberts owns it? My legal department said it belongs to some sort of nature conservancy—God's Creatures, or something like that."

"They didn't look deep enough. God's Creatures is owned and operated through a dummy corporation funded exclusively by one Bartholomew Roberts."

"Holy shit." Mac leaned forward and planted both hands on the table. "You're saying he followed me up here? That there could be some sort of really long-term revenge thing going on?"

"Was Zianne actively involved in his brother's death?"

Mac nodded. "You might say that." He tried to sound matter-of-fact, but he couldn't stop the smile. "She turned into a column of energy, hauled the bastard to the edge of the third-floor landing in front of my place, and tossed him off. That was after she'd already thrown the first guy over the edge. Then she came inside and saved my friend's life. That's the night I discovered who and what she really was."

"Hookay." Morgan stretched the word out on a low whistle, then chuckled softly. "I had no idea she was so bloodthirsty." He shuffled his notes. "I'm just running with ideas here, but what if Bart was there that night? What if he saw Zianne in her energy form, and knows you weren't the one who killed his brother? That it was something or someone totally inhuman? What if he knows more about this array than you're giving him credit for? Knows about the Nyrians, or at least that you're dealing with an alien life-form? What if he's after Zianne, not you?"

"Shit." Mac stared at Morgan. "That's a lot of 'what ifs,' but it could mean this religious crap is just a cover."

"Could be. But I think the real danger is tied to what happened last night. Those armed intruders trying to break in through the back fence? We have no proof he was involved, but it seems pretty obvious to me, especially since he's behind the protests out front, and his property abuts yours in back."

Mac shoved his chair away from the table and stood up. He felt like he was going to explode if he didn't move. "What could they possibly hope to achieve by coming on site?"

"We never got a good look at any of them. For all you know, they could have been carrying explosives. Maybe they want to destroy the array to prevent you from contacting aliens." Morgan shrugged. "The point is, we need to keep an eye on him and his activities. I think it's a lot more than just a quasi-religious group protesting you as the great Satan."

Mac nodded. "Dink might be able to help us with Roberts."

"Who?" Rodie scowled. "Why do I know that name?"

"I've mentioned him before. Dink's an old friend, the only one outside of you guys who knows about Zianne and the Nyrians. You might know him as Nils Dinkemann."

"Shit." Kiera stared at Mac with her mouth hanging open. "You mean that drop-dead gorgeous newscaster? The one that's all over the world covering crap and getting shot at?"

"The same. We've been friends for years. I called him this morning and asked him to come out here. He should arrive some time tonight."

"But why?"

Mac let out a long, slow breath as he curled his hands into fists. "Because, Kiera, this whole thing with the Nyrians is going to blow wide open, and soon. I've been hoping we could rescue them, then bring them in quietly. Get the papers they need to stay here in the U.S. without anyone knowing the truth, but I'm afraid that's not going to happen."

"Why not?" Kiera glanced at the others. "That would be the

safest way. Bring them in undercover and quietly assimilate them into the general population."

"It would be, in a perfect world. But I want Dink here covering the story. He's a respectable member of the established press, and he loves Zianne almost as much as I do. If everything goes to hell, I want him here to spin it to give the Nyrians the best chance at acceptance. And if Bart Roberts is Patrick Randle's brother, we're going to have to be ready to counteract whatever he has to say."

An earsplitting *whoop, whoop, whoop* drowned him out. Kiera slapped her hands over her ears. Rodie and Morgan shot to their feet, and Mac raced for the front door of the lodge. "That's the fire alarm!" he yelled. "Ralph? What's going on?"

The handyman was running for the garage beside the employee barracks. "Fire. Down by the front gate. I've called it in."

Mac turned around. "Finn? Get to the dream shack, stay with Lizzie and Zianne. There's a fire by the front gate and it's windy out here. Morgan, Rodie, and Kiera, if it spreads, if it looks like it's getting close, make sure the decks and walls stay wet. Roofs are all tin exactly for this reason. There's nothing around the array to burn, power lines are underground, so the dishes are safe. Hoses are by all the buildings. Ralph's contacted CDF. Worst-case scenario, get to the exercise room below the lodge and shut the door. It's a fireproof bunker with its own power and water supply. Cam? Protect that schematic. We're going to need it."

He took one last look as they all jumped into action. Then he shut the door and headed toward the fire.

Kiera looked blankly at Morgan. "Who's CDF?"

"California Department of Forestry. They handle fire protection up here." He left his notes on the table, grabbed Rodie's hand, and glanced at her short pants and flip-flops. "You need long pants and boots. C'mon. Crap. I wonder how it started?"

"Give ya three guesses, and the first two don't count."

"My thoughts exactly, sweetheart. Let's go."

Cam grabbed the schematic drawing of the ship. "I'll stick this downstairs. Then I'll be out to help." He raced toward the stairs that led to the exercise room.

The rest of them ran outside. Finn headed for the dream shack. Morgan hauled Rodie behind him and raced toward her cabin. He was already wearing jeans and hiking boots and so was Kiera.

She kept pace with the two of them. "You're not leaving me back there! Shit. It looks like it's spreading really fast."

Dark, boiling columns of smoke in shades from rusty brown to gray to black billowed above the trees below them, and the crackling of flames grew louder by the second. A brisk wind blew hot embers along the ground and overhead.

Racing across the short stretch between the lodge and Rodie's cabin, the three of them hit the steps and got inside. Morgan slammed the door against the smoke-filled air. Rodie stripped off her shorts and pulled on jeans and heavy socks while Morgan found her hiking boots in the closet. He knelt in front of her, tying one while she did the other.

He had to bite back a grin. When she'd pulled off her pants, he'd noticed black bikini panties with legs cut high on the sides.

Just like his fantasy. But damn, now was not the time to be sporting a boner. He finished tying her boot and stood up. By the time they got outside, the air was thick with smoke and burning embers swirling all about. Squinting through the ashes, Morgan shouted at Rodie. "We need water on the bunkhouse and lodge. I'll take care of the bunkhouse first. You guys grab the hoses at the lodge and wet down the walls and the deck. Then Liz's and Finn's cabins. They're closest."

Kiera grabbed the hose by the front of the lodge and began spraying the wooden deck. Rodie went after one on the side facing the woods. Remembering the security guys from the night shift, Morgan raced across to the bunkhouse and banged on the door. "Anyone in there? Wake up. We've got a fire out here. Wake up!"

Still yelling, he grabbed the hose down below and turned it on. After a couple of minutes, the door flew open and two men stumbled out, half dressed and still half asleep. The first guy was hardly more than a kid. He stared at the smoke, rubbing his eyes and blinking. "Shit. Need clothes." He turned and went back inside. The other man, a bit older, stared at the billowing smoke.

"Those bastards." He glared at Morgan. "You know who started this, don't you?"

Morgan shot a stream of water at a small patch of grass where a burning ember had landed. "I've got a damned good idea." He glanced at the guy's bare feet. "You'd better get some clothes and heavy boots. If it goes out of control, Mac said to take shelter in the exercise room. It's fireproof and has a filtered air supply."

"Thanks." The man disappeared inside the bunkhouse. Morgan sprayed down the entire area around the building, soaking the deck and walls. The trees had been cut back and the ground was hard and rocky, so there was very little vegetation to burn. The roof was tin, as were the roofs on all the buildings, but the structures themselves were made of logs.

He kept water spraying on the flammable areas and kept his eye on Rodie.

Finn slipped inside the dream shack.

Lizzie waved from her chair. "Thanks for coming. I looked out the door when I heard the siren. Saw the smoke, but I figure the dream shack is probably the safest place on the whole site."

"I think you're right. It'd take a hell of a fire to burn concrete blocks. This place is like a damned bunker."

"Mac told me it's to protect the equipment—if there's a power failure, the temperature remains stable because of the thick concrete walls. It can get really cold up here, and just as hot in the summer."

She stopped talking and took a deep breath, tilted her head, and frowned. "Finn . . . ?"

"What's the matter, Liz? You're safe here." He leaned against the console and folded his arms across his chest.

"It's not the fire I'm worried about." She glanced at the tote in the corner with Zianne. "What if it doesn't work? What if we can't save them? Have you thought about that?"

Finn stared at the skylight overhead, at the thick clouds of smoke blowing by. Everything he'd ever thought was important to him had taken a huge one eighty since last night. He hadn't been able to get Tara and Duran off his mind. Somehow, in just the short time they'd been together in the early morning hours, he'd lost his heart.

Or maybe he'd just lost his mind. "That's all I have thought of. I wish I could think of something else." He stared at Liz and tried to recall the women he'd had sex with. He couldn't call it making love. In fact, until he and the Nyrians—no, make that Tara and Duran, because they were more than just aliens from another world—until he'd been with them, Finn didn't think he'd ever known what making love even was.

It was weird, really, when he let himself think of it, but he was thirty-three years old. He'd gotten his first piece of ass—an eighteen-year-old neighbor girl—when he was thirteen, which meant he'd been screwing women for twenty years. The same twenty years Mac Dugan had been working toward rescuing Zianne and her people.

While Mac had focused his time and energy on saving lives, Finn had focused on getting laid.

What did that say about him as a man?

Certainly nothing he could be proud of.

Last night when Tara and Duran had come to his cabin, the experience had been unique on a number of levels, but the most important was actually pretty pathetic. It had been the very first time he'd ever connected with a bed partner on any level beyond his dick inside a warm pussy.

Hell, what he'd shared with Duran had been more intimate than with all the women he could recall. He and another man had made love. When Finn thought about the way it had felt to suck Duran's cock, to taste him, it made his hands tremble. When he'd submitted, when Duran had entered him, Finn hadn't been embarrassed; he hadn't felt really stupid. No, he'd felt loved, which was just weird.

The thought of sex with any other man didn't interest him at all, but he wanted to hold Duran again. Wanted to make him smile the way he had when they'd made love.

And Tara. There were no words for the way she made him feel. He'd made love to her, and just thinking of the soft slide of his cock into her warm, wet sheath made him hard. Made him want.

Made him finally understand what he'd been looking for. What he'd never expected to find. "Last night was a game changer for me, Liz. Something I never thought would happen to me did, and I'm still not sure how to deal with it."

She watched him, but she didn't say a word. Finn chuckled. "I think my predatory days are over."

"You?" She laughed. "Why do I find that so hard to believe? I haven't even gotten to show you my fuzzy handcuffs yet."

"Save 'em for someone else." He shook his head, as if he could shake off the sense of his life having irrevocably changed. "It's hard to explain, Lizzie, but after a whole lot of meaning-less sex over the years, I think I finally know what's been miss-ing."

"And what's that?" She grinned, probably expecting a smart-ass comment.

"A connection with my partners. The knowledge that I matter, that they matter. That what we shared was special, something so wonderful that I'll never find it with anyone else but them."

Lizzie's eyebrows crinkled up in that familiar frown again. "This doesn't even sound like you. In fact, you sound like you've been blindsided, Finnegan. You gonna be okay?"

A loud roar overhead shook the sturdy building. Finn glanced up, identifying the noise. He returned his attention to Lizzie and slowly shook his head. "I don't know, Lizzie. I wish I did, but I just don't know." He pushed himself away from the console. "You and Zianne going to be okay? I want to go out and see how they're doing with the fire. That was the CDF chopper. I'll check back with you in a bit, and if there's any danger, I promise to come for you."

"Thanks, Finn." She smiled warmly. "If you'd said that two days ago, I don't think I would have trusted you to come back for us. For some reason, now I don't have that problem. Be careful."

"You're probably right." He leaned over and kissed her, and she kissed him back, lips every bit as warm as her smile.

And when he headed outside, Finn realized that he'd just kissed a woman he thought of as a friend. One he had no intention of putting the make on, no desire to take to bed.

It should probably make him very nervous, but it didn't. No, it just made him feel really good about life in general.

Once again they met in the lodge, all but Morgan sitting quietly at the big table. Meg had served their dinner tonight, which felt oddly formal. Once she left the room, Mac gazed at his team, all freshly showered after dealing with what the CDF captain had described as "a fire of highly suspicious origins."

He glanced up as Morgan walked in carrying Zianne's tote. "Was anyone able to give her energy?"

Morgan set the bag on the floor beside Mac. "Yeah. A couple of people shared with her, but she's still weak. It's not helping as much as it did at first."

Mac nodded as Morgan took his seat beside Rodie. Zianne had been days now without her soulstone, and he knew she was barely hanging on. "How many Nyrians still need a human form? Any idea?"

Lizzie raised her hand. "I had three—a man and two women—come during my shift." She glanced at Kiera.

"I did a full shift and Lizzie's three got the word out. There were five gorgeous men who showed up during mine. Morgan? Your shift was pretty short. Did you have any new ones?"

"Three I've not met before." He grinned at Rodie. "All women. Believe me, my shift absolutely flew by."

Rodie elbowed him in the side and he grunted dramatically.

"Two of them shared energy with Zianne. They're worried about her, Mac. We need to take action as soon as we can."

"I agree, but we still have seven Nyrians who haven't been down here yet. Until they have bodies, we can't do anything."

"I'm heading for the shack as soon as I eat." Morgan picked up his fork as he talked. "Between Rodie and me, I'm hoping we can get the last of them covered by midnight. They understand the need to hurry, and they're all on board for the plan."

"Nattoch came to my room just before I left to come here." Cam focused on Mac. "He said the Gar plan to start ramping up power day after tomorrow for the move against Earth. Once that happens, it's going to be hard to get any of the Nyrians free with their soulstones because they're all needed. The Gar will know some are gone as soon as they discover they can't bring up enough power."

"Then we've got less than forty-eight hours to put this into motion." Mac let out a frustrated breath. "I don't know if Zianne even has forty-eight hours, but she's said more than once that her survival isn't important as long as we save her people."

He glanced at the sleeping squirrel. "You know I don't agree. I can't imagine coming this far only to lose her, but I will honor her wishes." He took a deep breath. This was so hard to say, as if speaking the words aloud doomed Zianne. "Whether Zianne lives or dies, we're sticking with the plan."

He blinked, clearing his eyes. This was not the time to lose it. Not while there was still hope, so he took another deep breath and continued. "Is there any one of you who has reservations? Do any of you, for any reason, feel that what we're doing is wrong? Tell me, please."

He wiped the back of his hand across his eyes. "Obviously, I'm not as clearheaded right now as I should be. This is a huge decision. Lives could be lost. We know we're condemning the Gar if we succeed. My feeling is, they deserve it, but I need your thoughts. Morgan? Finn? Your risk is huge. You're sure?" He looked at each of them, but there was no sign of doubt. None.

"Cam? Okay. Kiera? You're an attorney. Give me an argument."

She shook her head. "I can't, Mac. I'm sorry, but I think it's worth any risk to help them. They've suffered enough, and we know that if the Gar aren't stopped, we could all end up dead." She shrugged. "Personally, I think it's a no-brainer."

The others were nodding. Mac realized he was nodding in agreement, right along with them. "Okay. We'll do what we can for the Nyrians. Unless someone's got a better idea, we go with Cam's plan. Get as many Nyrians down here with their soulstones as possible before sending anyone to the ship. We'll have to time it during a shift change and hope like hell everything works."

He couldn't say any more. Not without losing it, but he took another deep, controlling breath. "I'm not a religious man at all, but Zianne swears her goddess still lives, that she's the reason they've survived this long. Tonight, and until this is over, I'm putting my faith in Nyria."

He glanced at the plate Meg had set in front of him before leaving the room. "Well, the goddess Nyria and Meg's excellent cooking." The others laughed softly and attacked their dinners. Grilled tenderloin, roasted potatoes and veggies, crusty French bread with olive oil and balsamic vinegar on the side—a perfect meal.

He stared at his plate and thought of the meals he'd shared with Zianne. Thought of the dreams they'd had, the long talks about everything under the sun in those few short, unbelievably special months they'd spent together.

He wanted that again. Wanted her. Hell, he wanted all of it. Was that too much to ask?

Mac felt a stirring, as if something in the room had changed. He raised his head and realized everyone was looking toward the front door. Mac turned just as Dink stopped beside his seat.

"Do ya think you could get me a plate like that?"

"You're here." Mac stood up and held out his arms. Dink enveloped him in a hug, and it was all Mac could do to hold back the tears. "Thanks, man. Thanks for coming."

Dink stepped back but kept his hands on Mac's shoulders. "Couldn't keep me away. You know that." He grinned, and there, in front of everyone, leaned close and kissed Mac full on the lips. Claiming him. And without hesitation, Mac kissed him back.

"Now," said Dink, smoothing his hands over Mac's shoulders, as if he couldn't stop touching him. "How about that plate?"

Dink sipped his drink and stared at the squirrel sleeping in the tote bag in Mac's lap. "I can't believe you've gotten this far and yet you could still lose her. God, Mac. I've missed Zianne so much. That time when she was with you, when I was still in town—that time was pure magic."

Mac nodded. "I know. I've thought a lot about those months these past couple of days. We're so fucking close, and yet there's too much that can still go wrong."

He really needed to take Zianne back to the dream shack in case anyone else showed up who could share energy with her, but he couldn't bear to let her go. He'd brought her up to his rooms along with Dink, just to keep her close.

She'd not awakened all evening, but he knew she was still alive. The subtle scent of vanilla and honey lingered.

"Uh, Mac? I think we've got company."

Mac turned as a column of energy materialized across the room. "It's okay. We'll know who it is in a moment."

An older man stepped out of the fading sparkles of energy. He looked directly at Mac and bowed his head.

"You are Zianne's Mac. I am Nattoch. I've come to share energy with Zianne."

"Thank you. She's here." He looked down at the squirrel. She was awake now, blinking her dark eyes and staring at Nattoch. "Should I take her out?"

"On the floor, here, where we have room." He leaned over and touched her as Mac set the squirrel down. "She's very weak. We have no idea how long she can survive without her stone, but we'll do everything we can to keep her with us." He raised his head and looked at Dink. "I know you," he said, smiling. "You are the other one Zianne loves, the one whose life she saved."

Dink nodded. That night twenty years ago when Patrick Randle died, Dink had been stabbed. A mortal wound until Zianne became a creature of pure energy and healed Dink from the inside. Dink hadn't known the story then. Now he did. Mac wasn't entirely surprised to see the damp trails of tears on his friend's cheeks.

"I am," Dink said. "I only learned a few days ago that she was the one who saved me, which means I not only love her, but I am forever indebted to her."

Nattoch dissolved into a small cloud of sparkles. Spinning slowly, he covered Zianne with a blue-and-gold light, pulsing over the squirrel for at least a full minute before the sparkles took on form and he was once again a very human-looking man kneeling beside a small gray squirrel.

He held out a hand and Mac helped him to his feet. "Thank you. My age begins to wear on me." He sighed. "I grow old and very tired, but you and your dream team have given me hope."

Mac couldn't take his eyes off Zianne. She was awake, watching him now with bright eyes. But for how long?

Nattoch followed his gaze. "One thing about my advanced years is that my energy is strong. This should hold her through the night if you wish to keep her here, with you."

"Thank you." What else could he say? He wanted promises, wanted to know that everything was going to be okay, but no one, not even Zianne's elder, could promise him the impossible.

Nattoch stepped back. "I must return before I am missed, but the rest of our people will have a human form by the end of this night. It will take less energy if they wait until nightfall to make their final escape to Earth. Expect the first group to begin arriving as soon as it turns dark tomorrow night, when the shift changes. They'll have their soulstones, and they will be staying. And never doubt that we have Nyria watching over us all."

He bowed to both Mac and Dink. Then his form wavered and dissolved once again into energy that slowly disappeared. Dink turned to Mac with a look of total disbelief on his face. "Well, fuck. Great newsman I am. I have a camera in my pocket and I forgot to take a picture."

"You'll have a chance." Mac got down on his knees on the floor. "Zianne? Is there anything you need? You've slept so much—does your squirrel need food or water? I've got it here for you."

She began to sparkle and grow. Within seconds Zianne stood next to the sleeping squirrel. A heartbeat later, she was in Mac's arms. He held her close, amazed at how healthy, how strong she looked. "But how?"

"Only for a while," she said. "Nattoch's energy is powerful." She leaned over Mac's shoulder. "Dink, hello."

Dink stared at her as if he were seeing a ghost. Mac almost laughed at the grin slowly spreading across that inscrutable newscaster's face of his. "Zianne? I don't know what to say."

"Now that's a first." Mac kissed Zianne. She was in his arms, a woman, alive and whole, if only for a short while.

She sighed. "I am growing weaker, Mac. If I don't survive, I don't want my last hours with you to be spent as a little gray rodent." She kissed him again. "I need to tell you how much I love you. And how much I love Dink as well." She looked at Dink, and her beautiful violet eyes sparkled with tears. "You two are the best of my memories, and you, Mac, will always be my beloved hero, whether this crazy plan works or not."

She wrapped her arms around him and kissed him again. Then she slipped out of his embrace, pulled Dink to his feet, and kissed him as well. "It's good that you're here, Nils Dinkemann. Mac needs you. And if this scheme works and my people are saved, we will all need you. You will be our spokesman and tell your world about us." She stood beside Dink with an arm around his waist and smiled at Mac, and for a moment he was back at Sloan's Bar, drinking cheap beer and laughing about nothing and everything with the two people he loved most.

He promised himself then that they'd go back to Sloan's together. They'd have those drinks and celebrate when this was all done, because Cam's crazy plan was going to work. He refused to accept anything else.

"How long can you hold this form?" Mac stepped up behind Zianne and wrapped his arms around her waist. She leaned her head back against his chest and sighed.

"Long enough. As long as Dink's not too tired. If we screw up and the plan doesn't work, I want my last night to be a good one, and I want to share it making love with both of you."

Dink raised his head and stared at Mac as if he couldn't believe he was here, that Zianne was here. That any of this was really happening, but Zianne was unbuttoning Mac's shirt, and it appeared there was an excellent chance, at least for now, they were going to spend this night building more dreams, more hope, and a whole lot of love.

Mac lifted Zianne and headed toward the bedroom as she continued working her way down the buttons on his shirt. He paused in the doorway and glanced over his shoulder. "Dink? This way. Unless you've forgotten how this works."

Laughing, Dink followed them into the bedroom. Mac refused to think of this as their last night. No, it was only the first of many in a lifetime to come. You just had to believe, but it helped, knowing they had Nyria on their side.

16

Finn sat alone in his room, waiting. He needed to see Tara and Duran. Had to know they were safe, to see what they thought of this plan for their rescue. So many things could go wrong, and it terrified him, to think he'd finally found something that truly mattered, and now he might lose it.

He pictured Tara with her gorgeous red hair and those emerald-green eyes, and he thought of her, not as she'd looked beneath him last night when they'd made love, but the way she'd stood there beside his bed, smiling at him as if he mattered. As if she'd chosen him because she cared.

But how the hell could she, or Duran, either, for that matter? They didn't know him. They'd only wanted him for the power of his mind, not the kind of man he was.

"You're wrong, Finn."

He wasn't startled this time. He raised his head and she was there, standing hand in hand with Duran. Both of them wore the same simple clothing as the night before, though he noticed that tonight Duran didn't hang back. He stood beside Tara, as if he'd somehow developed a bit more confidence.

"How so?" Lord, but he wanted to pull her into his arms and hold her until this whole fucking mess was over and he knew for sure they were going to be safe.

"Duran and I searched all the minds here, not just yours, but you are the one we wanted." She stepped closer until she was standing between his knees, but she kept her hands clasped at her waist. "You are a good and honorable man and there is nothing you can't do. We know that you and Morgan have agreed to board the ship to help our escape. We will wait and be among the last to leave because we want to be there with you, should you need our help."

"No. Please." He took her hands and glanced helplessly at Duran. "Try to be among the first group to come to Earth; save yourselves. Don't throw away a chance. If we fail, if somehow this doesn't work, I don't want to think I've thrown my life away for nothing. Tara, you and Duran are the reason I want to be part of the final steps, to make certain the Gar are gone forever, that you and yours are safe. I don't want to be worried about getting you out of there."

Duran sat next to Finn on the edge of the bed and put his arm around Finn's shoulders. "It won't work, Finn. I've tried arguing with her for years. I've never won yet. You'll need us to help you get through the ship. It's a confusing maze when you're actually there, and if it comes down to it, Tara can just shift to her human form and argue the Gar to death."

Finn bowed his head, but he couldn't stop smiling. Finally, he turned and looked at Duran. "Do you think we have a chance? Does the plan sound like it might work?"

"Whether or not it works, the Gar's reign of terror will end and the ship will die, and that is a huge success. It's also a worst-case outcome. I prefer to think positive—that we will retrieve our soulstones, we will find Zianne's, and all of us will make it home to your world, to our refuge, safely."

"Finn?" Tara knelt between his knees and rested her hands

on his thighs. "We have been inside your mind. We know who you are, we know your memories, and most of all, we know your dreams. They're all good. You are good. I already love you, and I hope that one day you will love me as well. That you will love Duran."

She smiled slyly at him and winked. "Though it will probably take longer with him. He can be so difficult at times."

He didn't know when he began to cry, but there were tears on his cheeks, dripping off his chin, and Tara was a beautiful blur in front of him. He felt like a fool, sitting here in his knit boxers, weeping while a beautiful woman knelt between his knees. There was something terribly wrong with this picture, but for the life of him, Finn couldn't figure out what that was.

He only knew that somehow, over the past couple days, he'd changed, and he'd changed because of these two people who weren't even human. No, they were so much more, and yet they had faith in him. They were entrusting their lives, the lives of their people, to Finnegan O'Toole.

When Tara crawled onto his lap and slowly pushed him back against the mattress, it felt right. When Duran lay down beside him and wrapped his arms around Finn, not for sex, but to hold him close and talk about their hopes for the future, he knew he'd made the right decision.

There were no guarantees that any of them would survive. None at all, but he felt absolutely no fear, no sense of indecision. They were making the right choice for the right reasons. Choosing to risk everything to give people who mattered a chance to survive.

And maybe, this was a choice that was giving Finn a chance as well. It felt like a whole new world was out there waiting for him. All they had to do was free the Nyrians and destroy the evil aliens. Yeah, he could do this.

There was too much at risk not to succeed, and he loved and

trusted the people he was doing this for as much as he already loved and trusted the ones he was doing it with.

Mac had spent twenty years in pursuit of a dream, and he'd been generous enough to include Finn and the others in the very best part of it. There were no doubts left. None at all, and a good four hours before his shift began.

Tara caught his wayward thoughts and grinned. Duran was smiling as well, and Finn almost laughed out loud. He hadn't been thinking about sex, not tonight. He'd been thinking about love and commitment and risking all for something bigger than himself. But as long as they were both here, and there was plenty of time, and they were interested . . .

Never in his wildest dreams had he imagined anything like this. Life was good. It might end up being shorter than he'd planned, but for now it was damned good.

"Hey, Cam." Rodie slipped off her mesh cap and tucked it into the drawer in the console. "I'm glad you're here. I'm really tired tonight."

"Me, too. Couldn't sleep very well." He moved out of Rodie's way so she could get out of the chair. "I keep thinking of all the things that could go wrong."

"It's a good plan, Cam. It's simple and straightforward. The fewer details, the less room for screw-ups." She leaned close and kissed him. "I feel good about it, so quit worrying. Which reminds me—between Morgan's shift and mine, we've covered all but two of the Nyrians who still need to make the trip for their body images. I imagine you'll get them before your shift is over."

"I'm ready. I've spent my shifts getting visions of Nyria and talking with Nattoch to gather details about the ship. I've yet to experience even one good sexual fantasy. The last time I tried, I just got Nattoch back with more details."

He grumbled, but Rodie knew he was teasing. She patted his arm. "Well, tonight you're on. There's two left, and I leave them in your expert care. Try thinking about sex instead of the next painting."

"Yes, sir." He saluted and settled back in the chair with the mesh cap in place.

Rodie paused at the door to look at him—like Finn and Morgan, Cam was so good-looking he was beautiful. And, even though he was quieter than the other guys, he was obviously brilliant and a really nice guy.

No wonder all the Nyrian men were gorgeous. They had excellent prototypes. As she left the shack, Rodie saw her favorite prototype waiting for her. Morgan stepped out of the shadows and took her hand.

"I didn't want to worry about you walking back to your cabin alone."

She smiled at him. "Is that the only reason you waited? To protect me?"

He shrugged. "No. I waited because I missed you. I wasn't in your fantasy tonight, and it was lonely without you."

Rodie stopped and looked at him. Morgan was everything she could ever want in a man, and he'd actually missed her? She stretched up on her toes and kissed him. "It felt wrong having a fantasy without you in it, but I wanted to bring as many in as I could."

"So, did it work?" He took her hand again and they walked the short distance to Rodie's cabin. He stopped at the bottom step, but she made him wait for her answer.

"Well?"

"Yes. It worked. Two men and a woman. There are just two left after your three, so I left Cam with orders to get the final ones covered."

"And he took your orders well?"

She shrugged. "Well, he did salute. Morgan? Are you coming in with me?"

"Am I invited?"

"Oh, yeah. Definitely." She tugged his hand and he followed her up the stairs, pleased with herself, that she'd been able to ask him in. Something about being involved in an interstellar rescue operation appeared to be giving her confidence.

As soon as the thought entered her mind, she had to bite back a laugh. None of this felt real, except that the people she'd met tonight had been amazing. And they'd thanked her.

"Did the ones who came during your shift say anything about the rescue?" She closed the door behind Morgan and locked it, like that was going to keep a Nyrian out of her room. She wondered if Bolt would make it here tonight.

Morgan leaned against the door and shoved his hands into his pockets. "Yeah, they did. It was almost embarrassing, but I guess they've been without hope for so long."

"What if we fail them? What if it doesn't work?"

"My two guys acted like that wasn't what counted. They're more concerned that someone cares enough to try. It sure puts a huge burden on us to get it right."

The air seemed to shift and shimmer, and Bolt appeared in the doorway to the bedroom. "There shouldn't be a burden on any of you for trying to help. The burden is ours, for being foolish enough to allow ourselves to be captured in the first place."

He walked out of the bedroom and brushed Rodie's tangled hair back from her face. "I wasn't invited, but I had to see you tonight. Both of you. Is that all right?"

"Of course it is." Morgan rested his hand on Bolt's shoulder. "You're all ours, Bolt. I'm glad you're here. It'll give us a chance to talk about the rescue. I want to know what you think of the plan."

"Morgan's right, Bolt. You are ours." She glanced at Morgan. "But as much as I would love to discuss logistics, I've got a few other things on my mind."

"Oh?" Morgan raised one very expressive eyebrow.

Bolt merely grinned. "We can talk later, if you prefer."

"I prefer. I'm not really sure what Morgan wants, but it is my cabin."

Bolt glanced at Morgan and shrugged. "The lady had a point."

Rodie grabbed Bolt's hand and Morgan's and tugged. Both men meekly followed her into her bedroom, and it was all she could do to keep from laughing out loud.

Who would have thought that she, Rodie Bishop, would have two amazing men taking her to bed? Two men who had chosen her, who seemed to think she was pretty special.

It was like a fairy tale, and she was the princess, though she knew that there was an excellent chance this particular fairy tale might not have the guaranteed happy ending.

She wasn't going to worry about that. Not tonight when things seemed to be going so well. The protestors were still out there, probably thinking of new ways to cause trouble, the Gar's star cruiser was still hiding behind the moon, planning to rape and pillage the planet, and the Nyrians were still slaves aboard their ship.

But they had a good plan, they had all the money and brains of MacArthur Dugan at their disposal, and a world-famous newscaster ready to tell their story to the world.

And Finn and Morgan, bravely volunteering to go aboard an alien ship to help free the Nyrians. Rodie was proud and heartsick at the same time. This was so dangerous. She could lose the man she'd just begun to love, but she couldn't imagine Morgan failing at anything. Or Finn, either, for that matter.

And as Morgan worked his way down the buttons on her blouse and Bolt discovered the intricacies of zippers and snaps,

Rodie decided they had a pretty darned good chance of actually pulling off this entire thing.

It had to work, therefore it would. If will could make things happen, then there was no reason to doubt their success. And if a life as screwed up as hers had been could suddenly be this spectacular, then Rodie figured anything was possible.

Bolt's tongue traced a line up her inner thigh, and Morgan had discovered her breasts beneath her clothes. No doubt about it. She lay back on the bed and turned herself over to the men in her life. Tonight and forever she would believe anything and everything were possible.

EPILOGUE

Mac sat in an Adirondack chair on the deck outside his room and sipped at the glass of Jack in his hand. The waning moon cast a silver glow over the satellite array, glistened off the skylight in the dream shack, and slanted sharply across the two figures lying amid the tumbled covers on his bed just beyond the sliding glass door.

Dink slept soundly, jet-lagged and well loved. Zianne had returned to her squirrel form and was curled up on Mac's pillow. Her fluffy gray tail curled over the top of Dink's head.

The two people Mac loved most in the world, here beside him to take on the greatest challenge of their lives. He gazed at Dink and Zianne, blinking back tears as the sense of their love hit him like a punch to the heart.

Damn.

Then Mac gazed toward the array and opened his thoughts.

His telepathic abilities seemed to be growing stronger. He sensed Finn and his Nyrian lovers and the strong well of emotion that felt so new to the Irishman. Then he shifted his search to Morgan and Rodie. Bolt was still with them, but he'd be leaving shortly. As would Finn's two, all of them going back to their prison aboard the Gar ship.

Mac took another sip of his drink, savoring the strong bite as the whisky rolled down his throat. Nyria willing, that prison would no longer exist a mere two days from now.

He focused on the dream shack. Cameron was there with the last two Nyrians. Both of them had taken on physical bodies.

It was almost time. Tomorrow evening the first refugees would come to Earth with their soulstones. The culmination of a twenty-year plan was almost here.

Smiling, Mac tossed back the last of his drink, took one final look at the array, and headed inside. Dink was right. He was too damned stubborn to fail. At this point, it wasn't even a possibility.

But he was sure gonna feel a hell of a lot better once this rescue was over.

Turn the page for a sizzling preview
of Kate Douglas's next novel
in her brand-new erotic romance series . . .

DREAM UNCHAINED

An Aphrodisia trade paperback
on sale November 2012!

1

It wasn't until a tangerine slice of sunlight flashed above the sharp edge of the plateau that Mac Dugan realized he'd spent the whole damned night on the deck outside his bedroom.

Sitting in a hard, wooden Adirondack chair, freezing his ass off while the woman he loved and his best friend were curled up together in the big bed in the room behind him.

He imagined the two of them—snuggled warm and cozy in a tangle of twisted bedding—and didn't know whether to laugh or cry at the visual. Dink, all long, well-formed male with a sexy mat of dark blond hair across his chest, washboard abs, and a strong, sharply masculine face darkened with morning stubble.

And Zianne? Fluffy little gray squirrel.

Last time he looked, she'd had her tail curled around the top of Dink's head and one tiny paw resting on his ear.

It wasn't supposed to end like this.

He took a deep breath, pushed back his fear and the sharp burn of frustrated tears, and focused on what they'd shared last night. Mac, Zianne, and Dink, together as they'd been so long ago. Zianne had held on to her human shape long enough for them to make love—the three of them connecting in a way they'd not been able to do since her abrupt disappearance so many years ago.

Twenty fucking years. Twenty years wondering if she still lived. Worrying whether or not all of his creative energies, every spare penny he'd been able to raise, and the combined technological advances of the entire research and development team at Beyond Global Ventures would be enough to rescue Zianne and the few surviving members of her species from slavery.

Twenty years, sixty million dollars, and a lifetime of focusing on an impossible rescue would all come down to the next thirty-six hours or so. Fewer than two days for Zianne to live or die, for her people to survive. Or not.

They were so damned close to success, even as the entire project balanced on a razor's edge of failure.

Shit. He hadn't allowed himself to consider failure. How could he, and still work toward such an impossible goal? What fool would even attempt the rescue of a small group of slaves imprisoned aboard a spaceship—held by another alien race preparing to plunder the earth of all its natural resources?

It sounded ridiculous no matter how he phrased it, so he did what he always tried to do when the fears surfaced. Mac pushed the negative thoughts out of his head. Refused to consider failure. Reminded himself it was not an option.

Call it denial, call it what you will, but it was the only way he'd survived the past two decades. Focus on the desired outcome. Ignore the rest. Plan for everything that can possibly go wrong, and then put those plans aside and go with the one that assured success.

Failure is not an option.

Clichéd, but still the only acceptable outcome.

Mac sucked in a deep breath, centered himself, and locked away his fear. He consciously refocused his energy, squinting at the growing brilliance of the sun as it slanted across the huge array of satellite dishes. He gazed at them a moment, taking comfort in the fact that they worked perfectly, that they had indeed allowed his small team of young men and women to make contact with Zianne's people.

Then he shifted his attention and glanced across the quiet yard at the square cinder-block building they'd labeled the dream shack—the center of operations for his team, the place where his telepaths focused their amazing sexual energy on the Nyrians now in orbit behind the moon. It was barely six, which meant Finnegan O'Toole had a couple more hours to his shift.

Now there was a guy who'd proved first impressions weren't always correct. Finn had come across as a class-A jerk—brilliant but still a jerk. Then he'd shown more character than Mac or any of the others had suspected when he'd volunteered to go aboard the Gar star cruiser to help with the rescue.

A brave and foolish request by a man who was no one's fool.

What kind of man would willingly step into danger like that?

Me?

Yeah, Mac'd knew he'd do it in a heartbeat, except he was needed here. This was, after all, his quest, for want of a better word. The culmination of his twenty-year mission to find Zianne, to save her people, to destroy the Gar—alien creatures with a record of plundering untold worlds.

It sounded like a grade-B movie when he spelled it all out, except it was real. Terrifying, beyond belief, yet all too real.

Who in the hell, in their right mind, would think he had a prayer of success? Of course, no one had ever accused him of being in his right mind. Even Mac's strongest supporters figured he had more than a few screws loose.

In all fairness to himself, what genius didn't march to a different drummer? It was probably a very good thing that the world didn't know the truth—Mac Dugan didn't follow a drummer.

Hell, no. He'd been following the directions of a beautiful

alien who drew her physical form from his sexual fantasies. A woman who wouldn't even exist as other than pure energy without the drunken visual of a twenty-six-year-old postgrad student back in the early days of the computer age.

Only a handful of people knew the truth—that his whole career had been based on a four-month relationship with an inhuman creature he'd fallen in lust and then in love with. The same creature now trapped in the body of a little gray squirrel.

Shit. What a fucked-up mess. What chance in hell . . .

"Mac? I thought you came back to bed. How long have you been out here? Good lord man, it's fucking freezing out here."

Mac leaned his head against the back of his chair and stared upside down at the man shivering behind him. "G'morning to you, too, Dink. Couldn't sleep. Didn't want to disturb you guys." He straightened up and waved at the chair beside him. "Have a seat. You don't by any chance have coffee, do you?"

"You're kidding, right? Me? Make coffee?"

"One can only hope." He chuckled. A famous investigative reporter, Dink had never been known for his culinary skills. "I was afraid of that, but yeah, I know. I lost contact with my toes a few hours ago." A thick down comforter settled over him, still warm from Dink's body heat.

"Okay. This works." Mac drew his feet up under the blanket and tucked all that soft warmth around him. "Damn, that feels good. I think it's even better than coffee."

A moment later, Dink flopped down in the chair beside Mac's, wrapped head to foot in another blanket. "I heard some rattling and clanking downstairs," he said. "Sounds like your cook's putting some fresh coffee on. I'll get us some in a few minutes."

Mac grunted in assent. He turned and glanced toward the sliding glass door, but Dink had closed it and the glare of the growing sunlight reflected off the glass.

He couldn't see Zianne. "Is . . . ?"

"She's asleep. Still a squirrel. I left her wrapped in your jacket."

"Thanks." He sighed.

"You okay?"

Mac rolled his head to the right and stared at Dink. "You're kidding, right?"

Dink grunted.

Hell, no, I'm not all right. "We'll know in approximately two more days, I guess."

Dink grunted again.

Two more days and Mac would know if all his efforts might actually pay off. And if they didn't?

He sucked in a deep breath. Exhaled. "Cameron was scheduled to meet the last two Nyrians during his shift last night, which means that by now all of them should have access to functioning human bodies. The first group will be coming to Earth tonight—once they have their soulstones—as soon as it turns dark."

"So what happens today?"

Mac glanced at Dink. There was none of the investigative reporter about him this morning. No, he just sounded like a very concerned friend. Right now, Mac figured he needed the friend more than the reporter. "Today a couple of the stronger Nyrians are going to show Finn and Morgan how to disincorporate and move through space."

"Holy shit." Whispered softly, more a prayer than a curse.

Mac shrugged. "That's the only way to get them on the ship. Breaking down to molecular particles and traveling with a host Nyrian through space. Sounds good in theory."

"I can't believe you actually got volunteers."

"Morgan Black and Finn O'Toole. Both good guys, physically strong, very sharp. The Gar shouldn't be expecting an attack, but they're always well armed. According to Nattoch, the Nyrian elder who's sort of their leader, the Gar carry weapons that can disrupt the Nyrians' energy field. Doesn't kill them,

272 / *Kate Douglas*

but can effectively immobilize them. It shouldn't affect humans, though. Once Finn and Morgan arrive on board the ship, they'll have to rematerialize and disarm the guards so the Nyrians can retrieve their soulstones."

And, Nyria help them, Zianne's soulstone as well. She was dying. Would die within the next few hours without an infusion of power from one of her fellow Nyrians, but even their generous gifts of power couldn't hold her here forever.

Not without her soulstone.

Mac sighed. So much could go wrong. So damned much.

Dink reached across the narrow gap that separated them, took hold of Mac's hand, and squeezed it tightly. "This is the one thing I hate most about being a reporter. Learning the plans, knowing the danger, and realizing there's not a fucking thing I can do to alter the outcome."

Mac squeezed back. "You're here, Dink. That matters more than you realize." He gazed into his friend's silvery eyes, but there was too much emotion, too much to even consider right now.

Mac glanced away as the sun broke free of the horizon in a blinding blaze of orange and pink against a cerulean sky. It was easier to blame the tears in his eyes on the brilliant flash of sunlight shimmering off row after row of white satellite dishes, marching west across the array with inexorable certainty.

The sun would continue to rise, the days would pass, the world would go on.

But life? Not such a sure thing. Not anymore. This might be the last day for Zianne, but if things went wrong with their plan for rescuing her people, it could be the end of more than the few remaining Nyrians.

If they couldn't stop the Gar, if the Nyrians were somehow compelled to continue powering their huge star cruiser, it could very well mark the end of everything, at least as far as Earth was concerned.

Zianne and Mac's love wasn't even a blip on the radar, not compared to the ultimate risks they faced.

It wasn't like humans had been such great stewards, but they hadn't totally fucked things up yet. If the Gar had their way, once they moved on to other worlds, they'd leave nothing but a smoldering chunk of rock where civilizations had once risen and fallen. Where humans had grown and evolved.

Where Mac had met an impossible, improbable woman, where he'd fallen in love and followed a dream.

A dream that had all the signs of transforming into a nightmare.

He didn't want to think about it. No, he had to believe in success. As Dink kept reminding him, it was the only acceptable outcome, and he said it again, whispering the words to himself as he sat there on the deck, his hand tightly clasped in Dink's.

Failure is not an option.

Cameron Paisley's hand shook so badly he couldn't get the damned paintbrush into the jar of paint thinner. This had never happened before. Not to this extent, this total loss of self while painting.

His fantastical landscapes of imaginary worlds had always come to him through dreams, but he'd generally been wide-awake while he painted them. The amount of money they brought in certainly kept his eyes wide open, but this canvas was something else altogether.

It was haunting. Beautiful. Terrifying. Even more frightening? He couldn't remember painting a single stroke. It was a world he'd never seen, and yet he knew exactly what it was. Where it was. And he knew, without a doubt, that it no longer existed as it once had. As he'd painted it.

He finally managed to drag his gaze away from the mass of dark and fearsome images, focused his attention on the jar of thinner, and jammed his brush into the solvent.

His attention was drawn back to the painting. Critics had

asked over the years if his work was more than his imagination. He'd always said his paintings were the product of dreams.

This was no dream. This hadn't come to him during his shift in the dream shack. No, this had taken him over like a bad drug trip, had caught him up for . . . He glanced at the clock on the wall. Two hours?

Stunned, he stared once again at the canvas. He worked quickly, but this painting was filled with such detail that it should have taken him much, much longer.

It hurt to look. To realize what he saw in the bold strokes.

Forcibly turning his back on the art, Cam grabbed a rag and wiped his hands clean. Somehow he had to clear his head; he needed to make sense of this.

Tossing the rag aside, he quickly slipped out of his clothes and left them in a pile on the floor in front of the easel. Naked and shivering in the morning chill, he walked quickly through the bedroom to the bathroom.

He caught a brief glance of himself in the mirror. As always, he quickly averted his eyes and turned on the tap in the shower. So stupid, the way he always reacted to his own image.

Someday he'd probably wish he still looked like an over-grown teenager, but for now, it would be nice to look his age. It was hard enough getting the established art world to take a thirty-year-old man seriously. A guy who looked about seventeen got absolutely no respect.

Did it really matter? Shit, no. If Mac's project failed, there wouldn't be a fucking art world to worry about.

Cam grabbed a washcloth off the rack beside the shower, stepped beneath the spray, and tried to empty his mind of everything but the welcome heat of the water, the way tension slowly eased out of tired muscles. A more welcome thought intruded, that he'd finally experienced what the other members of the dream team had known all along—sending sexual fantasies to Nyrians had one hell of a payback.

After two nights of fantasizing about his art and the pending rescue of the aliens, he'd finally gotten on track during last night's shift.

Had he ever. The thought had barely registered when a coil of arousal shocked him into immediate awareness. His balls drew close to his body; his cock throbbed with new blood.

"Down, boy." Chuckling, he smoothed his hand over his taut shaft, paused a moment to slip his foreskin over the broad head and back again. A shiver raced along his spine. A shiver of pure carnal pleasure. He turned his dick loose and brushed his wet hair out of his eyes. Even without stroking himself, his arousal seemed to be growing, just from remembering last night's shift in the dream shack.

And to think he was getting paid for this! Being a member of Mac Dugan's dream team definitely had good bennies. Using his imagination to broadcast sexual fantasies to aliens who gained power from his wild thoughts might sound totally impossible, but when those fantasies were combined with Mac's powerful satellite array to boost their energy, the results were beyond amazing.

He thought of the two women who'd come to him during his shift, the last of the Nyrians to make the journey to Earth for the combination of sexual power and visual images necessary to create their own corporeal bodies.

He'd certainly liked the bodies his two visitors had chosen, and he'd definitely loved what they did with them. Once the Nyrians had a solid form, they seemed to delight in the sensual pleasures their new human bodies allowed.

Granted, everything had happened in his head-sort of—but it had felt like so much more.

Sort of like the painting. He wondered if Mac was awake, if maybe he ought to show it to him. Shit. He let out a huge breath. He could be wrong, but he was positive the damned thing was . . .

Oh. Fuck. The soft brush of something warm along his inner thigh jerked Cam out of his convoluted thoughts.

Out of his thoughts and right back here, to what could only be a dream. "Mir? Niah? What are you doing here?" He blinked furiously, clearing the water out of his eyes. Both women, his Nyrians from the night before, here? In his shower? He was awake, damn it. He wasn't fantasizing.

"Hello, Cam." Mir gazed up at him, all bright smile and gorgeous, naked body. She and Niah knelt at his feet, almost mirror images of one another except for coloring. Where Mir was all sultry and dark with long black hair, dark coffee eyes, and skin the color of polished oak, Niah was her opposite. Platinum hair, eyes of molten silver, and skin so fair and fine as to make her look like a carefully constructed porcelain doll.

Yet her lips were red—deep red, slightly parted, and at this moment approaching . . . no. Oh, crap. They were sliding deliciously over the head of his wide-awake, *please-play-with-me* dick.

Groaning, he braced his hands against the slick walls of the shower and prayed his knees wouldn't buckle. There was no thought of stopping her—last night he'd quickly learned that Mir and Niah did exactly as they pleased.

Mir stood and slipped around behind him, tugged the wet washcloth from his nerveless fingers, and slowly swept it across his shoulders. She stroked his back, his buttocks, the backs of his thighs, while Niah slowly took him deeper and then deeper still, sucking his full length into her mouth, down her throat.

Oh. Fuck. He tightened everything—his buttocks, his thighs, the muscles across his stomach. Tightened and prayed for control, but he could feel it slipping, even as Mir dropped the washcloth and pressed against his back.

She was tall enough that her breasts hit just below his shoulder blades. Her nipples were beaded up so tight he felt them, twin little bullet points of sensation. Then she was sliding, sliding down, slowly dragging her breasts down his back, running her fingers over his flanks, dropping to her knees behind him.

This was so much more intense than last night when he'd slipped between fantasy and reality, and he'd wondered then if he'd survive their curious explorations. Now, Niah knelt in front, sucking his cock, and Mir had gone to her knees behind him, pushing his legs apart, licking the sensitive curve of his butt and then wrapping long fingers around his sac.

He might have whimpered. Knew he was cursing steadily, though if he'd been asked exactly what words he used, Cam doubted he could have given an intelligent answer. Mir forced his legs farther apart, somehow twisted around so that she had her mouth on his balls and her tongue doing something that had to be illegal in most states.

Probably on the planet.

Did it matter? Hell no. Hell. No. No . . . shit.

He tried to stop it. Honestly, he'd never fought so hard for control in his life, but there was no way. Not any way at all to stop what these two women had set into motion.

Lips and tongues everywhere; fingers on his balls; a hot, tight mouth and throat taking complete control of his dick. A finger teasing his ass, pressing, entering, sliding deep, pressing . . .

He cried out. Cursed. Shouted.

Climaxed.

Cam struggled to stay upright but gravity won and he slowly gave in. His knees buckled and his hands slipped along the wet tiles until he was half sitting, half lying on the floor of the shower with the water beating him in the face, with both Mir and Niah giggling with utter delight.

He opened his eyes and stared at both women. "What are you doing here? I thought you were going back to finish your shift."

"Nattoch wanted us to gather more energy." Niah licked her lips. "You weren't fantasizing enough to provide energy. We decided to help you along."

"You were sad," Mir said. She stood and offered him a hand. He wrapped his fingers around hers and she tugged him to his feet. "Your sadness distresses us. Come. Let's dry off and do it again. This time with laughter."

Cam thought of the painting in the other room. Thought of what it might be, what it meant. Then he looked at the women— two absolutely beautiful, wet, naked women—waiting impatiently for him to make up his mind.

He shut off the water, grabbed a towel off the rack, and ran it over Mir first, and then Niah. They preened like glossy, well-loved cats.

Cam dried himself. His legs had stopped trembling. His erection hadn't subsided a bit, and it was still awfully early in the morning. The painting could wait. He'd talk to Mac later. Tossing the wet towel over the shower door, he followed the women into the bedroom.

He glanced out the window as first Mir and then Niah crawled into the middle of his big bed. The sun was barely up. Mac was probably still asleep. Cam turned his attention to the bed.

To the women on his bed.

It was still made up from yesterday. He'd never gone to sleep at all last night. Not that he intended to sleep now.

At least, not for a while. Mir held out her hand. He took it, let her tug him close, and for some reason thought of the painting in the other room.

The dark, angry landscape with its familiar pattern of canals and lines, only they weren't canals at all, but highways. Cities and forests in the midst of terrible upheaval. A living planet under attack. He felt a terrible pain in his chest and thought of waking Mac, of telling him what he'd seen.

Then he caught the scent of vanilla and honey, and the painting slipped from his mind. Gently, he pressed Mir back against the pillows and parted her thighs with both hands. A quick smile for Niah. "You next," he said. Then he winked as Niah settled beside them to watch.

He knelt between Mir's legs with his palms beneath her firm, round buttocks, lifted her for his pleasure, and discovered that yes, she did taste exactly like vanilla and honey.

Morgan Black lay beside Rodie Bishop and watched the first rays of the morning sun cut across the tumbled blankets. Their Nyrian lover Bolt had returned to the ship at some point during the night, though Morgan had slept through his departure.

Still so hard to believe, that in just a few days he had not only interacted with aliens, he'd had some pretty mind-blowing sex with them. His thoughts drifted to the five Nyrian women he'd called with his fantasies—women who now had the human forms they'd need when the DEO-Map team put their rescue into action.

Five Nyrian women, one Nyrian man. And then there was Rodie.

She'd caught him by surprise, and yet it was as if she'd always been there, always a part of his life. The feelings he had for her, the woman herself . . . Hell, it still felt like a dream.

He'd never had a steady relationship with a woman before, and nothing all that serious with men. How could so much have changed? Now he had Rodie, he had Bolt and the other Nyrians, creatures he'd known for such a short time, and yet . . .

They mattered. Mattered to him in a way that was almost impossible to describe. As if the forms they'd taken from his mind had left an indelible imprint on his soul.

Essentially, they had become family. His family. And not just the Nyrians—no, the entire dream team was closer than those few he could claim by blood. They were the ones who mattered. Finn and Cam were the brothers he'd never had. Kiera and Liz were like little sisters. And Mac? How did he describe his feelings for Mac Dugan? Not just a friend, not even a brother. More a mentor, a trusted male, someone Morgan actually admired.

There were very few men he'd ever admired in his life.

And oddly enough, Finn O'Toole was one of them, which was almost laughable when he thought of his first impression. He'd pegged him as a jokester without a serious thought in his head, a guy who was more concerned with bagging another woman, adding another notch to his proverbial bedpost.

It appeared he'd been wrong about Finn O'Toole. At least he hoped so, since he'd be trusting him with his life. Today, he and Finn would learn how to dematerialize, or disincorporate, as the Nyrians called it. Essentially, he'd be reducing himself to the molecular level and hitchhiking within the energy mass of an alien creature in order to travel from Earth to the Gar ship that was currently in orbit behind the moon.

Yeah. Sure . . . and it was a good thing he didn't have a clue how this was going to happen or he'd probably be scared to death, but somehow, doing something that was so far beyond belief didn't seem to actually register.

Rodie let out a soft snore and snuggled against his side. He tightened his arm around her shoulders. She was just as far beyond belief as dematerializing. Rodie Bishop was someone else he'd underestimated.

He'd thought she was interesting and kind of cute.

He had no idea she'd totally rock his world.

Of course, when he'd signed on to this project, he really had no idea what he was getting into. Definitely a good thing being so ignorant or he'd never have agreed.

And then, just think what he'd be missing.